One Last Thing Before I Go

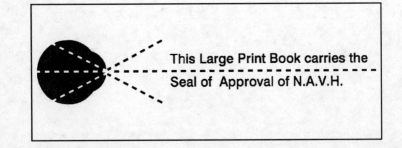

ONE LAST THING
BEFORE I GO

JONATHAN TROPPER

THORNDIKE PRESS
A part of Gale, Cengage Learning

GALE
CENGAGE Learning

Detroit • New York • San Francisco • New

Copyright © 2012 by Jonathan Tropper.
Thorndike Press, a part of Gale, Cengage Learning.

Thorndike Press® Large Print Core.
The text of this Large Print edition is unabridged.
Other aspects of the book may vary from the original edition.
Set in 16 pt. Plantin.

LIBRARY OF CONGRESS CATALOGING-IN-PUBLICATION DATA

Tropper, Jonathan.
    One last thing before i go / By Jonathan Tropper.
        pages ; cm. — (Thorndike Press large print core)
    ISBN-13: 978-1-4104-5183-5 (hardcover)
    ISBN-10: 1-4104-5183-6 (hardcover)
    1. Men—Fiction. 2. Domestic fiction. 3. Psychological fiction. 4. Large
type books. I. Title.
PS3570.R5885O54 2012b
813'.54—dc23   2012025127

Published in 2012 by arrangement with Dutton, a member of Penguin
Group (USA) Inc.

For Spencer, Emma, and Alexa,
who make all of my work
a labor of love

BOOK ONE

CHAPTER 1

This is Tuesday, just under three weeks before his wife will be getting married, and a few days before Silver will tentatively decide that life isn't necessarily worth living when you've been doing it as poorly as he has. It is seven years and four months or so since Denise divorced him for a host of valid reasons, and roughly eight years since his band, the Bent Daisies, released its only album and became rock stars overnight on the strength of their solitary hit, "Rest in Pieces." For one blessed summer it seemed as if the entire world was singing that song. And then they weren't, and then he couldn't get arrested — although, actually, Silver did get arrested twice; one DUI and once for solicitation, and he would tell you about it if he could, but he was, at best, fuzzy about the details back then, and now it's like an oral history long forgotten. Then, with a little back-channel manipulation from the record label, Pat McReedy, their lead singer, quit the band to launch his now epic solo career, dropping Danny (bass), Ray (lead guitar), and Silver (drums) back home in Elmsbrook to stare down the barrel of the rest of their painfully unglamorous lives. With nowhere else to go, Silver went back home to discover that Denise had already changed the locks and retained counsel.

But that was then, and this is Tuesday, eight years and countless mistakes later. Silver is forty-four years old, if you can believe it, out of shape, and depressed — although he doesn't know if you call it depression when you have good reason to be; maybe then you're simply sad, or lonely, or just painfully aware, on a daily basis, of all the things you can never get back.

And, this being Tuesday, Silver and Jack are on their way to jerk off.

"Is that a wedding ring?"

They are speeding down the highway in Jack's ten-year-old BMW convertible when Jack notices the band on Silver's finger. Jack is blasting hip-hop music and pretending to know the words, while Silver absently taps along on his knees to the automated beat. They are the same age, seasoned veterans of epically bad decisions and poor follow-through.

He forgot to take off the ring. God only knows how long he's been wearing it. Hours? Days, maybe. His finger still bears the groove from when he was married, and whenever he slips it on, it slides into place like a machined part, and he forgets about it. Chagrined, he pulls it off his finger and sticks it into his pocket, to jingle around with his other loose change.

"What the fuck, Silver?" Jack says. He has to shout to be heard above the din of the interstate, the hip-hop, and the incessant ringing in Silver's ears. Silver suffers from a moderate to severe case of tinnitus. There is no cure and, as far as he knows, no one is running any triathlons to raise awareness or fund research. He suffers alone.

"I was just playing with it."

"Is that your actual wedding band?"

"As opposed to what?"

"I don't know, I thought maybe you went out and bought one."

"Why the hell would I buy a wedding ring?"

"Why would you wear your old one, ten years after your divorce?"

"Seven years."

"Sorry. Seven years. I stand corrected."

Jack flashes him a sly little smile, the one that says *I know you better than you know yourself,* the one that generally makes Silver want to plunge his index finger through Jack's eye socket, around the back of his nose, and out the other eye, creating an effective handle with which to rip his face off.

"Something wrong there, Silver?"

"What could be wrong? I'm a forty-four-year-old man on my way to masturbate into a cup for seventy-five dollars. Living the dream."

Jack grins. "Easiest money you'll ever make."

A good amount of his time with Jack is spent wondering whether Jack actually believes his own particular brand of bullshit. They are two middle-aged divorced men, their friendship born of mutual inconvenience, because they happened to live on the same floor of the Versailles. Jack thinks Silver is depressed and Silver thinks Jack is an idiot and, at any given moment, both of them are generally right.

They are on their way to a satellite office of the Blecher-Royal Medical Research Facility, where they will check in, submit to the prick of a blood test, then submit their own pricks to a quick, sterile flurry of self-abuse and gracelessly come into specimen jars. They will accomplish this without the aid of any chemical lubricants, in the name

12

of science, and for the weekly seventy-five-dollar stipend.

The drug trial in which they are enrolled — Jack found it online — is purported to be a new nonhormonal treatment for low sperm motility. Possible side effects include mood swings; dizziness; and, strangely, decreased libido, a fact the test administrator told them during the twenty-minute orientation without the slightest hint of irony.

You don't want to hear about his deposit, about the small room overwhelmed by the liberal spraying of industrial-strength disinfectant, about the weathered porn magazines he won't touch because of all the sticky hands that have already handled them. About the depressing little television on its teetering IKEA stand, and the small stack of DVDs, each case marked with either an *H*(etero) or a *G*(ay). Or about how he doesn't sit in the chair or watch the discs, but just kind of stands in the center of the room with his pants around his ankles, calling up the images of girls he slept with back when he was young enough to be wholly consumed by a deep, passionate kiss, the sight of a freshly unsheathed breast, the smoky half-closed eyes of a girl in heat, looking up at you as she hungrily takes you in below.

But as always, just before his ejaculate hits the bottom of the specimen cup with a soft plastic burp, no matter how determined he is to avoid it, he sees Denise, frowning at him with her customary scorn, depleting the moment of whatever lingering molecular pleasure it may have retained.

A last sad grunt and squeeze, the cold damp of the baby wipe, and then the warmth of his semen against his fingertips through the thin plastic walls of the cup, more alive than anything coming out of him has any right to feel.

CHAPTER 2

Out in the lobby, Jack, already finished, is
chatting up the receptionist. She isn't his
type — mousy-looking with a light smattering of adult acne across the edge of her jaw
— but Jack likes to stay sharp. You never
know who might be in the market for a
house.

Jack is a real-estate agent, always with a
business card tucked between two fingers,
slipping it into your hand like a reverse
pickpocket before you even realize he's done
it. He carries himself with the cocky swag-
ger of someone who is always closing,
whether he's trying to talk someone into
bed or a center-hall colonial. In fact, he is
somewhat famous for often accomplishing
both simultaneously. This went on back
when he was still married, so it was only a
matter of time, really. There was a Puerto
Rican bartender. She showed up to his
house at dinnertime, cursing at him in

Spanish. His wife went after him, first with a meat tenderizer, and then with a team of lawyers from her father's white-shoe law firm.

"There he is!" Jack says, announcing Silver's presence to the entire office. "What, did you have to buy yourself dinner first? I was about to send Vicki here in to expedite things."

Vicki smiles, embarrassed, maybe even offended, but somehow flattered too. That is Jack's gift.

"I'm fine." He hands Vicki his deposit without making eye contact, she hands him his check, and just like that, he has sold his seed. The cup is opaque, but still, the act of handing your sperm to a woman is one of those things that will never stop feeling creepy.

"Good job," Jack says, slapping his back as they step out of the office into the afternoon sun.

This is my life, Silver thinks to himself, and, as always, tries like hell not to panic.

Mistakes have been made.

It's hard to know where to start. Things have been a mess for so many years that trying to pin down a starting point is like trying to figure out where your skin starts.

16

All you can ever really know is that it's wrapped around you, sometimes a little tighter than you'd like.

But clearly there have been some mistakes. Bad ones. You can tell that just by looking at him.

For one thing, he has gotten fat. Not obese, not *People* magazine fat, but still. He has been on an extended hiatus from any kind of physical fitness. Do they even say "physical fitness" anymore? He isn't sure. He hasn't quite fallen apart yet, but the cracks are fast becoming fissures: an increasingly pronounced gut, incipient jowls, and the strategic application of baby powder in the warmer seasons to avoid chafing.

So as not to smell like baby powder, he uses excessive amounts of deodorant and generous helpings of Eternity, by Calvin Klein. He applies the cologne by spraying it into the air and then walking through the vapor, like he saw his mother do when he was a boy. So, yeah, now he's the fat guy who smells like baby powder and too much cologne, who sits alone in Manny's Famous Pizza leaving greasy fingerprints all over the book he isn't actually reading while blotting the oil off his poorly shaved chin with a napkin, keeping an eye on all the pretty girls who come in.

You could be excused for thinking he is somewhat pathetic. Or maybe a pedophile.

Which is why lately he has gotten into the habit of wearing his old wedding band. Not because he misses Denise — he doesn't at all, which is maybe a sad confirmation of what she always suspected about his overall emotional wherewithal — but because that gold band around his finger alters the whole picture, confers upon him some faint glimmer of respectability. It implies that he goes home to someone who finds redeeming qualities in him, who is ostensibly not averse to at least occasional physical contact with him, and that makes all of his obvious flaws seem more superficial, less ingrained. It could complicate things if he happens to strike up a conversation with an attractive woman, but the women he tends to engage these days are not, generally speaking, the sort who are going to blanch at a wedding band.

CHAPTER 3

His habit is to while away the depressing afterglow of his sperm deposit at The Last Page, a large independent bookstore in the quiet downtown area of Elmsbrook. He generally sits in the store's small café, reading *Rolling Stone* and drinking a large soda, replenishing his fluids while he waits.

Lily arrives at a quarter to three, her long hair haphazardly tied into a loose ponytail knot that is already coming undone, blondish wisps spilling out and trailing her like a comet's tail. Her hair has been dyed different shades of blond for so long that it has lost all genetic memory, so that her visible roots aren't so much dark as confused. Her black tights are tucked into black cowboy boots, and her lean torso swims in a loose-fitting cardigan the color of dirt. She wears her guitar on her back, neck up, in a soft black case, like a ninja sword.

Silver watches her closely from his perch

in the café. Imperfections abound: her prominent forehead, her small fighter's nose, a misaligned lateral tooth. But the overall package has a pleasing composition to it, a fractured beauty that lingers for him even after she has moved past him into the Children's Books section.

He loves her as much as any man can love a woman he's never spoken to, which is significantly more than you'd think. It's a pure love, epic in its own way. If the situation called for it, he'd step in front of a speeding bus for her. The only other person he would ever do that for is Casey, his daughter, whom he imagines might actually enjoy the spectacle. In eighteen years, he hasn't exactly proven himself in the father department. The sad truth is, dying for Casey might be his only shot at redemption, and even then he doesn't think it would help his case very much. Any idiot can die, right?

He moves furtively through the aisles of books like a shoplifter. He can already hear the soft sounds of Lily's guitar, punctuated by the occasional hiss of the espresso machine in the bookstore's café. She plays this gig twice a week, for the handful of three- and four-year-olds who sit in a small circle around her low styrene chair, sipping at their juice boxes and singing along while the assorted mix of nannies and au pairs chat softly amongst themselves in island dialects.

Silver stands in the Self-Help aisle, where he can listen without alarming anyone. *Thirty Days to a Flat Stomach, Eating Your Way to a Thinner You, The Self-Esteem Workbook* — a billion-dollar industry built on the questionable notion that people can be fixed. He pretends to browse while he watches Lily play. Her whole body moves as she strums, her light hair falling over her face like a curtain, and then she looks up at the kids and starts to sing.

The cat came back / the very next day / The cat came back / we thought he was a goner / but the cat came back / He just wouldn't stay, away away away yeah yeah . . .

There is no way to explain this. It's an inane kids' song. And her thin voice wavers on the high notes and occasionally runs flat. But she sings with passion, like it's a raw and earnest love song, her deepest pain set to music. The ridiculous song is much too small to contain her energy, and so it spills over, filling the room, filling him. The kids sing along tunelessly with the chorus — they've been here before — but her voice rises above them and floats around the ceiling fans of this scrappy little bookstore still

21

clinging fiercely to life in the digital age. He can feel the familiar lump forming in his throat, the paradoxical sense of having lost something he never had. By the time she hits the third verse he is undone.

The man around the corner swore he'd shoot the cat on sight / He loaded up his shotgun with nails and dynamite / He waited and he waited for the cat to come around / Ninety-seven pieces of the man was all they found . . . / But the cat came back . . .

Every so often, clarity washes over him in a wave, drenching him with realizations and reminders of what he's lost and who he has turned out to be. He lurks there, beyond help in the Self-Help section, a middle-aged mess of a man with restless legs, ringing ears, and an aching heart, fighting back the tears elicited by a woman he's never met singing her heart out about the attempted murder of a cat.

The way he sees it, he's teetering on that edge. By his estimation, he's got maybe one last shot at any kind of real and lasting love, and that's before you take into account his warped and deeply compromised faculty for it to begin with. He has loved more women than any man should. He doesn't so much fall in love as dive-bomb it like a kamikaze pilot, fearless and at full throttle. He used to look at this propensity as a gift, then a curse, and now understands it to be just another way in which he is broken.

He's been alone for a long time now, more than seven years. At some point, loneliness becomes less a condition than a habit. In time, you stop looking at your phone wondering why you can't think of anyone to call, stop getting your hair cut, stop working out, stop thinking that tomorrow is the first day of the rest of your life. Because tomorrow is today, and today is yesterday, and yesterday beat the shit out of you and brought you to your knees. The only way to stay sane is to stop hoping for something better.

But there's still something in him, a small pocket of insurgency that hasn't fully conceded. There's a part of him that still believes she's out there, the woman who will see the man behind this shifting, splitting land mass, the woman who knows exactly what to do with the hopeless paradox of a kamikaze lover like him. And he knows that's the part of him that has to finish dying if he's ever going to sleep soundly again.

The first girl he ever loved was Sofie Kinslehour. She had a pixie haircut and a pink, horn-shaped birthmark on her neck, and the first time they kissed, she let out a small moan that conveyed a world of carnality he had only vaguely intuited up to that point. They were sixteen years old, in a dark corner of the parking lot behind the high school — there was a game of some kind going on — and when she moaned, he heard himself answer in kind, like she'd woken something up in him he didn't know was there. She pressed the full length of herself against him, opening her mouth to accept his tongue. For the next few weeks, she occupied him like a conquering army. At home he tugged on himself so furiously and so often that at one point he feared real and lasting damage. When they were together they kissed themselves raw, until their lips were swollen, flaking husks, their tongues charley-horsed. And then, one day, it ended. He doesn't remember the salient points, but statistical evidence and the cold spasm of regret in his belly whenever he thinks about it assure him that it was he who blinked first, who found a random flaw in her to cling to until it swallowed him whole.

CHAPTER 4

It's summer, the air thick with that virulent East Coast humidity that shortens your breath and dampens the back of your shirt as soon as you step outside. He is sitting with Jack and Oliver in their usual chairs by the Versailles pool, trying, like everyone else, to look like he isn't looking at the college girls.

Or maybe they are college women? He doesn't know. They defy categorization, this gaggle of bronzed, bikinied students, stretched taut like pulled taffy on lounge chairs near the deep end of the pool. He is sitting in his usual spot between Jack and Oliver, catty-corner to the girls, pretending to read a magazine. All around the pool, other men sit, alone and in clusters, and they are all the same, all sad and depleted, abusing themselves with stolen glances at forbidden fruit.

"Will you look at those girls," Jack says,

probably for the third time. Silver tends to tune him out.

They don't need him to tell them. They are men after all — not the men they once might have been, and not the men they maybe could be — but men, after a fashion. And these girls, these women . . . well, they glisten with nubile perfection under their SPF 15, baking their soft, unblemished skin to a honeyed glaze as they read from textbooks and tabloid magazines, tap away at texting devices encased in pink and red rubber, or listen to their iPods, their bare, manicured feet twitching to the music. They do that thing with their lips that girls do when they feel the music, puckering their lips, kind of kissing the air as their heads bob up and down.

The pool is supposed to be exclusively for residents of the Versailles, an efficiency hotel just off the interstate, but the girls come daily as Jack's guests, and no one ever complains. They come from Hudson College, situated just four blocks away on the other side of Route 9. The semester is just starting up again, and the proximity of so many young, ripe women to a place like the Versailles is like keeping your matches and blasting caps in the same drawer.

Yes, he is living in an efficiency hotel.

Mistakes.

The Versailles, a drab monolith that rises like a tombstone fourteen stories above the sailor's knot of parkways and connecting ramps that feed into I-95, is the only apartment building within the Elmsbrook city limits. Years ago, it was converted into a residential hotel, where rooms can be rented at a weekly or monthly rate. As such, it has become the inevitable destination of all the sad, damaged men of Elmsbrook, banished from their homes in the wake of disintegrating marriages. An aura of failure hangs over the place — middle-aged men living on their own in small, sparsely furnished, subdivided hotel rooms. "He's living in the Versailles, now," people say, and everyone knows exactly what they mean. It is *that* building. The pool, the gym, the concierge, the plush lobby furniture; none of these amenities can obscure the fact that this is a place where broken men come to lick their wounds as the battles over marital assets and custody arrangements are slowly lost at a rate of roughly six-fifty an hour plus expenses.

In the framed architectural drawing that still hangs in the lobby, the building is rendered in a soft white that glints in the sun, surrounded by emerald lawns and a lush canopy of ash and oak trees. But the zoning board required a larger parking lot, so the lawn and trees and the little kids flying their red and yellow kites never made if off the drawing board, and the diesel exhaust rising off the nearby expressways has gradually turned the Versailles into a vertical slab the color of a thunderhead. It's hard to fathom the logic of displaying this picture of the building in all its unrealized splendor, someone's idea of a cruel joke, maybe, a blunt metaphor designed to effect a kind of subliminal torture on the residents.

Back when Silver was married, the building, in better shape then, was still something of a punch line, fatuously tacked onto the end of arguments. *"If I'm so horrible, why don't you just move out? I'm sure there's a vacancy at* the Versailles . . ." Like that. Cut to seven years later and here he is, the sum total of his existence confined to a two-bedroom efficiency eight floors up, alongside his brothers in arms, the men exiled from Elmsbrook's tree-lined residential streets, from the carpeted and curtained warmth of solid, creaking Tudors and colonials, stripped of marriage and family but still paying for it in ways large and small. Paying the mortgages on houses in which they are no longer welcome, paying for their ex-wives' new wardrobes and haircuts and facials and body waxings and gym memberships, all to tone, smooth, and buff bodies that they no longer get to touch, paying for the personal trainers who are probably fucking their wives and for their wives' lawyers who are fucking them, and for their own lawyers who seem powerless to do anything about any of it except explain in lay terms exactly how they've been fucked. Paying for Little League and soccer and piano lessons and ice-skating and karate and Gap Kids and private school and speech therapy and tutoring and after-school programs and health insurance. Standing in the lobby, you can feel the building vibrating with the collected agitation of desperate men living in a constant state of subdued panic, in a permanent frazzle, avoiding bank statements, selling off dwindling assets, knowing that they can only keep this colossal mess aloft for so long before the whole thing comes crashing down in a miasma of courtroom vitriol and bankruptcy.

And so the men of the Versailles, brothers in disgrace, reach out to one another in the invisible ways that men do, and small, fragile friendships of convenience form like desert moss. They bitch and moan to sympathetic ears, preaching to the choir about

the courts, the antiquated laws, the goddamn fucking lawyers, and this new, en-
forced, seemingly insurmountable poverty
in which they have all landed. And when
they aren't bitching, they try like hell to
believe that this isn't a permanent state of
affairs, that they can and will find love
again, that they won't die alone, that they
will have some version of sex in the near
future. But in the meantime, they will mope,
drink to excess, and stare at women of an
inappropriate age, searching for the silver
lining, wondering when the perks will finally
kick in.

Which brings us back to the college girls.

"I mean, just look at them, would you,"
Jack says.

Jack is handsome in a manner that allows
him to get away with this unabashed leer-
ing. He is tall and slim, built for shirtless
lounging, with dark, wiry hair and the
dimpled chin of a superhero. He and Silver
had been casual acquaintances in their old
lives, part of a loosely associated ring of
husbands and fathers connected less by
genuine friendship than by the friendship of
their wives. And now they are connected by
their absence. No one was happier about
Silver's divorce than Jack, who practically

friend's daughter.

"Hey there," Casey says with that jaded nonchalance she reserves exclusively for him. As always, in the first instant he sees her, he can feel his heart suddenly shut down, the way you do in those first moments after impact, or, he supposes, when you're drowning. Love or panic. The two have always been fairly indistinguishable to him.

"Hey, Casey." He sits up in his lounge chair, suddenly self-conscious of his rolling gut, his unshaved face, the haircut he's been meaning to get. "What are you doing here?"

She smiles as if his question has triggered a private joke. "What indeed?"

It will surprise no one to learn that he has not been anyone's idea of a model father. In the seven years since his divorce he has missed, by design or neglect, more than his share of birthdays, recitals, varsity games, and more dinner dates than he dares to recall. His relationship with Casey gradually evolved from playful to strained to distant, and once puberty had had its way with her, her once habitual forgiveness became somewhat more elusive. He knows this is all his fault, knows he deserves far more contempt from her than she is capable of, but still, there's something about hearing your little girl look down her nose at you and say "What indeed?" that makes you feel fractured beyond repair.

Casey looks them over, and he can see them through her eyes; Jack, the aging lothario, coasting on a witless charm that started to fade sometime in the late '90s; Oliver, doughy and dour and old enough to be her grandfather; and himself, sweating through an extra-large T-shirt commemorating a band that stopped being cool before she was born. Her eyes briefly flit over to the college girls, then back to them with a cynical gleam and they are busted for being the sad, drooping ball sacks that they are.

It's hard to get up smoothly while simultaneously straddling a lounge chair and sucking in your gut. He achieves verticality, but only after some graceless jostling with inertia, and somehow this simple effort leaves him flushed and breathless. The Versailles has a decent gym, and with all the time on his hands, you'd think he'd have wandered in there by now.

He kisses her cheek. She doesn't cringe outwardly and he is ridiculously overjoyed.

"Look at you," Jack says to her. "How old are you these days?"

"Eighteen."

"Wow, that makes me feel old."

36

"No, I think it's probably your age that's doing that."

"Shazam!" Jack says. He does that sometimes. They don't know why.

Casey rolls her eyes, essentially negating Jack's existence, and looks at Silver. "I need to talk to you."

"Is everything OK?

She appears to contemplate that for a moment. "Everything is peachy."

"You want to go sit by the cabanas?" he says.

"Sure."

As she walks ahead of him, he catches a glimpse of color, a flash of red on her shoulder.

"What's that?"

"It's just a rose," she says defensively.

As far as tattoos go, it's fairly restrained; a bloodred rose, with a single leaf, tattooed onto her scapula. Even shitty fathers can cry from something like that. But he has long since squandered any rights to paternal indignation, so he figures he might as well score a point.

"Nice."

Casey smiles wryly, on to him. "You should see the one on my ass."

"Jesus."

"Focus, Silver. We've got bigger fish to fry."

"Such as?"

She turns to face him, still smirking, but her eyes are wide and he can see her trembling.

"Such as," she says, "I'm pregnant."

There are moments when you can literally feel the planet spinning beneath you, so much so that you instinctively need to hold on to something. He gently grabs Casey's arm and looks into her eyes and they stand there, with the world coming apart around them, both of them waiting to see what it is that he is going to say.

CHAPTER 5

"Wow."

That's what he says. She doesn't know what she was expecting, really. Drew Silver is not exactly famous for knowing what to say in a pinch. Or out of one. Ever, really. But in his defense, here are the things he didn't say:

"Are you sure?"

"Who did this to you?"

"You're not the girl I thought you were."

He doesn't get angry, he doesn't yell, and he doesn't look away. If there's a perk to having such a fucked-up father, it's that he's in no position to judge. Silver looks right at her and takes hold of her arm, which normally would piss her off, but right then, having just said the words out loud for the first time, she kind of needs someone to grab her arm. And as soon as he touches her, she feels something, some long fossilized knot inside of her, shift and loosen.

He says "Wow" again. He doesn't yell it, his jaw doesn't drop, nothing like that. The "wow" is just filler as he absorbs this sad fact and all the secondary information that comes along with it, like someone who has spent a good part of his life absorbing sad facts, and she understands now that this is why she came to him.

And even though he's a lousy father, and she knows he'll almost definitely disappoint her sometime in the next five minutes, in this moment she could cry from how much she loves him, even as she hates herself for it. So she does. She cries. In front of these sad broken men and the half-naked hotties lying out over at the shallow end — and who lets those girls in here anyway? That Russian doorman acts like he's guarding the White House, for God's sake. It just goes to show you how far you can get if you're rocking a nice set of tits.

And Silver, he pulls her into this kind of one-armed hug, like he's not sure how to do it, like he's scared he might break her, and how the hell do you go through life without learning the basic mechanics of a hug? Usually she hates it when her pity for him interferes with her anger, and she compensates with extra nastiness, but now she closes her eyes and disappears into the rough, weathered cotton of his T-shirt for a few moments while she gets her shit together. She breathes in his familiar smell, the one she thinks of as Eau de Deadbeat, a mixture of aftershave and talcum powder. And even as she holds on to him like she's drowning, she can feel the familiar anger returning, like an old song that you've heard so many times it's not even a song anymore, just a wasted pathway in your brain that you can never reclaim.

She feels the anger rising up inside her — at him, at herself — and she shakes herself out of his inept embrace, maybe a little more roughly than she'd intended. He takes a step back, confused. She knows this expression well — that dumb, startled look, like the world is simply moving too fast for him to keep up. It's pretty much how he's looked at her ever since puberty, like, once an ice-cream cone won't do the trick, he's out of his depth. She assumes it's a look her mother got to know pretty well in the years before they divorced, although they've never really talked about that. As much as she despises Silver, she doesn't let her mother talk shit about him anymore, not because she feels any loyalty to him, but because her mother is on a lifelong mission to exonerate herself with regard to the fucktrap of her

41

first marriage, and that's a bone Casey is just not ready to throw her. Even though she's pretty sure her mother is right.

Case in point: After she gets the waterworks under control, she looks up at Silver, this man she's come to in her moment of need, in defiance of all conventional wisdom. And Silver, he runs his fingers through his long, messy hair, rubs his jowls thoughtfully, and then says, "You want to get some ice cream?"

If being the valedictorian and the only girl in her grade to get into an Ivy League school isn't irony enough, there's this: Up until three weeks ago, Casey was a virgin. She didn't even have a boyfriend.

She had one earlier in the year, the somewhat implausibly named Jake Prudence, but he broke up with her in March for a needlessly complex network of reasons that could all be summarily boiled down to the fact that she wouldn't have sex with him. They'd get naked in his Jeep, or his bed when his parents were out, and he'd stick his fingers in her even though she'd hinted repeatedly that on worked better than in. Then he'd lie between her legs, grinding on her, and just as she began to feel the hot stirrings of something, he'd moan and she'd feel the sticky wetness explode across her belly, and that would be that.

"Did you have one?" he would say afterward.

"No," she'd answer as she cleaned off her stomach with a baby wipe, the smell of his semen reminding her of the indoor pools where she'd spent so much of her free time over the last few years competing on the swim team.

And Jake would flash her this wounded look that said he wished she'd just be a sport and fake it once in a while. "You would have if I was inside you," he would declare.

Somehow, she suspected that would be even less satisfying, if that were possible. In any case, she didn't feel like surrendering her virginity to find out.

It was in these supposedly intimate moments that Casey found she liked him least. Jake was funny and honest and had a softness to him that she found endearing. But once they'd progressed to naked petting, their entire relationship seemed to become colored by his campaign to deflower her, and she found herself cast in the role of the reluctant prude, which seemed grossly unfair considering his lectures on the topic often came while she held his throbbing dick in her hand.

At some point, it became an unspoken ultimatum, and Casey opted out. Two weeks later Jake was with Lucy Grayson, who'd been a JCPenney model when she was younger, and who'd been with so many guys in their grade she was practically a rite of passage.

But somehow, despite holding the line with Jake, Casey still managed the trick of being, as far as she knew, the only valedictorian in the history of Washington Irving High School to deliver her speech not quite twenty minutes after peeing on a stick in the girls' locker room. And two pages into her speech, she realized that she was still clutching the EPT stick in her hand up at the podium. And every time she looked down at her text, there they were, those two pink lines that laced everything she said with a secret irony. "And as we head out into the world, the only certainty is uncertainty. . . . Ultimately, we will become the sum of our choices, and our mistakes. . . . We can already see this life we hold so dear fading behind us, to be rediscovered one day as a memory to share with our own children. . . . Blah, blah, blah . . . the friendships made, the lessons learned, the experiences shared . . ." et cetera, ad nauseam.

And all the while, that stick of doom in her sweaty hand, tapping the podium as she turned the pages, and the thing inside her, that convergence of lust, apathy, and biology that even now must have been splitting and multiplying in her uterus like there was no tomorrow. She fantasized about tossing her prepared remarks, holding up the EPT, and issuing some heartfelt confession that would earn her the respect and sympathy of everyone in the room. *You think you're scared? Check this shit out!* And after she finished, and Justin Ross came up with his black eye shadow and his guitar to sing Green Day's "Good Riddance," there wouldn't be a dry eye in the room, and she would become something of a local legend.

When she was done, the auditorium erupted into the standard canned applause, and she saw her mother and Rich beaming at her. And way in the back of the room, against all odds, Silver, in jeans and black button down, standing against the wall, clapping. So when the tears came, as she made her way back to her seat, she couldn't be quite sure exactly what she was crying about. Take your pick, right?

CHAPTER 6

"How'd your mother take it?"
"She's OK."
"Really?"
"I haven't exactly told her."
"Ah. Smart move."
"You're the only person I've told."
"OK."
"How does that make you feel?"
"You sound like my therapist."
"You still go to therapy?"
"Nah. I gave up years ago."
"Mental health isn't for everyone."
"Neither is contraception."
"Well played, Silver."
"Have you made a decision?"
"I decided I'm an asshole."
"How far along are you?"
"Not very. When do you count from?"
"I don't know. Conception, I think."
"So, three weeks or so."
"OK. So you have a little time."

"What do you think I should do?"

"I think you should probably have an abortion."

"Wow, Dad. That didn't take very long, did it?"

"You asked me what I thought —"

"I mean, just come right out and say what you think, Dad."

"I just did."

"No thought at all to the life I have growing inside me."

"Is that how you see it? As a life, I mean?"

"Yes. No. Sometimes. I don't know. How do you see it?"

"How I see it doesn't matter. You have to do what feels right to you."

"What feels right to me is not being pregnant."

"Don't cry, honey."

"Don't tell me not to cry. I hate that."

"I'm sorry."

"I mean, Jesus, Dad. This is like, the perfect time to cry. I'm fucking pregnant."

"You're right. I'm sorry."

"Can you tell me something?"

"Sure."

"Does it upset you that I'm not a virgin?"

"It upsets me that you're not seven years old anymore. It upsets me that I blinked and you're already a woman, and I've missed a million moments I can never get back. It upsets me that I was a lousy father. You deserved better than that. But as for your virginity . . . I guess I just assumed that you were active by now. So no, that doesn't upset me."

"OK."

"Are you crying again?"

"A little."

"You don't have to decide today."

"I don't want to decide. I want someone else to decide for me."

"What does the, um, father say?"

"There is no father, because there's no baby. Just a cluster of cells that, left to its own devices, might turn into one."

"OK. So you don't feel the need to tell him."

"Look at you, identifying with the father. Seriously?"

"You just said there is no father."

"There isn't. It's an immaculate cluster."

"I'm not identifying with anyone. I'm just trying to keep up."

"Well, try harder. Hey! Where are you going?"

"I'm going to get another ice-cream cone. You want one?"

"Two ice-cream cones in one sitting? Seriously? What's your cholesterol like?"

"It's a special occasion, right?"

"Yeah. I'm going to go now."

"Did I say something wrong?"

"Well, in your defense, there is no right thing to say."

"Will you let me help you?"

"I might. Maybe you already have. I don't know. I have to go be by myself and process all of this."

"If you decide on an abortion, I'll take you, OK?"

"There you go, stumping for the abortion again."

"I'm just saying, if you don't want to involve your mom and Rich."

"Yeah, it would suck for you if Rich got to take me."

"I'm sorry I offered."

"Don't be. I'd have written you off for good if you didn't."

"Then why are you giving me shit for it?"

"Because you deserve shit, Dad. Because you're a shitty father, and just because you get to bail me out of this now, that doesn't change anything."

"So I do get to bail you out?"

"I was speaking hypothetically. In the event that you do."

"I understand. Can I at least drive you home?"

49

"You don't have a car."

"I use Jack's."

"It's OK. I have my own wheels."

"Since when?"

"Mom and Rich got me a G35 for my graduation."

"That was nice of them."

"Mom's still compensating for you. I milk it a little."

"I would. Can I ask you something?"

"Sure."

"Why'd you come to me?"

"Really?"

"Yeah."

"I care less about letting you down."

CHAPTER 7

When she's gone, he sits there, gutted like a fish. Casey has always been like that, so quick with the blade that only after she's gone does the blood start to flow. They'd been sitting in Champs, the small coffee/ sundry shop shoehorned into a kidney-shaped alcove in the back of the lobby. The shop is run by Pearl, a buxom Hungarian widow in her fifties who applies her makeup with a paintbrush and whose every move is punctuated by the rustle of nylons rubbing together and the Christmas jingle of a thousand golden bangles.

"Your daughter," Pearl says in her almost comically accented English as she re-arranges the inventory of headache remedies behind the counter. Aspirin is a big seller at the Versailles.

"Yes."

"Beautiful girl. Nice legs. She's going to get herself in trouble with those legs. My

Rafi, he was more of a tit man." She pauses to indicate her own massive cleavage, bolstered by an unseen system of pulleys and straps that must have long since carved permanent tracks into her back. "But fashions change. Now it's all about skinny girls with the legs. You better watch out. A boy sees those legs, all he thinks about is spreading them. Right?"

"I'll watch out."

She shrugs. "Nothing you can do. Kids going to do what they want, right?"

"Right."

Through a quirk they could never trace, instead of calling him "Daddy," Casey called him "My Daddy" when she first learned to speak. He can see her now, marching joyously across his and Denise's bed in nothing but her diaper, her small, round belly poking out like the world's tiniest beer gut, saying "My Daddy!" over and over again, her high, excited voice pealing with laughter when he made a grab for her ankles.

"Hey, Silver. You okay?" Pearl asks him.

Even if he could suck in enough oxygen to speak, he would have no idea how to answer.

He has lost so many things: his wife, his

52

home, his dignity, and, most famously, his job as drummer and co-songwriter for the Bent Daisies. Pat, Ray, Danny, and he had begun playing together after high school; punk, post-punk, and then something a bit more full-throated, skating up to the edge of pop. They played the rock clubs up and down the East Coast, cutting demos whenever they could scrape the money together for studio time.

Silver couldn't remember a time he hadn't been drumming. His mother always said she'd been able to feel him banging out beats in her womb. When he was four, he built himself a drum set out of buckets and boxes, setting it up next to his father's stereo speakers, and he would drum along to the Beatles and Crosby, Stills & Nash using chicken skewers. They bought him a drum set when he was six, and started him on drum lessons, figuring he'd move on to something else within a few years. But the drums, it turned out, was the single lifelong commitment Silver would make. When he sat behind his kit all the restless parts of him — his throbbing legs, his fluttering heart, his racing mind — all came together under one unifying rhythm. It wasn't something he understood consciously, but drumming was the only time Silver was at rest.

After Casey was born, there was a noticeable change in Silver's songwriting. His ballads became grittier, more passionate. He was seeing the world differently. The Bent Daisies began to mature, and the roving A&R guys they'd been meeting for years took note. A year or so later, they were finally signed, in a small deal with a major label. Their first single, "Rest in Pieces," rode one of those perfect accidental waves up the charts, and they were international rock stars for a few weeks, as these things go. Long enough to taste it and never forget.

Then Pat McReedy came down with a fatal case of front man's disease and decided he would do better with a solo career. The three remaining Daisies, Danny Baptiste, Ray Dobbs, and Silver met for drinks to decide their next move, but they could see the truth in each other's eyes. The only thing worse than not having your dream come true is having it come true for a little while. Ray moved down South to work for his brother-in-law and they never heard from him again. Silver still ran into Danny on gigs once in a while — they overlapped in some of the same wedding orchestras — where they would share a rueful grin, a lazy man-hug, and would occasionally, when the band heated up, throw old familiar riffs at each other that no one else could hear.

It would have been easier to swallow, he suspected, if Pat had crashed and burned, as they all expected (hoped) he would. But years later Pat is still out there in Los Angeles, winning Grammys and sleeping with movie stars, and Silver's only consolation is the shrinking residual check he still gets every month for "Rest in Pieces," which sadly remains his greatest source of income, his orchestra gigs and professional masturbation notwithstanding. Publicly, Danny and Silver wish Pat well. Quietly though, at gigs, when they've had enough from the open bar to loosen their tongues, they are not above expressing the sincere hope that Pat is, right at that moment, snorting that fatal cut of blow off some model's ass, or sliding the business end of a shotgun past his pouty, front-man lips to the back of his throat. If Pat did kill himself, they'd both find it in themselves to say generous things when the VH1 film crew showed up.

Tonight he is playing a wedding with the Scott Key Orchestra. Silver slaps away at his kit, pretty much on autopilot, ignoring the one or two drum geeks that always stand on the side to watch. Every so often at these things, someone figures out who he is and he draws a slightly bigger crowd, but after a while they all come to realize that there's nothing any more exciting about watching a once-famous drummer than any other drummer, and they go back to their arugula salads and filet mignon entrees.

They are seven pieces and two backup singers tonight. You do this long enough, it isn't even music anymore, just trained monkeys being put through their paces. Scott stands at the mike, singing "The Way You Look Tonight" with too much lounge lizard lilt in his voice, compressing the lyrics and stretching the odd vowel for effect, and you just have to be thankful that Sinatra isn't alive to hear it. Baptiste grins at Silver and rolls his eyes. Silver nods back and tosses in an offbeat fill that throws Scott, who misses his mark. Scott turns to glare at Silver, who smiles vacantly, playing dumb. Baptiste laughs. We are all losers, Silver thinks, each in his own way.

Once in a while, after a gig, he can get laid. If he hasn't sweated too much, if he is wearing the larger tux, the one that manages to streamline his gut, if they've played a good set and the energy is up and there has been ample time for bar breaks, so that everyone in the band is feeling happier than their personal realities would normally dictate, if all of that has happened, then there are backup singers, dance motivators, waitresses. It all turns on a complex sliding scale of how badly everyone doesn't want to go home.

Dana is one of the backup singers. It takes Silver three trips to load his drums into the back of Jack's car, and when he's done, Dana is still smoking in the parking lot. She is thirty-five or so, and a knockout at fifty feet; slender, with great legs and a luxurious mane of auburn hair. Only up close do you see how tired her eyes are, and a hardness in her features that has set in over time as life failed to live up to her expectations. One of life's unassailable truths is that no one sets out to be a backup singer.

She takes off her shoes in his car. She's been standing and swaying in six-inch heels for six hours. As he wordlessly steers them to the Versailles, she puts her feet up on the dash and cracks the window, her hair fluttering wildly around her. He can see in her profile the cheerleader she once was, the homecoming queen. There was a time when she had the world on a string; friends, the quarterback, and whatnot. Now she is going home with the fat marching-band geek just to feel alive, or at least less lonely.

Maybe she doesn't see it that way though, because if she did, she'd wait until the car had gathered enough speed, then throw open the door and hurl herself onto the thundering blacktop.

Once in his apartment, Silver rejoices invisibly. He has not had sex in quite some time, and getting them through the door is half the battle. He takes a quick shower, tending to his nethers with a bit more care than usual. Once out, he overapplies his deodorant and attempts to make sense of his untamable mess of hair. When he emerges, in boxers and T-shirt, she is lying on his bed, still in her short black dress, aimlessly channel surfing. She takes slow sips of the whiskey she's poured herself, absently sucking the lone ice cube into her mouth then dropping it back into her drink again. In the blue light of the television she is beautiful again, and he experiences a surge of affection that has no place in these utilitarian proceedings. Although he's known her for a while, he knows nothing about her. For instance, he made up the part about her being a cheerleader. For all he knows, she wore a scoliosis brace and stuttered.

She rolls into him as he lies down beside her, either voluntarily or because the mattress has shifted under his weight, and rests her head on his shoulder, her hair tickling his chin. He closes his eyes to inhale her shampoo, falling briefly but deeply in love even as he knows that tomorrow, in the light of day, he will have trouble making eye contact with her.

"You smell nice," she says, her sung-out voice just above a whisper. "Like autumn."

"Irish Spring."

He watches her chest rise and fall with her breath, the soft roundness of her breasts gathering at the top of her dress, and he can feel things starting to stir down below. Then she turns her head to look up at him, and he could cry from the desolation in her eyes.

"Is it okay if we just lie here for a bit?" she says.

Not really, no. "Sure."

Teenage vampires skulk on cable. Outside, a truck horn blares. He watches Dana's toes as they curl against his comforter and experiences what might be best described as homesickness, but he'll be damned if he knows what or where it is that he's missing. Tomorrow morning, with the skies still pink from the inevitability of sunrise, he will drive her back to the catering hall, where her small car will be sitting marooned in

the vast empty lot like something lost, waiting to be claimed. The sight of it will sad-
den both of them in ways they couldn't
begin to explain.

CHAPTER 8

"When was the last time you emptied this fridge?" his mother, Elaine, says, holding a plastic covered tin of what looks like congealed brain at arm's length.

"I don't know, last week maybe?"

"I don't think so," she says, tossing the container into the garbage. Once the fridge is cleaned to her satisfaction, she will fill it with fruits and vegetables that will slowly go bad until her next visit.

"Please, Mom, you don't have to do that."

"I don't mind."

Elaine disappears into the fridge, leaving his father and him to make small talk.

"You getting enough gigs?" his father says.

"Yeah."

"That's good."

"How are things at the temple?"

"The God business is pretty much recession-proof."

"If it wasn't, that would raise some pretty

interesting theological questions."

"Would it?"

Someday his father will be gone, and Silver will still be able to have these conversations, word for word, from memory.

His father, Ruben Silver, is the rabbi of Temple B'nai Israel. When Silver was a boy, he and his younger brother, Chuck, would sit up on the stage with their father during the Sabbath services, facing the congregation. Silver would pretend that his father was their king, and he and Chuck their esteemed princes. Ruben would sing along with the cantor — he had a gruff but melodic voice — and he would put his arm around his boys, pointing to random Hebrew words in the *siddur,* which they would dutifully read aloud to him. At some point, as his encroaching maturity bred a certain self-consciousness, Silver stopped sitting up there with them, he can't remember exactly when. It wasn't something they ever talked about. It was just one of those things you quietly outgrow and only realize it after the fact.

His father whistles "Penny Lane."

"Whistling," Elaine says unconsciously. He stops. They've been married for forty-seven years.

Ruben knows many other songs, but if he's whistling, it's "Penny Lane." For all Silver knows, he's been doing it ever since *Magical Mystery Tour* came out. The first time Ruben heard the song, the opening bars wrapped themselves around his cerebral cortex and that was that.

They come by every other Sunday, Elaine and Ruben, because he is their son and they love him, and because they think he's lonely. These visits kill him, because he loves them too, and because he knows his sad little life hurts them, maybe even more profoundly than it sometimes hurts him, which means these visits probably kill them too. So every other weekend they spend an hour or so together that leaves them all depressed and depleted, but they never miss it, and if that's not the best definition of family, then he doesn't know what is.

"So," his father says, somewhat awkwardly, while Elaine is out in the hall on her third or fourth trip to the incinerator. Silver generally refrigerates his Chinese leftovers and subsequently forgets about them until they've congealed into something beyond the help of his microwave. "Any women worth writing home about?"

"Have you gotten any letters from me?" Silver says.

His father shrugs, ignoring his sarcasm. "You should come to temple."

"Dad."

Ruben raises his hands defensively. "I'm not selling. I'm just saying, plenty of single women."

"Are you really pitching temple as a dating service?"

"Best one there is. Do you really think all those people are coming to pray? I pray. The cantor prays. They mingle. Welcome to organized religion."

"And what about God?"

"God doesn't want you to be alone any more than I do."

"I'm trying, Dad."

Ruben nods. "If that's true, I'd hate to see what happens when you stop."

Silver is about to retort, something unnecessarily biting, and so he is relieved when his mother reenters, cutting off the conversation. She looks at them inquisitively, Silver sprawled on the couch, his father perched on the edge of the kitchen table, and can tell she's interrupted something. "What are you boys talking about?"

"Women," Ruben says.

Elaine nods meaningfully. "Any worth writing home about?"

When his parents leave here, they'll swing by Chuck's house for a barbecue. There, amid the aroma of homemade marinade, the shouting of boys and pissing of babies and dogs, life will reassert itself around them, and they will be whole again.

When they leave here, Silver will go down to the Blitz and drink himself numb, then fall asleep in front of the comforting flicker of his television. Hopefully, he'll remember to take off his shoes. There's nothing more depressing than waking up in your shoes.

CHAPTER 9

The Lockwoods had been Casey and Denise's neighbors for about ten years. Denise and Valerie played tennis together twice a week, and once Rich arrived on the scene, he and Steve Lockwood would sometimes sit out in the backyard in the evenings and have a scotch together. Casey, who had lettered in swim, was given carte blanche to swim her laps in the Lockwoods' pool whenever she wanted, which was what she'd been doing on the night in question. She was feeling anxious about Princeton, and she'd always found something soothing about night swimming.

Around fifteen laps in, she realized she was no longer alone. She looked up to see Jeremy Lockwood sitting on one of the lounge chairs, drinking from a silver flask as he watched her swim.

"Hey," he said when she stopped, waving to her with the flask. "Don't stop on my account."

He was two years older, had just gotten back from Emory to work at his dad's firm for the summer.

"I heard you were back," she said, climbing out of the pool. With anyone else, she might have been self-conscious in her bikini, but she'd known Jeremy long enough to have dared each other to show their privates in his basement back in second grade, and so the rules were different.

Casey grabbed a towel and sat down at the foot of his chair. He leaned over to kiss her cheek, a method of greeting he'd picked up in college that still felt a little strange to her. "Look at you," he said appreciatively.

"What?"

"You got hot."

"Shut up."

"I heard you got into Princeton."

"I heard you changed your major."

"I heard you were valedictorian."

"I heard you broke up with Hailey."

"Hadley."

"Well, it doesn't matter now, does it?"

Jeremy smiled and took a sip from the flask. "With moms like ours, who needs Facebook?"

"I know, right?"

He offered her the flask, and she took a

sip. He had filled it with some of his father's scotch. The good stuff, Steve called it, even though to Casey it tasted like acid, burning her throat but warming her belly. When she handed it back, Jeremy took another long swallow.

"She broke up with me, actually."

She looked at his face, trying to determine if he was starting a conversation or just stating a fact. In all the years their families had been friendly, she and Jeremy had never had a serious talk. They were more like cousins than friends.

"I'm sorry," she said.

He shrugged. "It was just sex, anyway. And not even that good, really."

Something in the offhanded way he talked about sex thrilled her. In the booze, the sex talk, the kiss on the cheek, she sensed the ways in which her world would be expanding in a few months. When he passed her the flask, she drank two swallows.

"Easy there, tiger," he said, grinning.

It was, quite suddenly, and for no real reason, a sexy grin.

Jeremy had always been good-looking in a bland, generic way — tall, lean, with thick dark hair that he wore short and unbrushed. Handsome, Casey thought, rather than hot. But now there was an edge to him, something a little darker and jaded, and it occurred to her that if they were strangers, she'd be checking him out. And the steam was rising off the water and swirling in the glow of the pool lights, and the moon was full and low, and Jeremy was giving her this look, maybe, over his whiskey flask, and the whiskey was making her feel flushed and tingly, and suddenly, everything felt electric.

Jeremy told her about his breakup, and Casey told him about hers, and then he showed her Hadley's Facebook page on his iPhone. She wasn't exactly pretty, Hadley, but you could see why guys would think she was hot. Hadley had updated her status to read "blissfully single," and had posted photos of herself partying with all these greasy *Jersey Shore*-looking guys. Jeremy thought the "blissfully" was uncalled for, so they went to Jeremy's page and changed his status to read "Free at last." It was Casey's idea to add a picture of him and her canoodling. Hadley and Jeremy were still Facebook friends, and she'd have no idea that Casey was just his neighbor. So they started clowning around, doing a whole photo shoot with his phone, and somewhere in there Jeremy took off his shirt, and his skin was hot against hers, like the scotch in her stomach, and a few minutes later they were making out like there was no tomorrow. And somewhere in there, when they were coming up for air, gasping and grinding against each other, he mentioned that his parents were away for the weekend.

And the moon, the hot summer air, this boy she'd known for her entire life, it all just felt right to her. And so, when the moment of decision arrived and he pulled back a little to say *Are you sure,* she reached down decisively, sliding her hand between the slick wetness of their crotches, grabbed hold of him, and guided him into her.

Afterward they skinny-dipped and horsed around in the pool, the moonlight bathing them in a silvery hue, and she thought to herself that she couldn't have planned a better way to lose her virginity if she'd tried.

CHAPTER 10

Sad Todd is in the lobby, trying to get his twin boys to simmer down. They are five-year-old terrors with flaming red hair and plastic lightsabers, which they are swinging wildly as they jump on and off one of the leather lobby couches. They have spent the weekend mainlining all the sugared crap that is forbidden in their mother's house, the cereals and ice cream and soda and candy that Sad Todd stocks his shelves with so that they'll love him back. And so now they run circles around their hapless dad, performing dropkicks off the couch, clambering up and down the two stairs that bisect the lobby into two levels, caroming off passersby, and knocking over the potted ficus trees that grudgingly stand in every unfurnished corner. They bounce frenetically around the room like a couple of Jedi houseflies, standing still only long enough for everyone to see their unbrushed hair, mismatched shirts, and the white stains on their faces that Todd will try to pass off to his ex-wife as milk, but which are obviously the remnants of the boxful of powdered doughnuts they had for dinner.

They call him Sad Todd because he has been living in the Versailles for more than two years and no one has ever seen him smile. He has still not bought a stick of furniture or hung a picture in his apartment, has not been on a date or made a friend. He suffers from what Jack refers to as Little Orphan Annie syndrome. He still believes his family is going to come for him one day, so there's no point in getting comfortable.

It's Sunday evening, and Sad Todd looks like something so much more than exhausted. He is unshaven, unkempt, and borderline suicidal. He has brought the twins down to the lobby well in advance of their mandated pickup time, probably because they've already laid waste to his apartment and he didn't know what else to do.

"This could be the day that Sad Todd finally snaps," Jack says, his voice conveying that unique mixture of sympathy and contempt they all feel for one another here.

"Someone should buy that man a coke

habit," Oliver says, nodding sadly.

It's Sunday evening, and they are on their way out to have dinner and too many drinks at the Blitz, a rundown sports bar on Route 9 famous for its overstuffed burgers and its absurdly attractive waitresses. Sunday nights are particularly depressing; you either didn't have your kids for the weekend and you feel lost and alone, or you had your kids and now they're gone and you feel exhausted and inadequate. Either way, drinks and ogling are called for and, this being America, both are within walking distance. Jack, as usual, is overdressed, in a black blazer and dress shirt, taking his cues from whatever he last saw George Clooney wearing. Oliver is wearing inadvisable cargo pants and a baseball cap. Silver would like to think he falls somewhere in between, in jeans and a dark knit polo shirt, but next to Jack, he just fades into the background like a passing extra.

Out in the driveway, Jack and Oliver sit down at the edge of the fountain to smoke cigars, which is more complicated than it sounds. First, Oliver takes two tin tubes out off his shirt pocket and cracks the seals. Then Jack pulls out a little guillotine and studies the cigars, under Oliver's watchful eye, making sure to circumcise them properly. All the while, Oliver prattles on about where he got these particular cigars, about their relative superiority to certain other cigar brands, about their overall relevance in the cigar world, if you will. This never fails to prompt Jack to tell one of his Best-Cigars-I-Ever-Smoked stories, complete with names, dates, and locations that mean nothing to anyone else, while Oliver lights up with the blue jet from his monogrammed butane lighter and Silver tears his hair out, going quietly insane with boredom.

Cigars are all the rage these days, on both sides of the marital divide. The married men smoke them to somehow feel less fenced in by their lives, the divorced men smoke them to stave off the encroaching desolation on sad Sunday evenings, and neither group can shut up about it. Because of a tossed salad of latent Freudian inadequacy issues, middle-aged men will perform fellatio on a clump of cured leaves and somehow feel more like men because of it, which, if nothing else, is a colossal triumph of marketing. And you would think that, phallic or not, a habit that involves plugging your mouth would be a quieter affair, but you would be wrong.

Great works are written and empires crumble in the time it takes for these two to finish with the cigar bullshit, so they are all still there in the driveway to witness the arrival of Sad Todd's ex-wife, who pulls up in a silver minivan. She is a drab sliver of a woman, with paper-thin lips and the harried expression of someone who has long since resigned herself to being the only competent person on the planet. She inspects the twins while haranguing Todd at the same time.

Look at them! They're a wreck! How can you let them out of your apartment like this? Is that powder on their faces? You gave them doughnuts? Did it occur to you to bathe them, even once in three days? Jesus Christ, Todd, I could leave them at a kennel and they'd be better cared for!

Sad Todd does not respond. He stands there with his head bowed, absorbing the abuse like a tree in a storm. When she finishes chewing him out, she shakes her head for a moment, then leans in and straightens his folded collar, and, to Silver's great surprise, gives him a quick peck on the cheek before getting back into her minivan and driving off. Love, Silver thinks. The twins wave to their father from the back window of the van, and Sad Todd stands in the middle of the driveway, waving back absently until they turn a corner, his face twisted with a grief so raw that Silver has to look away.

He loved a girl named Megan Donahue. She had a tiny waist, feline eyes, and was a passionate vegetarian. They wrote each other long love letters, citing proofs from the lyrics of lesser-known rock bands, which they would slip into each other's lockers. When she wore white turtleneck sweaters, the fuzzy kind, she looked like Christmas morning. They were seventeen, juniors in high school, both virgins, and she was the first person he said "I love you" to. Actually, what he said was, "I love you, too," but that's just semantics. They were doomed by the endocrine system. His hormones, which were doing all of the heavy lifting back then, would not be denied. She wanted to stay a virgin every bit as much as he didn't. Or maybe he just wanted to enjoy a burger now and then without being made to feel like a murderer.

CHAPTER 11

Lily is wearing a gray hooded sweatshirt today, with shadows where the letters of her alma mater used to be ironed on. It's the kind of sweatshirt she would have worn endlessly in those first years after college — maybe it belonged to a former boyfriend and for a while had retained his scent. Silver imagines her back then, sitting in a small apartment, listening to music that brought her back, and absently pulling at the ironed-on letters until they came loose and had to be pulled off. There's a metaphor in there, he thinks. Maybe even a song. But it's been years since he wrote a song, and he knows that his creative impulses have been worn down to just that, impulses. The idea of actually writing something now is so alien to him that he can't remember what it even felt like when he could.

Lily sings songs about birds and bugs and rain and cars and John Jacob Jingleheimer

Schmidt. When the little kids sitting around her on the floor sing along, she closes her eyes and smiles, banging the strings of her guitar with the flat of her hand to generate percussion. When she hits the high notes, they buzz like static in his ear, his tinnitus deeply sensitive to the upper registers. This gig can't pay very much at all, Silver thinks, watching, as always, from a safe distance. She either does it because she enjoys working with kids, or because she's that broke, and while both scenarios are appealing to him, he hopes it's the latter, because he doesn't do well with nurturers. He could not say what it is he finds attractive about her — maybe it's her coltish grace and her open expression, or maybe it's the way her voice emanates from her, clear, thin, and waveringly melodic; he hears a sweetness in it that he thinks reflects her personality.

All of which is rendered completely moot by his utter inability to so much as make eye contact with her. He watches as she packs up her guitar, collects her check from one of the two hyperathletic lesbians who own the bookstore, and heads for the door. She will walk right past him, and their eyes will meet briefly, as always, before she dismisses him in much the same way he probably appears to dismiss her.

He has always been somewhat shy when it comes to approaching women. Alcohol helps, but they don't tend to serve it in bookstores, and he doesn't think a flask at three in the afternoon would do much to enhance whatever appeal he might still possess. He watches Lily stopping to thumb through a magazine on her way out, and he cannot come up with a thing to say, a single conversational gambit, that won't feel like he is coming on to her. To approach a strange woman is to reveal your intentions before the first word has been spoken, and he has always found such transparency to be paralyzing.

He has been alone for so long now. He has nothing to lose, and everything to gain. She might be lonely too. He's pretty sure she is, he can hear it in her singing. Maybe she'd welcome the conversation, the possibility of possibility. Maybe it would change both of their lives. The risk of a quick rejection should be insignificant in the face of all of that. But somehow, it isn't. And as he watches her leave the bookstore, the bells on the door ringing as it swings shut, he decides it's simply another facet of the same general malaise that has informed the countless wrong turns that have shaped his life.

CHAPTER 12

Casey's Infiniti is white, with dark seats that fill the air with the smell of new leather. The drums and bass coming from her stereo are as smooth as the ride, and they throb softly beneath his skin, just like they should. It is a thing of beauty, this car of his daughter's, and Silver tries not to think about the fact that it was bought for her by the man who isn't her father but who does a much better job of it.

The thing about living alone is that it gives you a lot of time to think. You don't necessarily reach any conclusions, because wisdom is largely a function of intelligence and self-awareness, not time on your hands. But you do become very good at thinking yourself into endless loops of desperation in half the time it would take a normal person. So, sitting there in her car, as the Japanese engine thrums along with more horsepower than any teenage girl could ever possibly need, his dark thoughts rise up and fan out before him at record speed.

He thinks about the fact that the lives of everyone close to him seem to improve dramatically once they leave him behind. Denise found herself a better husband, Casey a better father, Pat McReedy a better career. He is a stepping-stone to a better life. No, that would imply that he somehow helped. He is the nonessential ballast that you toss out of the plane to achieve flight.

He looks over at Casey, who is humming along lightly to the ridiculous, mechanical song on the radio. Fucking Auto-Tune. She still looks so young to him; too young to have been through what he and Denise put her through, too young for this $40,000 car, and too young to be driving to an abortion clinic with her poor excuse of a father riding shotgun, only because she loves her mother too much to involve her in this sad and tawdry business.

Early Intervention is in a corporate park off I-95, just a few miles north of Elmsbrook. Their sign, a simple "E.I." set against a pink clover-shaped background, is discreet and strangely cheerful. Casey parks and they walk through a small outdoor plaza where corporate smokers have ritualistically gathered, greedily inhaling their first- and secondhand smoke.

"Do you like my car?"

"Sure. It's a great car."

"What? I said, 'Did I lock the car?' "

"Oh. I don't remember."

She gives him a funny look. "Are you OK there, Silver?"

He wishes she would call him Dad.

"Sure."

He doesn't think he's ever told her about the tinnitus. Right now it is ringing like a siren in his ears, wrapping her voice in a fuzzy static shell.

"You look a little . . . off."

"I'm fine. I'm just having some ear issues."

She looks at him for another moment, then jogs back across the plaza holding out her keychain until she is in range to lock it. As he watches her run, something in his chest catches, and with no preamble, a short, guttural sob bursts forth from his mouth. A random memory: It's a snowy evening and Denise, Casey, and he are walking back from somewhere, he doesn't remember where. Casey is running ahead, up the slope to the front door of the small Cape Cod they bought, somewhat impulsively, a few years earlier when Denise told him she was pregnant. Casey, two and a half feet high, lifts her knees like a soldier, marching around in the snow with unfettered delight. "She's beautiful, isn't she," Denise says. He looks at Denise, her hair glittering in a crown of dissolving snowflakes, and in that moment he is more in love than he's ever been; with this woman, with this little girl, with this family they've made. Casey's tiny boot prints surround them, and as she squeals with delight, he thinks to himself, This is the most perfect moment I will ever know.

"Silver?"

She is back, smiling uncertainly at him.

"You sure this is what you want?" he says, not because he sees an alternative but because it just feels like the kind of thing that, in hindsight, you'll need to know you said.

"Do you have a better idea?"

"No."

"I'm early enough that they can use the aspiration method, which is basically the equivalent of inducing a period. There's no pain and no recovery. I won't feel a thing."

"OK."

"And this will stay our little secret, right?"

"Right."

He has to admit, it feels good to share a

secret with her.

"Thanks."

"For what?"

"For not telling me I'm an idiot for having unprotected sex."

"I guess I thought that was obvious."

She laughs. Neither of them has made a move toward the front door of the clinic yet.

"Have you had a lot of sex?" he says.

She is momentarily surprised by the question, but seems to welcome it. "This was my first time."

"Shit."

"Yeah."

"How was it?"

She takes a long time to answer. "It was actually very lovely," she says, and then bursts into tears.

There aren't a lot of forms to fill out, since E.I. doesn't take insurance. And Casey wouldn't have used insurance anyway, since she wants no explanation of benefits showing up in Denise's mailbox. The price of an early intervention turns out to be six hundred and twenty-eight dollars. He supposes a round number would seem equally odd. He's brought the cash with him, reducing his checking account roughly by half and giving the whole enterprise a whiff of the illicit. After paying, he joins Casey in a small private waiting room furnished with two leather couches, a water cooler, and two end tables covered with pamphlets, all trying to put a happy face on the situation.

Casey grabs a pamphlet and reads aloud to him. " 'The entire procedure takes less than ten minutes. Cramping during the procedure is tolerable, and only lasts for a few minutes. There is no recovery period. Women leave the office ready to resume their everyday activities.' "

"Sounds great," he says. "Why doesn't everyone do it this way?"

"You have to be between five and ten weeks. After that, you have to go hard-core."

They sit in companionable silence for a few moments. He leans back on the couch and closes his eyes, experiencing a sudden, crushing wave of unearned exhaustion.

"Can you tell me something?" Casey says.

"What?"

"Anything. Just talk to me until they're ready."

"I don't know what to talk about."

"Are you lonely?"

"Right now?"

"In general."

"I don't know. Sometimes."

"Do you have a girlfriend?"

"No."

"A fuck buddy?"

"I did bring a woman home the other night."

"Go, Silver. How was it?"

"She just wanted to be held."

"Oh, well."

"It's OK. Sex isn't always what it's cracked up to be . . ."

"He said to his pregnant daughter in the waiting room of the abortion clinic."

Silver smiles. Despite his best efforts, she has emerged as a bright, witty, beautiful, and largely well-adjusted kid. Sometimes when he is with her, the sense of what he's lost is powerful enough to flatten his lungs, which may be why he's been so bad about being around in the years since the divorce.

The room is too warm, even sitting right beneath the central air vent, and the ringing in his left ear has reached the point where it is starting to crackle like a fire. He holds his breath and presses his palms to his ears, emitting a low hum from deep in his throat to counteract the whine in his ears. After a few moments, the whine recedes and then, to his surprise, it fades altogether. Blessed silence explodes across his head.

"Dad!"

She called me Dad, he thinks.

He opens his eyes to find Casey standing over him, looking panicked.

"What's wrong?" she says.

He opens his mouth to tell her he's fine, just a little tired. He can feel the words forming in his throat, but nothing comes out. Casey disappears for a second then returns with a middle-aged woman in a white doctor's coat.

"Mr. Silver?" she says. "Can you hear me?"

"Of course I can hear you," he says, and moves to stand up. But nothing happens. He can't feel his limbs, can't move his lips, can't make a sound. He closes his eyes for a second. He can't get over how quiet it is in his head, no buzzing at all. He hasn't heard silence like this in years. He wants to wrap it around himself like a blanket and weep with relief.

When he opens his eyes again, he's in the hospital.

CHAPTER 13

If there's a good thing about waking up in a hospital it's that, even with your brain still flickering like a loose bulb, it takes only the faintest germ of lucidity to figure out where you are. The beep of the heart monitor, the smell of industrial disinfectant, the overly starched sheets, and your wife sitting in the chair beside you.

Ex-wife.

Right.

Denise is squinting into her magazine in much the same way she used to squint at him, peering into his workings like a mechanic trying to find the frayed wire, the loose connection responsible for his host of malfunctions. This sense memory of her habitual contempt serves as a toehold for his short-term memory, which doesn't so much come back as reveal itself to have been there all along, temporarily camouflaged against the sandy texture of his brain.

Denise looks up from her magazine. "You're up."

She doesn't look terribly concerned, which might be a good sign or might be because she doesn't particularly give a shit either way. His death, at this point, wouldn't have much in the way of ramifications for her. Or anyone else, really. This realization is enough to get him to close his eyes and try to reconnect with dreamless oblivion. He hears the high-pitched wail of dry hinges, and then footsteps.

"Dad?"

He opens his eyes to see Casey standing over his bed, holding a bottle of Diet Coke with a chewed straw sticking out of it.

You called me Dad.

"Can you talk?"

I'm fine, Casey.

She turns to Denise, alarmed. "Why can't he talk?"

Denise leans over him and says, loudly, "Silver, can you talk?" like he is a three-year-old. She used to talk to the Mexican gardeners like that too.

Of course I can talk. This is me, talking.

Denise stands up and positions her face right in front of his. "Blink if you can understand me."

What the fuck, Denise?

90

"I'm going to get Rich," Casey says, running out of the room.

"You're OK," Denise tells him, but she's looking at him with that old familiar gaze, the one that says that, to no one's great surprise, you've gone and shit the bed again.

They met at his cousin Bruce's wedding. She wasn't the most beautiful bridesmaid, that was Andrea Lumane, whose plum-colored gown clung to her like shrink wrap, and whom the photographers followed around the reception as much as they did the bride herself. Neither was Denise the runner-up. That honor went to Hannah Reece, who could have sailed through on her unassailable cleavage alone. But Denise was a strong third place, maybe a bit plain-looking, but her soft features had a certain understated elegance, and her smile was full and honest. She seemed like someone who could laugh at herself, which was a trait he looked for in the women he attempted to date. It made it less likely that they would laugh at him.

So he downed a few shots to tranquilize his innate introversion, fixed his wild mane of hair as best he could, popped a breath mint, and then boldly sat down in the empty seat beside her.

"You look like you could be having a better time," he said.

She had been a bridesmaid one too many times, and was drinking more than she generally did, more than he would ever see her drink again. She was tipsy, funny, and he knew, within the first ten minutes of talking to her, the way a man knows only when a woman lets him, that if he listened and nodded sympathetically, and danced all the slow dances with her, that she'd let him be the one to peel off that ridiculous dress when the wedding was over. The reception was at the Hilton, and for the sake of convenience, she had booked herself a room for the night, which meant no car ride during which she might sober up and reconsider.

So they danced, and he made her laugh with his moves, and refreshed her drink just the right amount to maintain her buzz without crossing over to staggering drunkenness, and a few hours later, after only some minor awkwardness, they were in her hotel room, where she fucked him with a drunken energy that bordered on anger before passing out facedown on his belly. And seeing her like that, vulnerable and spent, awoke something in him, and he studied the graceful slope of her spine down

92

to the roundness of her ass, the smoothness of her skin, the way her small breasts held their own in pretty much any position, and he decided that hers was a beauty that revealed itself in stages, and congratulated himself on discovering it and getting laid at the same time.

He had planned to leave in the morning before she woke up, but by the time he opened his eyes she was already in the shower, and it seemed inexcusably rude to leave while she was there, somehow not at all the same as her waking up to find him gone, although he couldn't have said why. So he stayed for breakfast, and she told him she was getting her real estate license, and he told her about his band, and he was inordinately touched by the fact that she wasn't bemoaning their night together and saying things like "I never do this" or "I was so wasted," which he would have taken personally. So sex led to a relationship, and the relationship led to a marriage, and the marriage to a baby, and only after it was too late did he realize the die had been cast all because she woke up before him, and that he'd fallen for her largely because she didn't regret sleeping with him. Which, in time, she most definitely would.

CHAPTER 14

The doctor who tells him he is going to die is the same man who will be marrying his ex-wife in two and a half weeks, which is either poetically just, or at least the sort of karmic fart that is emblematic of his life these days.

Rich Hastings is a tall, thin man, with a narrow face and bushy eyebrows that offset his receding hairline and make him look like a thoughtful owl. He is the one who bought Casey her car and will be paying her college tuition. He has not only replaced Silver as husband and father to his own family, but clearly fills that role better than Silver ever could. And yet Silver finds it impossible to dislike him, and not for lack of trying. He has expended no small amount of energy trying to cultivate a healthy disdain for Rich. But there is just something too innocent about him, something that defies cynicism. Also, he just seems to like Silver so damn much, and that is a rare trait indeed. And even now, as Rich tells him he is going to die, Silver can't find it in himself to resent him.

"You have an aortic dissection," Rich says, his voice low and grave.

"I don't know what that means." Silver's ability to speak has returned, although the words still sound a bit funny to him, alien, hanging in the air until they lose their meaning.

Rich holds up his scans, not so much to show him the colorful nonsense as to hide behind it.

"There's a tear in the inner wall of your aorta."

"Well, that can't be good."

"It's not." Rich puts down the papers. "Your blood rushes into the tear, filling the wall, causing the layers of your aorta to separate and expand. This is also called a dissecting aneurysm."

"Don't people die of aneurysms?"

"Yes, they do. But you caught a break here. The TIA tipped off the ER doctors, who did an MRI and found the dissection."

"Rich."

"Yes?"

"You have to stop speaking doctor."

"Shit, I'm sorry, Silver." And he is. The

95

remorse cuts deep furrows in his wide forehead, making his eyebrows flex like caterpillars. When Casey was little, Silver would read a book to her about a caterpillar. The caterpillar would eat its way through fruits and vegetables and, ultimately, through the hard pages of the book. Casey found it hysterical. Silver never really got it, but he loved the unfettered way she laughed.

"A TIA is a transient ischemic attack. A ministroke. It's why you briefly lost the ability to speak."

"Oh."

"The blood running into the tear has distended your aorta, which can sometimes cause small clots to form. When those clots break off and get up into your brain, they can impair various functions."

Silver takes a minute to absorb this news. He imagines his aorta, like an unspooled garden hose, bent and torn. It feels right to him.

"So, am I going to die?"

"No!" Rich says emphatically. He gets to his feet. "We caught this in time. You need emergency surgery, but when we're done you'll be good as new."

"Just like that."

"Well, I don't mean to minimize the risks

of surgery, but you're young and healthy —"

"I have an aneurysm. I just had a mini-stroke. I don't feel healthy."

"Well, yes, obviously. What I meant was, you're a perfect candidate for the surgery. I'd like to operate first thing tomorrow morning."

"You'd be the one operating?"

"Yes." He considers Silver for a moment. "Would that be an issue for you? If it is, I could refer —"

"No."

"You sure?"

"I wouldn't want anyone else."

"I'm glad to hear it."

"If I was having the surgery. Which I'm not."

That shocks Rich, almost as much as it shocks him. Rich's eyes grow wide with concern. Rich is a good person. Silver would like to punch him.

"Silver, without this surgery, you will die."

"When?"

"That's impossible to predict. But your aorta will ultimately rupture, I guarantee it."

"I understand. Thank you."

"I don't think you do."

"I'm smarter than I look."

Rich looks around the room, at a loss. Without realizing it, he turns in a complete circle, looking for an answer. He wasn't on call today. He has come in for this.

"You have a daughter, Silver."

"And she has you."

Only when he sees Rich shake his head sadly does Silver realize he said it out loud. There is something about being around nice guys that brings out the asshole in him.

"I'm sorry, Rich. I didn't mean it like that."

Rich nods, accepting the apology. "Listen," he says. But Silver can't. He knows Rich is still talking, but his words are congealing into gibberish and fading to background noise. All he can hear is the ringing in his ears, scrambling his brain, and he closes his eyes and disappears into the soft angry noise.

He loved a girl named Emily. A lifeguard. She had wavy dark hair that always looked like she'd just stepped out of a light wind, and the first time they kissed it happened like this. They were in his car, hugging good-night. They had already established a manifesto of reasons why they could not get involved, reasons based largely on geography and chronology that they'd already talked to death. So she kissed his temple, and he kissed her cheek, and then they hugged some more. He could feel her shaking, could feel her smooth face moving against his rougher one, her fingers moving in his hair, their lips sliding along skin until their searching mouths could feign surprise at stumbling upon each other. And then, with gasps and groans, they surrendered to the hot wetness of their bad idea. There were reasons they could never be together, insurmountable obstacles he can't recall anymore, but all they could have were those sweet, urgent, endless kisses, night after night, tormenting him with a perfect, unsullied love he would never be allowed to keep.

CHAPTER 15

He is vaguely aware, over the next few hours, of the quiet bustle of a small crowd swelling and dispersing in the hospital room. His parents are there, perched against the windowsill, quietly watching, as if from the balcony seats. His perfect brother, Chuck, three years younger, moves in and out of the room, distributing snacks and refreshing his parents' coffee. Denise stands out in the hall talking on her cell phone, maybe dealing with final wedding arrangements. And Casey sits alone in the corner, curled up into the only available chair, one leg slung haphazardly over the armrest. She is staring sullenly at him with red eyes and a poker face. He feels the need to apologize to her for something, but then, isn't that how he always feels when he sees her? Still, the general sense he gets is that he has pissed everyone off. Again.

"He's up," Casey says.

Ruben and Elaine perk up. Chuck puts down the packaged sandwich he was about to eat. "Hey," he says. "We were worried about you."

"Why are you here?" Silver says.

Chuck looks concerned. "You're in the hospital," he says, slow and loud, like Silver is an elderly man.

"I know that," Silver says. "I'm just wondering why you're here."

"You're my brother," Chuck says.

Silver shrugs. "We're not really that close."

Chuck looks instantly offended, and Silver wonders to himself why he just said that. But before he can think it through, Denise comes back into the room with Rich in tow. She looks good, Denise, in her simple black sweater and jeans. Even in his benumbed state, he feels a pang, a dull blade scraping him somewhere soft.

"So," she says sternly. "Are you with us, Silver?"

Something is different. He can't isolate it, but everything feels fresher, more immediate. The sound of Denise's voice, the hospital smells, the hum emanating from the fluorescent lights in the fixture above his bed.

"I could use some water," he says.

"You could use some surgery," Denise

101

says. "Tomorrow morning, at eight. I've canceled our dinner plans so that Rich can get a good night's sleep."

"I'll be in top form," Rich says with a smile.

"That was nice of you." Denise is tan, and her skin seems to be glowing in the stark whiteness of the room. Her teeth look whiter than before, and he can't tell if it's the contrast to her tanned skin, or if she maybe had them whitened in anticipation of new wedding photos.

"So, you'll have the surgery?" his mother says.

"No."

Denise snorts and shakes her head, on behalf of the room. "You're being an ass-hole, Silver." To the untrained ear, she might sound pissed, but he can hear the concern in her voice, the residual love that still pisses her off and pathetically warms him.

Casey brings him a plastic cup of ice water. He drinks it down in two greedy gulps and then savors the feeling of a few smaller ice cubes melting against his tongue. He has never really appreciated the way things can melt in your mouth, effortlessly altering states with the heat of your tongue.

He looks at Denise. "Did you have your teeth whitened?"

"What?" she says, blushing through her tan.

Her teeth are white, her skin is tan, and her eyes are bluer than they are in his memories. She's beautiful in a way that hurts.

He notices that everyone in the room is staring at him, their expressions a mix of chagrin and concern, as if they can hear what he was thinking, and that's when he understands that he has said these things out loud.

"What the hell is wrong with you, Silver?"

"I have an aortic dissection."

"No, I mean, why are you saying these things?"

Rich clears his throat. Then he steps over and shines a penlight into Silver's eyes. "He may be having a TIA."

"That's a ministroke," Silver explains to Casey, who is standing beside the bed, looking worried. "Don't worry, honey. I'm fine."

"You're so not fine." Casey.

"Talk some sense into him." Elaine.

"You need this surgery, Silver." Rich.

Silver looks at Denise, who has fallen strangely silent. "I miss having sex with you. The way you would kiss me after you came."

"Holy shit!" Casey.

"Jesus Christ, Silver!" Denise.

"He can't help it." Rich.

"I always figured we'd end up back to-gether." Silver.

"Dad, stop!" Casey says, her eyes filling with tears.

He doesn't know why he's saying these terrible things. Or why it is they're so terrible. Something is different. On some level, he knows he'll regret the things he's said; he may already be regretting them some-where, but something has changed, he doesn't know what it is, and he's powerless against it.

"I'm sorry, Case. I'm sorry for everything. I was a shitty father —"

"Just stop talking!"

"Can't you give him a shot?" Denise.

"His vitals are stable. There's no reason to sedate him." Rich.

"Are you hearing him?!" Denise.

Silver looks at Casey, and now he can feel his own hot tears, running down his face. "I wasn't there for you, and you needed me to be. I wanted to be, but seeing you just hurt so much. I would look at you, and I would just want to be back there, and I couldn't be back there, so it just got easier to stay away."

"Silver, please . . ."

"And now you're all grown up, and my

little girl is gone."

"I'm still here."

"And now you're pregnant."

Casey closes her eyes, mortified. "Fuck, Dad."

She called me Dad, he thinks.

"What?" Denise.

There is a moment of stunned, blessed silence, and then the room explodes.

For a while there is a good deal of crying and yelling, worthless questions and regrettable responses that lead to more yelling. Then, during an accidental lull, Ruben clears his throat in a way that immediately commands attention; you spend enough time up on the pulpit, you develop these tricks. Within moments, he has ushered everyone out of the room and into the hall. He closes the door and pulls the chair over to Silver's bed, then fixes his son with a grave smile, rubbing his small black yarmulke back and forth across his head in a motion so familiar it instantly brings a lump to Silver's dry throat. Then he nods a few times, to Silver, to God himself, maybe.

"So," he says, offering up a strained smile. "At least there's no drama."

"It's all my fault."

"You share some measure of responsibility, yes. But I'd hardly say it's all your fault."

"Everything I've ever had, everything I touch . . ." Silver can't finish the thought. Something about talking to his father is making him emotional.

"They have shrinks upstairs, you know."

"Shit, Dad."

"I'm just saying. You're struggling with a major decision to make here, it might help to talk it out with someone."

"I'm not struggling. I've already made the decision."

"OK then. I'm struggling with your decision."

"Then maybe you should talk to someone."

He smiles. Then he looks at his son, really looks at him, the way people almost never look at each other, with naked love and concern, the way a real father looks at his child. Silver sees the burst capillaries tracking across his father's eyes, the folds of tired skin hanging off his jaw, and he can sense the deep weariness in him. Fifty years in the God business. He has seen some shit. And now this.

"Do you want to die?" Ruben asks, not challenging, just wanting to know.

"No. Not really."

"So what then?"

106

He doesn't want to answer, but he hears the words come anyway. "I'm just not sure I want to live."

Ruben closes his eyes as he absorbs this, then pats his son's leg as he stands. "Fair enough," he says. "I'll leave you to it, then." He moves slowly toward the door, then turns back around. "If my vote counts, I just want to be on record as saying you should have the surgery."

Silver watches him leave, feeling a fresh wave of shame and guilt wash over him. He is a good man and a good father, and I am neither, Silver thinks, wondering, not for the first time, what sort of quiet death his father dies every time he looks at him.

For the record, he only ever attempted suicide once. And it wasn't really an attempt, as far as these things go, more of a flirtation really, a brief dalliance with the concept. This was not long after Denise had kicked him out, and a year or so after Pat had quit the Bent Daisies and gone on to fame and fortune without them. He had no family, no home, no money, and in desperation had just crossed a line he swore he would never cross, and played a bar mitzvah with the Scott Key Orchestra. During the band's scheduled breaks, he drank heavily from the open bar, and then somewhere between the Electric Slide and the reprehensible butchering of Marvin Gaye's "Let's Get It On" it became clear to him that he had fucked up his life beyond repair.

He considered jumping from a bridge or slitting his wrists, but neither method seemed foolproof, and both carried the risk of painful failure, and he'd had just about enough of that, thank you very much. And even if he owned a gun, he wouldn't have trusted himself with it.

So, that night, after the gig, he sat on the floor of his still unfurnished apartment, put the Bent Daisies on his iPod, and began washing down over-the-counter sleeping pills with a half-finished bottle of Hennessy. At some point, he heard himself singing along loudly to "Rest in Pieces," and that's the last thing he remembered until he woke up thirty hours later, his face glued to the wood floor with congealed puke that had hardened like cement. When he finally managed to sit up, he discovered two things: he had shit his pants while he slept, and he had lost the urge to kill himself. It took him a half hour to crawl to the bathroom and get into a shower. Suicide is difficult, but it's nothing compared to the morning after.

■ ■ ■ ■

You lie in a hospital bed for long enough, you start to feel unqualified to walk. Not being qualified for much else, he's not about to let that one go. The linoleum floor is jarringly cold against the soles of his feet, but the air-conditioning feels like a cool breeze on his thighs and ass, exposed where the ends of his flimsy hospital gown don't quite meet. He stands still for a moment, taking stock. Everything feels creaky, but no more than it does when he climbs out of his own bed every morning.

His blood catches him off guard by spurting out of his wrist in a graceful arc when he pulls out the IV needle, painting a small red slash across his hospital gown before he can clamp his other hand onto the hole. Who knew there was so much life in him? He pulls a piece of gauze from a drawer and presses it against his wrist. After a moment, it sticks there.

He pokes his head out of the room and peers down the corridor. They are all gathered in a waiting area at the end of the hall, sitting and standing around two long couches and an easy chair. His perfect brother Chuck's perfect wife, Ruby, has arrived, and is now waiting on Elaine as if there's an inheritance at stake. It's an ungenerous thought. Ruby has never been anything but kind to him, and it's not her fault that kindness is just a different category of poison to him.

"The gang's all here, huh?"

"Hey, Jack."

He has come up quietly behind Silver, waiting to be noticed, a favorite maneuver of his. "What a clusterfuck."

They look down the hall at Silver's ex-wife and her fiancé, his pregnant daughter, his perfect brother and sister-in-law, and his aging parents. They are all here because of him, but they all seem to be getting along just fine without him. History has shown that people generally do.

"Oliver's parking the car," Jack says.

"Tell him to keep it running."

Jack raises his eyebrows and looks Silver over in his hospital gown.

"Are we cutting out?"

"We are."

"Is that wise?"

"No."

Jack shakes his head, then smiles and pulls out his cell phone. "Cool."

CHAPTER 16

In the car, on the way home, Denise cries softly in the front seat. Casey wishes like hell she would stop. She loves her, but Denise's years of being a single mother have forged in her a finely honed martyr complex, and she tends to view everyone else's problems as being there simply to increase her own immeasurable burden.

"Jesus, Mom, will you give it a rest?"

"I'm sorry that my teenage daughter's pregnancy is upsetting to me."

"Have you considered the possibility that it's upsetting to me, too?"

"Of course. I just . . . How could you do this? You know better."

"It was an accident, obviously."

"You accidentally had unprotected sex?"

"Would it make you feel better if I said I was raped?"

"Don't even talk like that."

"I'm just trying to figure out at what point

you might start feeling sorry for me and not yourself."

"I think we all need to take a beat here," Rich says.

"Trust me, I feel very sorry for you," Denise says in a tone that never fails to make Casey contemplate homicide by fire.

"Denise," Rich says quietly.

"Dad handled this much better than you," Casey says, watching as the remark lands like a grenade.

Denise turns around in the front seat to face Casey, her red-rimmed eyes wide with anger. "I'm sure he did. Fucking up is Silver's superpower. He must have been thrilled to see you're a chip off the old block."

"Well, he didn't make it about him, unlike some other people."

"So go live with him. I'm sure the two of you — I'm sorry, the three of you — will be very happy."

Casey presses her forehead against the window and draws a heart with an arrow through it in the fog left by her breath. The people on the sidewalk look impossibly, obnoxiously happy, like they're about to break into a spontaneous musical number.

"We're all upset . . ." Rich tries again.

"Rich!" Denise shouts at him. "For Christ's sake, just shut up and drive!"

CHAPTER 17

He is dying. Maybe. It's a gray area. He spends a few minutes trying to sort through the tangled morass of his crossed thoughts, trying to ascertain how he feels. He doesn't seem to be scared, or even terribly upset. He has regrets, certainly, but he had those when he wasn't dying, too. More than anything, the prevailing emotion seems to be one of relief.

He sits at his desk, surveying his shitty apartment, which consists of two bedrooms, an L-shaped living/dining area, and an exposed kitchen. The dirt-brown area rug is threadbare and stained, the exposed wood in desperate need of scraping and refinishing. The couch facing the television is permanently bowed from where he has spent the majority of the last seven years feeling sorry for himself and self-medicating with beer and television. The only decorations on the walls are a large painting of an oceanic vista in the living room that was left there by the previous tenant for obvious reasons, and a framed photo of him and Casey, taken when she was six years old. She is sitting on his lap, laughing — he'd been tickling her just before Denise shot the picture — and she's small and perfect in her shorts and tank top, and he is slim and still daring to be hopeful and hasn't let her down yet, and it hurts him to look at it so he tends not to. The second bedroom was supposed to be hers. He had painted it pink and bought a Tinker Bell bedspread, but Casey never got into the habit of staying over, and the room eventually became a depository for discarded drum equipment: old stands, cymbals, skins, drum frames, and pedals for which he no longer has any use. He finds it hard to part with these possessions, certain that he will miss them when he's gone. And yes, he's painfully aware of the irony.

His living room windows face Route 9, where at any time of day he can watch the suburban mothers pulling in and out in their minivans, picking up their dry cleaning, shopping at the Korean fruit stores, picking up Chinese or Japanese or Pad Thai. Would the suburbs even be possible without the Asians? And who's going to do it in twenty years, when all of their kids are doctors and hedge-fund managers? The mothers are gone by nightfall, home to serve dinner and do homework and pick up their husbands from the train, and there's always a lull in the action right around sunset, a moment of silence to mark the death of another day. Then Route 9 gets busy again, this time with bands of roving teenagers flipping their skateboards in parking lots and trying to score some beer from the supermarkets and convenience stores, and college kids hitting the garish chain restaurants and bars that come alive at night. He can spend hours just looking out the window, numbing his brain by watching these snatches of quotidian human drama being played out on sidewalks and in parking lots, people relentlessly going about the business of living even as his own life has ground to a complete halt.

He rubs the puncture on his wrist where he pulled out the IV needle and realizes that he is still wearing the plastic hospital bracelet. He tears it off and turns to drop it on the worn oak desk he bought at a yard sale a few years ago from an older couple who were selling their house to move closer to their grown kids and grandchildren. The wife, a petite wisp of a woman, had showed him how each corner of the desk bore a set of initials from each of her four children, who had carved them in themselves years ago. In her mind, this added value. Silver thought it was cause for a discount. They'd settled on seventy-five dollars, and a ride home for the desk and Silver in her husband's pickup truck.

He opens up the top drawer and pulls out a folded piece of paper. It is a printed e-mail, addressed to him.

FROM: Siobhan S.
TO: Silver
RE: Miss you

Just landed back in Galway, and I'm already missing you terribly. I miss your smile, your calm low voice, your skin against mine. The last few weeks were like a dream I wished would never end. I didn't think it was possible to fall in love like this anymore, but I have, and it fills me with joy, and, of course, a deep sorrow that I can't simply pack up and move to the United States to be with you. Between Mum and Isabelle, my place is here right now, just as yours is there. So there's nothing to be done but live for these annual trips, and pray that the time comes soon when our respective situations can allow for something more. Thank you for the best month of my life.

All my love,
Siobhan

He knows the letter by heart. He should; he wrote it. When you live alone, you take certain precautions. He could get hit by a bus, or drown in the pool, or have a sudden heart attack, or, let's say, an aneurysm. It will then fall to his parents to sift through his pitiful belongings, and should that happen, he feels a certain responsibility to make them feel that he wasn't quite as alone as he seemed.

He pulls out a notepad and a pen, then another pen that actually works. He thinks for a moment and then composes a small to-do list for himself.

1. **Be a better father.**
2. **Be a better man.**
3. **Fall in love.**
4. **Die.**

It seems simple enough, and maybe even noble in its simplicity. But it is not without its obstacles. He can devote himself to Casey, and he's pretty sure that dying will take care of itself. It is number two and three that give him pause. They sound good in theory, but with no practical experience, he has no idea where to even begin.

Chapter 18

When you know you're dying, everything comes into focus in a way it never has before. It's like the grimy world has been polished to a sparkling shine, and everything stands out, latching onto your stream of consciousness and sending it in every direction at once, and your brain becomes a puddle of free associations.

He lies in bed, studying his fingernails. He's always assumed they were smooth, but now sees that they're scored with a slew of vertical lines, each forming its own tiny shelf along the face of the nail, like the facet of a diamond. He's been biting them for years, never once noticing how much dimension they have.

The lightbulbs in the standard-issue fixture in the center of his bedroom ceiling actually emit a soft, audible hum that sounds like the first note of the kids singing *"We don't need no education"* in Pink Floyd's

"Another Brick in the Wall." When he was a boy his parents were out and the babysitter, some high school girl from around the corner, was playing that record downstairs on his father's stereo. Lying awake long after he should have been asleep, he imagined that she'd invited over a crowd of friends, that there was a gang of teenagers sitting downstairs in the living room, singing along to the record. He was too young to realize that it was a recording, that the singing kids had English accents . . . The babysitter — he can't remember her name — she had strawberry-blond hair, a smattering of freckles across her nose, and her calves never failed to generate what may have been his very first impure thoughts. . . . He can recall exactly what it felt like to lie in that bed, in his childhood home, the blue-and-red-striped comforter pulled up to his chin, the smell of his freshly vacuumed carpet filling the air with a warmly pleasant mustiness, the Morse code knocks of the radiator, the reassuring creaks of the downstairs hallway as his parents moved around, the soft, comforting hum of their voices, the whippoorwills that woke him in the morning with their plaintive cries of "Theodore," over and over again, the white plastic globe-shaped light fixture that hung in the center

121

of his bedroom, which he was always accidentally hitting with his spinning nunchucks during an extended Bruce Lee phase. . . . Victor Corolla, his next-door neighbor, had taught him how to use the nunchucks. He was three years older, with a speech impediment, a porn collection, and knotty, muscular arms that Silver would have given anything to possess. Vic spun a mean nunchuck, shoplifted baseball cards from the five and dime, and had the first VCR in the neighborhood. He only had two movies, *Star Wars* and *Grease,* and to this day, Silver still knows them both by heart. . . . And, speaking of hearts, he can feel his beating softly against the clasped hands on his chest. He taps out a series of jazz fills on the off beats, and imagines his frayed aorta, tearing microscopically with each beat, its swelled walls slowly expanding to their breaking point like a water balloon.

He rolls out of bed with a new energy — not happy or sad, but attuned to the universe in a way he's never been before.

In the shower, he celebrates the spray of water against his scalp, the winding paths it takes down his chest. He gets lost in the scented lather of his shampoo, in the smoothness of his shoulders, in the logo carved into the Irish Spring soap bar. He watches fondly as his morning erection grudgingly deflates, then closes his eyes and concentrates, the steaming spray penetrating his pores until, after an indeterminate amount of time, the water goes cold.

"There's something wrong with you," Oliver tells him. "Just have the damn operation."

"Take it easy on him," Jack says. "He just got out of the hospital."

"He had no business leaving that hospital."

"You drove him home, dipshit."

"I'd have never done that if you'd told me his condition."

"That was on a need-to-know basis."

"Asshole."

"Shithead."

And around they go. It's a cloudless morning, and they're sitting in their usual spot at the pool, just like always, just as if everything hasn't been turned completely upside down. The inertia of this place has always been disconcerting. Time lurches to a halt, even as they continue to grow older at an alarming rate.

A few chairs over, Ben Eisner, a laid-off investment banker, is rubbing suntan oil across his chest. He was briefly legendary for assaulting his ex-wife's boyfriend with a beer stein when they happened to end up in the same bar one night. But then her lawyers ran with it, and now he's gone into debt trying to regain some measure of custody of his three children, and he's not so legendary anymore. He spends his days either in court or looking for work in an industry that no longer has any, and it's hard to say what gets him out of bed in the morning.

"So," Jack says. "What's your plan?"

"I'm going to go see Casey," he says.

"She mad at you?"

Silver doesn't actually know. He hasn't heard from Casey, or Denise, since he snuck out of the hospital, but that's not indicative of anything since they never call him anyway.

"She's got bigger problems," he says.

"Like what?"

"She's pregnant."

That gets Oliver's attention. "Since when?" he says, sitting up in his chair, his belly fat folding in on itself, becoming a series of smaller, infinity-shaped bellies. We are meat, Silver thinks to himself, that no one wants to eat.

"I don't know. She told me a few days ago."

124

To their left are Eddie Banks and Jon Kessler, both still licking the wounds of fresh divorces. Eddie receives alimony from his wife, who is a stockbroker, and Jon still works for his father-in-law, which is its own unique bite of this shit sandwich the men of the Versailles share. Both men spend an inordinate amount of time on their smart phones, checking their various online dating sites and getting excited about women who have made contact based on the enhanced versions of themselves they've created online.

"Shit," Jack says. "Pregnant? You'd think by now these kids would be smarter than that."

"Says the proud father of Emilio Jesus Baker."

"Fuck you, Oliver. She had an IUD."

"I guess your sperm was too much for it. Ate through it like acid. Good thing she wasn't giving you head."

"If only," Jack grumbles.

Oliver turns back to Silver. "Will she get an abortion?"

"I think so," he says. There's no reason to think her plans have changed at all, and yet, when he says it, he feels a stab of uncertainty, and a vague sadness that has yet to take shape.

When Casey was three, she'd fall asleep holding on to Silver's arm like a doll. He'd lie next to her in her bed, both of her little arms wrapped around his forearm, her fingers playing with the small hairs on his wrists, and he would listen to her breathing slow down as her eyes closed. He'd stay there long after she'd fallen asleep, unwilling to untangle his arm from hers, knowing, even then, that the time was fast approaching when she'd be too big to wrap herself around him like that, when she wouldn't even remember that she had. And then, eventually, he would detach himself and head down the hall to his and Denise's bedroom, where Denise would already be in bed, reading a book, wearing the plastic, black-rimmed glasses that made her look like the sexy secretary in a porno. And she'd pull back the blankets for him to join her, and sometimes she was naked, and sometimes she wasn't, and either way, he never appreciated the luxury, the sheer bliss of moving from one warm bed to another like that.

Jack and Oliver are staring at him.

"Did I just say all that out loud?" Silver.

"Your inner monologue seems to have broken free." Oliver.

126

"You were having a moment. A soliloquy." Jack.

"Shit."

"You were very eloquent." Oliver.

"And by eloquent, he means depressing as shit." Jack.

Dan Harcourt has just shown up, limping in his space-age knee brace. He played ball in college and refuses to give up the ghost, still going to the park to play in pickup games with younger guys who tolerate his forty-six-year-old ass because he buys all the drinks. One day soon he's going to pull up for a shot (he stopped driving to the hoop more than a decade ago) and his tattered knee will finally pull free from that last worn ligament holding it in place, and he will hit the pavement hard and wish he'd made the switch to golf years ago.

And the first batch of college girls have just arrived, flitting about their chairs with weightless grace, young enough to be their daughters and old enough to make them feel even more pathetic than they already do.

"I feel like crying," Silver says.

"Please don't," Jack says. "I'm begging you."

CHAPTER 19

Denise and Casey live in North Point, a pleasant if somewhat cookie-cutter neighborhood on the north side, with curving streets and no sidewalks to speak of, in a small, redbrick Georgian with a beard of ivy crawling up the front walls that, like beards often do, makes the house look like it takes itself too seriously.

Rich opens the front door, looking none too pleased with him. He still owns a smaller house just outside Elmsbrook, closer to the hospital, but he moved in with Denise and Casey about two years ago, taking over the payments, a move that demonstrated a level of commitment and optimism that Silver will never understand.

"Silver," Rich says. People, once they've known Silver for a while, tend to pronounce his name with a certain weary inflection. It's not so much a function of the specific syllables of the name but more a tone, really.

Until now, he doesn't recall Rich ever having attained this level of familiarity, but it's clear now that he has. Silver feels a sense of loss. Rich was the last person in this house who liked him.

"Hey, Rich."

"You don't just walk out of a hospital."

"Mitigating circumstances."

"You're going to die."

"Not yet."

Rich shakes his head at him, disapproving of his cavalier dismissal of medical science. If he thought about it, he'd no doubt come to the conclusion that Silver's death would somewhat enhance his own quality of life, but after twenty years or so of saving lives, Rich doesn't think that way.

He is still standing in the doorway blocking the entrance, and Silver is acutely aware of their positions, on the porch, in the family, in the universe.

"Can I see her?"

"Which one?"

"Both." He thinks about it for a moment. "Either."

"Now is not the best time."

"That's why I'm here, Rich."

"I know. But they're . . . in the middle of it right now. Why don't I have Casey call you later."

129

"I might be dead later."

Rich opens his mouth to say something, but nothing comes out. Silver has stumped him. Doctors can be slow like that, he finds.

Rich looks tired, with a few more gray hairs than he had yesterday. He is supposed to be getting married in a few weeks. He is supposed to be dealing with florists and caterers and party planners or, more likely, making the right supportive noises as Denise handles the logistics. Instead, he's dealing with a pregnant future stepdaughter, a hysterical fiancée, and now his fiancée's somewhat unbalanced ex-husband. Silver almost feels bad for him. But then he remembers that it's his ex-wife Rich is marrying, and his daughter he's safeguarding from him, and he can feel the rage start to build inside of him.

"Rich," he says.

"Yes, Silver."

"You're a good guy. You're sleeping with the only woman I've ever loved, and that makes things uncomfortable between us, because sometimes when I'm talking to you, I picture you fucking her, and I picture her making the sounds she used to make when I fucked her, and then I picture myself fucking her, and I get jealous and upset and I hope like hell that you've got a small dick,

130

and that when she's underneath you, she has to be thinking of me. I mean, you can't have sex with someone for that many years and not, in some way, just associate them with sex in general, you know what I mean?"

He's gotten off point here. His brain is draining into his mouth at an alarming rate. And Rich, he looks like he'd like to punch Silver in the face, but he can't, because, like Silver, his hands are his livelihood.

"You need to shut up now, Silver."

"My point is this whole delicate dynamic we've been navigating like adults since you started dating Denise, it all falls apart if you start preventing me from seeing my daughter." Silver looks him straight in the eye, to underscore the seriousness of what he's just said. "The dynamic gets fucked."

"As I said, now is not a good time."

Be a better father. Be a better man. A better man, Silver thinks, would come back tomorrow.

Silver looks up at the house. "Casey!" he shouts.

"She can't hear you."

"Casey!"

"Silver, don't make me call the cops."

Be a better man.

Silver turns to say something to Rich when his legs suddenly buckle, and he falls

131

against the railing. "Christ," he says, his voice suddenly hoarse.

"What is it?" Rich says. He steps out onto the porch, alarmed, and right at that instant Silver ducks around him and slides into the house. He catches a glimpse of Rich's expression just before he slams the door and locks it, and he swears to God that Rich actually looks hurt.

It takes a moment for him to get his bearings. Like all houses that have been professionally decorated, Denise's looks cluttered, unlived-in, and, when you take in the throw pillows on the couch, the art over the fireplace, and the tasseled curtain valances, just this side of ridiculous. He leans against the front door as Rich bangs away on it, shouting his name. He is once again acutely aware of their respective positions. Yesterday he was hooked up to a heart monitor while Rich diagnosed his aneurysm. Today, he's locked him out of his own house. The universe can be flexible like that.

"Silver!" Rich shouts. "Open this goddamn door!"

"Now's not a good time," Silver says, heading for the stairs.

The dynamic is most definitely fucked.

CHAPTER 20

He figures he has roughly two minutes before Rich comes in through the garage, or a back door, so he's moving pretty quickly when he bursts into Denise's bedroom, which scares the shit out her.

"Silver! What the hell?" She jumps off of her bed instinctively. Casey, on the window seat across the room, jumps up as well.

"Dad?" she says. His daughter's voice, calling him Dad, his adrenalized assault on the house, it all packs an emotional punch he isn't prepared for, and suddenly he's crying.

"Hi," he manages to get out, after a stifled sob.

"Where's Rich?" Denise says.

"He's outside." He turns around and locks the bedroom door. Denise's eyes grow wide.

"What are you doing?"

"I just . . . I just need to catch my breath for a second," Silver says, leaning against the wall. Casey, her eyes red from crying, has moved across the room and is now standing in front of him. "Hi, baby," he says, and cries a little bit more.

"What's wrong with you?" Casey says.

"Nothing. I don't know." He can smell Denise's moisturizer. In all these years, she hasn't changed it. He used to rub it onto her arms and legs after she showered, her wet hair, longer then, dripping onto her naked shoulders, and he would think to himself, I will love this woman forever.

He looks down. There are patterns in the carpet. You don't see them right away because it's gray on gray, but they're there — little floral shapes repeating until they make no sense. She picked this carpeting out herself, furnished this room, this house, by herself, because she was alone. Because he'd made her that way.

"You're crying," Casey says.

"So are you," he says.

They look at him, these two women, his lost family, at an utter loss to understand him. He knows how they feel. "So," he says. "What did I miss?"

Casey laughs. Denise doesn't. "Why are you here?"

"My daughter is pregnant."

"And suddenly you're Father of the Year."

"I'm just trying to be her father right now."

"She has enough to deal with as it is."

He turns to Casey. "You came to me. I'm here for you. Whatever you need."

"Thanks, Silver."

She doesn't call him Dad. He guesses that that was a temporary thing. Still, it was something, right? Below them, the room shakes lightly as the motorized garage door opens. He's running out of time.

"Listen," he says. "This, right here, the three of us, we're a family. We're a screwed-up family, sure, and that's my fault, but still. There was a time when the entire universe was outside the front door, and it was just the three of us, in our house, happy. And we're still those people. That's not gone." He turns to Denise and he can see that she's crying now. He's made contact. "Please, Denise. I know you haven't forgiven me. But the thing is, I still love you, I still can feel us, how we were then. Let me help my daughter."

He can hear Rich's footsteps pounding up the stairs, and then his body hitting the door. "Denise!" Rich shouts. His body hits the door again. Silver can hear wood splintering.

Denise looks at him for a long moment.

He hasn't been nearly as coherent as he needed to be. He doesn't know exactly what he was hoping to accomplish coming here, but even though he can no longer recall most of what he's said, he's pretty sure he didn't accomplish it.

"It's OK," Denise says. "I'm just going to let him in."

As she moves past him to the door, he reaches out for her arm. She stops, and for one electric moment, he can feel her fingers come up and wrap themselves around his forearm, her nails digging into his flesh. He feels her connected to him, and once again, the universe seems to be shifting beneath his feet. But this all happens in a fraction of a second, and before it can settle into reality, before it can actually take on any weight, Rich, who is on the other side of the door and thus has no idea of the nature of things on this side, hits the door with his shoulder, hard enough to break the latch. And the door flies open with violent force, connecting solidly with the face of his bride, who flies back across the room, going down hard when the corner of the bed takes her out at the knees.

BOOK TWO

CHAPTER 21

Denise rides, pumping away fiercely as she hits the first incline. Lake Terrace Boulevard is a long, winding road with three major inclines, which makes it a favorite among the local cyclists, all gluttons for the punishing hills. Denise, in black spandex shorts and a yellow top, crests the first hill without the usual sense of adrenalized accomplishment to propel her. The sweat, originating beneath her helmet, is trickling down her forehead, stinging her in the thick scab that has formed at the corner of her eye.

It was the corner of the door that hit her, the effect both severely bruising as well as lacerating, and now she looks like the battered wife in a television movie. It's been three days since Silver stormed the house — that's how she thinks of it, in those exact words — and despite an aggressive regimen of prescription anti-inflammatories, the swelling is only now beginning to recede, the deep purple bruising starting to yellow at the edges.

As she hits the second incline, she hears "On your left" as another cyclist passes her. He's forty-five or so, riding a carbon fiber Pinarello, for God's sake, and wearing one of those absurdly colorful racing jerseys like he's training for the Tour de France instead of getting in a morning ride before putting on his jacket and tie and heading off to an office somewhere. The Pinarellos start at $5,000, like you need a bike of that caliber to ride Lake Terrace Boulevard. Men and their hardware. Rich is the same way about golf, always looking for the latest equipment. And she remembers teasing Silver about his constantly evolving drum kit. He couldn't walk into a music store without finding something to buy. She wonders about the nature of the hole they're trying to fill with all of this gear.

She is suddenly filled with a fury that makes her bowels clench. Rising off her seat, she leans into her pedaling, unwilling to let this brightly colored asshole beat her. She has had it with men, with their gear and their holes, their relentless cocks, and the messes they make.

The cyclist, sensing her approach, takes a look over his colorful shoulder and Denise sees his own ass rise from his seat. It's on. She shifts down one gear and speeds up her pedaling. Ahead of her, she hears the grind and click of his $5,000 gears, and she knows he's done the same. He's not about to let a woman pass him.

Fuck you, she thinks at him. Fuck your middle-aged, weekend warrior, veiny-calved, overcompensating, overspending ass.

She's barely spoken to Rich since the accident. He's been staying back at his house near the hospital, at her request. Denise told him she needed some one-on-one time with Casey, but she could see in his eyes that he suspected something more. She knows she's being irrational, that it was an accident, as much Silver's fault as anyone's, but something happened in that room, something she hasn't quite been able to wrap her mind around. In that instant just before Rich had broken through, she'd been looking at Silver, and she'd seen something in his expression — a passion and determination she hadn't seen in years. The dull, defeated expression that had become his default in recent years disappeared, and she'd seen, well, her Silver. For that one instant, she had felt her family around her, Silver and Casey, and something in her, some long-dormant protective instinct, had sparked to life. And it had thrown her, badly. So much so that when Rich burst into the room, she felt like he — and not Silver — was the intruder. And then the door hit her in the face.

They have reached the second crest. There's now a small straightaway, the briefest stretch of downhill, before the road curves sharply into the third and final incline. She is inches from his rear wheel. She bends over her handlebars and comes up one gear. "On your left!" she shouts as she starts to pass him. But the guy doesn't yield. He stays where he is so that they are neck and neck, their legs pumping just inches apart from each other. The bike lane is narrow up here, and it's nothing short of reckless to be riding abreast like this. She should let it go, give him his senseless victory, but something in her won't yield. She's on the left, closer to the passing cars, and as she leans in, she can feel their elbows tap lightly. She turns to look at him, sees the sweat sliding off his pointed chin, the long muscles of his forearm grinding as he presses forward. For the briefest moment they make eye contact. Fuck you. Fuck you. Fuck you.

She is filled with a fury she doesn't understand. Ahead of them, a large fallen bough lies across the bike lane. She'll pass it with no problem, but it's directly in his path. He will have to fall back to get behind her. Instead, he speeds up and tries to veer into her space. Are you kidding me? she thinks. She speeds up, forcing him back. The bough is a thick one, with numerous smaller branches that still have their leaves. He will not be able to ride over it, would be an idiot to even try.

He's an idiot. She should have known. The jersey was a dead giveaway.

She hears the sound of the leaves and twigs swallowed up into his spokes, the almost musical sound of his small metal components vibrating against each other as the bike thrashes and then goes over. He lets out a short, panicked bark as the bike goes down, and she hears it slide into the gravel along the side of the road. She looks back to see that he managed to click out of his pedals and take the fall on his side. She wishes him dead in the same instant that she hopes he's not hurt.

His voice fills the morning air like a call to prayer. "Cunt!"

Perfect.

She laughs and flips him a reverse bird, bends over her bike, and throws herself into the final climb, the wind whistling in her ears like a catcall.

Rich, sitting on her doorstep, stands up as Denise pulls her bike into the driveway. She leans the bike against the garage door and turns to face him.

"I got your message," he says.

"I figured."

She left him a message late last night after another marathon argument with Casey, apologizing for not calling him back for the last few days and suggesting, in a matter-of-fact tone, that they postpone the wedding.

"What's this about, Denise?"

He is dressed in what she considers his unofficial uniform; dark slacks and a button-down shirt with some element of blue in it. His hair is cut close, revealing a high forehead, tanned and slightly weathered from his days on the links. She can remember how his forehead had appealed to her on their first date, its sand-colored, textured surface like the side of a rocky mountain. There was something strong and solid about it, about him. It was funny how a little subliminal imagery could determine the course of love, she thought to herself, how small visual grace notes could trigger lasting emotional changes.

"You're so laid back for a surgeon," she'd exclaimed over dinner, sounding younger and so much less cynical than she'd become. And he'd laughed, and she'd watched that forehead crease and go smooth, and she knew right then that she would go home with him that night. And now here she was, three years later, sweating in her driveway, hating herself for not being able to summon up any kind of warmth for him.

"I just think we need to push the wedding off," she tells him now, unable to look him in the eye. "Between Casey's situation and my face . . ."

"It won't look that bad in two weeks."

"It will still look like someone beat the shit out of me."

He cringes when she says this, as she knew he would. His buttons have always been right there on the surface, just waiting to be pushed. She loves him for this readability, for all the time not spent wondering what he's thinking or feeling. And sometimes she hates him for it.

"I'm sorry," he says. "You know it was an accident."

"I don't blame you," she lies, once again picturing that single instant: Silver's hand on her arm, his eyes ablaze with . . . something.

"Then why am I sleeping alone?"

"Listen to me," she says. "My daughter is pregnant. Silver is dying."

"Silver is being an idiot."

"Silver has always been an idiot. The point is that I don't want to get married while my life is in turmoil. You don't want that either. You can't. And I want to be a beautiful bride." She chokes up at this, realizing that it's true.

He steps over to her and runs his hand down her sticky wet face. "You are beautiful. A little bruise can't even make a dent in that."

She smiles. She knew he would say that, and she wonders to herself when it suddenly became a crime to always say the right thing.

"I just need a little time," she says. "I need to focus on my family."

"You mean our family, right?"

"Right," she says, and can tell from his expression that he remains unconvinced.

CHAPTER 22

"Is everything OK?" the girl asks him.

She's pretty, topless, panting slightly, and right to ask, because she is holding, in the palm of her hand, his increasingly flaccid member.

They are lying on a twin bed in Jack's guest room. Beyond the closed door are the not-so-muffled sounds of throbbing dance mixes, laughter, and drunken conversation. It's been three days since Silver left Denise's house and turned off his phone. A few hours ago Jack invited the college girls back from the pool for what he called a spontaneous suicide party. He gave a brief speech about Silver's impending death, and then began pouring drinks. At some point Silver found himself pulled off the couch to dance. Everyone watched him for a while, until it became apparent that he wasn't going to go into convulsions anytime soon. He would have felt like an idiot even if he weren't wearing baggy Bermuda shorts and flip-flops. The girl dancing with him had long dark hair and wore a tank top and a pair of white short shorts under which her tanned legs shone in the phosphorous glow of the blue lightbulbs Jack had screwed into the fixtures.

Dancing with a pretty young thing can turn you on and make you feel like a potato at the same time. Silver surrendered to the moment. Someone handed out little red pills that looked like M&M's. The dancing girl swallowed hers gleefully and then offered one to him.

"What is it?" Silver said.

"Trust me."

She put it on her tongue and then opened her mouth, inviting. He trusted her. The waxy taste of lipstick and spearmint gum, a hint of sweat, the thrilling warmth of her tongue in his mouth.

"What's your name?" he said when he reluctantly came up for air. She told him, and he forgot it instantly.

And now, through a sequence of events he can no longer recall, they are here, in this bed, her impossibly buoyant breasts hovering inches above his face, his wilting dick in her hand.

He's never had erection problems before, but now seems as good a time as any to start. This girl whose name he can't remember is young and beautiful, but he is old enough to be her father, is in fact the father of someone young and beautiful just like her.

"Wait here," the girl says with a grin, and with no further ceremony, she goes down on him. It feels excruciatingly good for a minute, and then it doesn't feel like anything at all, like he's lost all sensation. He can hear the wet sounds of her working down there, but in the dark he feels utterly disconnected. After a moment she gives his dick one last, sorry kiss, like it's a mischievous but ultimately well-intentioned nephew, then comes back up to where he is.

"What's wrong?" she says.

Where does he begin?

After she's gone back to the party, he waits an appropriate mourning period and then takes matters into his own hands. And maybe it's all the practice he's had at the clinic, but within three strokes his dick is standing tall and proud. He wishes what's-her-name was still here to see it. It occurs to him that there might be something fantastically warped about being able to arouse himself better than the half-naked coed who just went down on him. There is, at least, a subtle metaphor to be divined in this unusual turn of events, but before he can wrap his scattered mind around it, the door opens up and Jack steps in with his arm around another pretty young thing. Jack is carrying two drinks, any one of which he manages not to drop as he and the girl come face to face with Silver, perched on the edge of the bed, clutching his manhood. The other glass shatters on the parquet floor.

And that's when things get weird. Because Silver can feel himself spinning and rolling, yanking up his shorts as he goes, offering muttered apologies as he flees the room. But on another plane, he's aware of the fact that he hasn't actually moved at all, that he's still sitting there, his fist wrapped around his member, staring up at them.

"What the fuck?" Jack says. The girl giggles, but not in a mean way. And then they're gone, with only the light of the bathroom reflecting off the broken glass on the floor to confirm that any of this just happened. Then Jack comes back into the room, alone this time, still holding the remaining glass in his hand.

"Jesus, Silver," Jack says. "Will you put

that away?"

And this time, his body seems to get the message from his brain, and he releases his confused dick and pulls up his shorts. Jack sits down on the edge of the bed and hands Silver the glass. Silver throws it back, and shudders.

"I probably don't have to tell you this, but generally speaking, the objective is to have your erection and the girl in the room at the same time."

"That's one way to do it."

Jack grins and then laughs, and then they're both laughing, hard, not because anything is funny, but because they're drunk and drugged and getting older faster than they'd like and really, what else is there to do?

"I'll miss you when you're gone, buddy," Jack says somberly.

"Thanks, man."

He looks at Silver until Silver looks back, and then quickly looks away. That's about as much intimacy as either of them can stand.

"You want to tell me what this is all about?"

"Not really."

Another look, another look away. Jack slaps his leg and gets to his feet. "Fair enough. You coming back out?"

"I'll be there in a minute."

"OK. Watch your feet, there's fucking glass everywhere."

"I thought you were using plastic cups."

Jack grins. "The glasses are for the grown-ups."

Outside, the party has reached a fever pitch. The girls are all buzzed and sweaty, gyrating wildly to the music. Two of them, stripped down to their bras, dance on Jack's coffee table. What few men Jack has invited are either dancing ridiculously with the girls or perched on the furniture that's been moved to the perimeter, downing hard alcohol and watching. Jack is in the center of the dance floor, sweating profusely as he dances pelvis-to-pelvis with a girl Silver recognizes from the pool. What he lacks in grace he makes up for with shameless enthusiasm, and even though he's an ass, Silver feels a warm rush of affection for him.

"Dead man walking!" Jack shouts, waving to Silver. He's been calling him that all night.

Sad Todd sits weeping into his whiskey on the arm of a couch. The girls on the coffee table get wrapped up in a passionate kiss, and the room applauds their open-mindedness with shouts of encouragement.

The girl who had come with him into Jack's guest room leaves the dance floor to embrace him with an enthusiastic hug, like a long-lost love. She is either trying to make him feel better about before, or else the little red pills are still pirouetting through her blood, painting the room pink for her. Either way, he can't remember the last time someone hugged him like that, and he feels his eyes grow warm and wet.

"You feeling better?" she says, her lips brushing his ear.

"Yeah."

She smiles. "Dance with me."

She pulls him into the tangled mass of undulating bodies, wraps her arms around his neck, and shimmies against him. He falls into the basic white man's two-step and tries not to get in her way. No one over the age of twenty-five should ever dance like this. As a drummer, he has an inherent sense of rhythm, but rhythm and grace are not the same thing. The girl purses her lips and presses her rocking pelvis against his. "You are feeling better," she says with a sexy grin. She runs her fingertips over his pants, up the length of his erection. Then she leans forward and gives him a warm, open-mouthed kiss. He closes his eyes, feeling the room spinning around him, the deafening music, this beautiful girl's warm, willing lips pressed softly against his own, and he thinks, If I'm going to die, now would be a perfect time to do it. Of course, if he did, he would haunt every kiss this girl ever shared afterward, but we take our immortality where we can get it.

"Come with me," she says, leading him off the dance floor, back toward the hallway to the guest room. Before he can decide whether or not he's up for another attempt, another girl squares off in front of them with an angry scowl on her face.

"Jesus, Silver. Are you kidding me?"

The girl holding his hand drops it and, after a moment of uncertainty, touches his shoulder in farewell and heads back to the dance floor to begin the healing process. He looks at Casey, who is drilling him with unforgiving eyes, and he thinks, for the second time in as many minutes, that now would be as good a time as any to check out.

Casey is wearing a short skirt, a backpack, and an expression that causes his internal organs to clench with regret. She opens her mouth to speak, and he knows that whatever she says will further pierce his already perforated soul, but he is spared from hearing it because right then, Jack's flimsy coffee table finally gives way, and a collective squeal rises up from the room as the dancing coeds come crashing to the ground in a tangle of limbs and underwear.

"Shazam!" Jack yells. Casey rolls her eyes and looks at Silver like it's all his fault, then storms out of the apartment.

CHAPTER 23

"Were you really going to have sex with that girl?"

"It was a strong possibility. She gave me this pill."

"So you were being date raped? Is that your story?"

"I don't need a story. We were two adults."

"It doesn't go by cumulative age, you know."

"She was legal."

"How do you know? Do you ask for ID before you have sex?"

"No, but that's probably not a bad idea."

"You're not charming, Silver. You're a creep. How would you feel if I fucked Jack?"

"Shit, Casey."

"No wonder you never remarried. You're too busy chasing skanks who only do you to get back at their fathers."

"Is that what you were doing? Getting back at me?"

"No. I actually had sex with an age-appropriate partner."

"So you figured a condom was unnecessary."

"You're an asshole."

"Tell me something I don't know."

"OK. I'm moving in."

"Where?"

"Here. This shithole. You got yourself a roommate."

"What are you talking about?"

"I'm pregnant and you're suicidal. We'll have a blast."

"I'm not suicidal."

"Yeah, and I'm not pregnant."

"Why are you here, Casey?"

"Isn't this where you come when your life goes to shit?"

"Your life isn't going to shit. I'll take you back to Early Intervention tomorrow. We'll get it taken care of."

"Yeah, about that. I've changed my mind."

"What? When?"

"Right around the time you decided not to have that operation. You inspired me."

"Casey . . ."

"I'm going to ride it out, just like my old man."

"You're an idiot."

"It runs in the family."

He met a girl in a bar, or a club, or a movie theater, or a fraternity house. The point is, there was loud music playing in the background. As soon as he saw her face, he knew what it would look like when she ended it. But he went in anyway, because he was eighteen and horny and years away from knowing how much there was to truly fear. Maggie Seals. She was taller than him, a long, limber playground of a girl, and in the black light of her dorm room, the silken mileage of her skin went on forever. He followed her around like a puppy for his entire freshman year, and went broke calling her long-distance over summer break, but she still showed up the next fall with a prepared speech and a new boyfriend. For a long time afterward, every girl he slept with felt just a little too small.

CHAPTER 24

He wakes up and thinks, *I'm alive.* This simple fact fills him with a sense of accomplishment. He didn't die in his sleep.

Last night he was filled with the electric certainty that he would. That at some point, mid-snore, that last bit of threadbare tissue holding his aorta together would finally snap, and he'd bleed out in his sleep and wake up dead. The thought made sleep impossible. That, and the knowledge that Casey was in bed a few feet away, in the second bedroom that, in spite of everything, he still thought of as hers. He was thrilled to have her there, but also terrified that she would be the one to find his cold lifeless body. He lay awake, picturing the scene: She comes in, calls his name a few times (he still cannot picture her calling him Dad), and then tentatively approaches the bed. Silver? she says. Then she prods him, his shoulder most likely, and in doing so feels how stiff and cold he is. Her eyes grow wide as she realizes what's happened. But then what? That's where he ran into trouble. It would have been nice to imagine that she is overcome with grief, but the truth is, Silver couldn't see it. And also, hadn't he put her through enough already? So maybe just a wry smile, as if to say "Good one, Silver," and then a quick phone call to Denise. But maybe not even that. Maybe an indifferent shrug — *Oh well* — and then back to normal for all concerned. She grabs her phone and posts a Twitter update: *Found my dad dead in his bed. WTF? #howwasyourday?*

But at some point, his racing mind must have run out of steam and allowed him to sleep, because here he is, waking up. And now he can hear voices coming from the living room, and he instantly recognizes his father's deep baritone laugh. It can't be Sunday already. He sits up in bed and falls back instantly as the room starts to spin. For a little while, he worries that he's having another ministroke, but then remembers the little red pill on that girl's tongue and realizes that he's just drugged and hungover. He gets up again, slower this time, and performs a kind of shuffle/stagger into the living room.

His father is seated on the couch, in his

customary all-purpose midnight-blue suit. Casey is curled up on the love seat, eating cereal from a bowl.

"He's alive," she declares dryly, raising an eyebrow at him. Her irony is unintentional, or else she's so good at it that he's just a bit slow on the uptake. He can't begin to remember the last time he woke up to her voice. And the situation is not what you'd call optimal, but still, the happiness he feels at having her in his apartment is so powerful that for a moment he finds himself forgetting that she's knocked up and he's down for the count. He wonders why he didn't fight for this years ago, which triggers a small but intensely powerful spasm of regret. She is wearing boxer shorts, one leg tucked under her, and he can remember watching her at four years old, in a pair of orange shorts, her thin, coltish legs climbing the stairs ahead of him, and wishing she could just stay that way forever. When kids outgrow who they are, you don't mourn them, but you should. That four-year-old girl is as lost to him as if she'd died, and he'd give anything to have her back.

"Are you crying, Silver?" she says.

"A little." He wipes his eyes and turns to his father, who is looking at him with unmasked concern.

"I'm sorry I disappointed you," Silver says.

Ruben gives him a funny look. "When?"

"I don't know. Always."

"Silver." There is a great warmth in his eyes. Silver wishes he knew how he did that. He would look at Casey like that, and then she'd just know.

"Know what?" Casey says.

"What?"

"You were saying 'Then she'd know.' "

Shit. He has to get a handle on this.

"I'm sorry. Just thinking out loud."

They're both looking at him funny now.

"Are you having another stroke?"

"Hard to say."

His father stands up, taking charge. "Do you own a suit?"

"No."

He nods, as if his worst fears have been confirmed. What kind of life requires no suit?

"I have some band tuxes."

"That will have to do, then."

"Where are we going?"

"I'll tell you on the way."

"Can I come?" Casey says.

"No."

"Come on, Pops," she pleads.

Her grandfather looks at her fondly, and if

there's sadness in his gaze, he hides it well. "One train wreck at a time," he says.

In the driver's seat, Ruben looks over at the ruffles on Silver's tuxedo shirt and grins.

"What?"

"Nothing."

"Can you tell me where we're going?"

"To a funeral."

"Who died?"

"Eric Zeiring."

"I didn't know him."

"Me neither."

Outside, the sky is cloudless. It's another scorching day. Silver turns up the Camry's air-conditioning, and it starts to whine a little. Ruben absently turns it back down. Silver can't remember the last time he was in a car with his father.

They pass Kennedy Park, where Silver watches a tall guy in gym shorts pushing his kid in a stroller and walking a large golden retriever. He looks totally cool with it. Silver pictures the guy's wife back at their house, in paint-speckled shorts, her hair up in a bandanna as she paints a mural on their little girl's bedroom wall. Her husband has gotten the baby and the dog out of the way so she can work. Later, he'll drop them off so he can get to his regular basketball game, and on the way home he'll pick up a nice bottle of wine, which they'll drink in their claw-foot bathtub after putting their daughter down for the night. They've given up nothing in their marriage. His athletics, her art, it all merged effortlessly when they came together. Silver is happy for him, for the life he's made, for the little girl who will grow up in that home.

". . . position on suicide?" Ruben is saying.

"What?"

"I was wondering if you were aware of the Jewish position on suicide."

"I'm guessing they don't come down in favor of it?"

He nods. "No, they don't. It's a grave sin. The tradition is that for a person who kills himself intentionally, there should be no mourning rites, no eulogy. None of the honors of burial."

"Is that supposed to be a disincentive?"

"Maybe. It's hard to know. In the entire Bible, there are only two instances of suicide. The most famous one, which has greatly influenced Jewish law, is the suicide of King Saul on Mount Gilboa. You remember that story?"

"He fell on his sword. They were losing to the Philistines. He knew what would happen to him when he was captured."

Ruben smiles, clearly happy that Silver has retained some element of Jewish knowledge. When they were little, every Friday night Silver and Chuck would walk home from temple, holding their father's hands. And as they hopped and zigzagged to avoid any sidewalk cracks, he would tell them a story from the Bible, a different one each time. Silver favored the miracles — the splitting of seas, manna from heaven, water from rocks, the ten plagues. Chuck loved the battles. It was either a testament to Ruben's storytelling skills or simply a function of the Bible's aesthetic that he could usually incorporate both.

"That's right," he says, now in full rabbinic mode. "The sages used Saul's suicide as a qualification, a separate status. If there were mitigating circumstances that distressed a person, then the rabbis could take a more lenient approach."

"And you can apply that to pretty much every suicide."

"That's true. I think that was the point."

"A loophole," Silver says. "Nice."

"Compassion," Ruben says.

"You say tomato . . ."

His father shakes his head, frowning. This is why they don't discuss religion. "The

165

point I'm trying to make is that suicide is, both morally and spiritually, a very tricky area. Forget religion, forget God, for that matter."

"Done."

Ruben flashes him an annoyed glance. "This is serious."

"Sorry. I know."

"You have a family. You have a daughter. And regardless of how lousy things have been, Casey is still quite young. You have a lifetime to be the father you want to be to her. To be the person you meant to become before . . ." His voice trails off. This is the closest he has ever come to acknowledging his view of Silver's life.

"Before what, Dad?"

"Before you got lost."

Silver wants to get angry, but the anger won't come. Instead, he finds himself fighting back tears. "I don't know what happened," he says weakly.

Ruben nods and pats his knee. Silver sees the age spots and wrinkles on his father's hand. We're all aging, he thinks, coming apart cell by cell at an alarming rate.

"Cheer up," Ruben says brightly as they turn into the cemetery. "We're here."

"Yeah, about this. Why are we here? I didn't know this guy."

"How do you think I feel? I have to give the eulogy."

"That is rough."

Ruben shrugs. "Could be worse." He looks over at me. "I could be wearing a tuxedo from the eighties."

Silver laughs. They both do. They have the same laugh.

Eric Zeiring was twenty-eight years old and lived alone in some shithole in Brooklyn until he died of a drug overdose. No one tells Silver this, but he infers it from the things people are not saying, from the way everyone who speaks is carefully couching their words. His father makes reference to Eric's struggles, to his parents' unwavering love and numerous attempts to help him. To the elusive peace he has now finally found.

A single, enormous white cloud unfurls out across the sky with enough texture to see any shape you'd like: a woman's boots, a weeping clown, Sigmund Freud in profile. It's a small funeral, maybe thirty people gathered graveside, mostly friends of Eric's mother. Eric's father, balding and feature-less, stands off to the side, looking impatient and out of place. Silver's guess is they've been divorced long enough to be strangers.

Eric's mother, petite and pretty, weeps and nods emphatically at everything Ruben says. He talks about Eric's mop of curly blond hair that made him look like a cherub when he was a boy, about how Eric loved to visit his nana in Key Biscayne, about what an athlete he was. He evokes the boy Eric was for his parents, to help them forget about the sorry man he became. No parent should ever bury a child, Ruben says.

It makes Silver wonder about his own funeral.

Because pretty soon, in a matter of days or weeks, his father will have to bury him. And maybe no parent should bury their child, but it's really a question of value. His father has a wife, another son, grandchildren, and people like the Zeirings who count on him for comfort and perspective, to put a spiritual spin on things when the darkness invades their ordered lives. His funeral will be crowded, but not with his people. The entire community will come out to comfort his parents, which is what they deserve.

But who will be there for him?

Casey, of course. She'll be there, maybe even shed a tear, he hopes, but the loss will be more theoretical than real, since she lost him years ago, really. Denise will be there, the self-conscious ex-wife, looking much sexier than she needs to. Definitely a low-cut dress and a push-up bra, stiletto heels that will punch small wormholes in the grass around his grave. Will she cry? For Casey, maybe. She'll stand between Rich and Casey, and they will leave the graveyard a whole family, no longer complicated by the phantom limb that was him.

Who else? Some of the guys from the band? Maybe. Dana? Depends on how empty her life really is. Do you go to pay respects to the drummer you occasionally hook up with? It's a judgment call. Jack and Oliver, certainly. Jack will be restless, scanning the crowd for sad, desperate women and saying inappropriate things too loudly while Oliver shushes him, also too loudly. Maybe a few other guys from the building, hoping for a similar courtesy if they too should die before getting their sad lives back on track.

Everybody dies alone. That's a fact. Some more alone than others.

He looks at Mrs. Zeiring. Her eyes are swollen from crying. She loved this fucked-up junkie with her whole heart, breast-fed him, carried him, celebrated his first words, his first steps, overlooked his flaws, wiped his tears, and lived for his smiles. Then something in him broke, something she couldn't see, and she watched her boy die slow and hard, and probably with a good deal of shouting and nastiness as he went. Her marriage is over, her boy is gone. There was a time when they all lived together, like Denise, Casey, and Silver, a time when she never could have seen this coming. He feels her pain.

Ruben finishes speaking and nods to the funeral director, who moves forward and flips a switch, and the coffin slowly begins to descend into the grave. The only sound is the small motor of the coffin-lowering device, and that shouldn't be what Mrs. Zeiring hears as her son is taken away from her. Someone should sing, Silver thinks, and then someone does — a low, somewhat hoarse man's voice singing "Amazing Grace" quietly but with great sincerity. Ruben's eyes grow wide, and almost in the same instant that it occurs to Silver that "Amazing Grace" is not sung at Jewish funerals, he recognizes the singing voice as his own.

But Mrs. Zeiring is looking at him, not with anger or surprise, but a strange half-smile, and he decides that the only thing worse than spontaneously breaking into a Christian hymn at a Jewish funeral while dressed for a wedding would be to not finish it. So he does, slowly, and with feeling, while Mrs. Zeiring closes her eyes and thinks some secret truths to herself, and up at the lectern Silver's poor father somehow achieves some measure of dignity as he quietly shits a hard square brick.

The sky turns threatening on the drive home. In this heat, quick, random thunderstorms are a daily occurrence.

"So," his father says, "what did you think?"

"I don't know. What was the desired result?"

"I'm not going to paint a bull's-eye for you."

"I thought maybe you wanted me to see what it looks like for a parent to bury a child."

He scratches his beard thoughtfully. "That would have been petty and manipulative of me, but I won't rule it out."

He sounds weary; not generally, like it's been a long day, but specifically, like Silver is sapping his energy.

"Are you mad about the 'Amazing Grace' thing?"

"Of course not," he says, and even grins a little. "But really, what in the world possessed you?"

Silver doesn't really know how to explain it. It's like he's been inexpertly rewired. Signals are being mixed, relays being tripped, power surging and waning, and he's acting on impulses before he knows he's had them.

"Me," he says. "I possessed me."

"Some might say it was God."

"Yeah, people are always getting us confused. I'm taller."

Ruben turns into the driveway of the Versailles, pulls over, and throws the car into park. "I have a plan," he says.

"Do you?"

"You're going to come with me to one of every life-cycle event I've got on my calendar. A bris, a bar or bat mitzvah, a wedding, a death."

"And we just covered death."

"Right."

"OK."

He gives Silver a tender look. "You don't look so good."

"I've been better."

Ruben smiles sadly, then leans forward and kisses his forehead. Silver can't remember the last time he did that. He feels his father's stubble scratching his forehead, can smell his familiar aftershave, and in that instant, he experiences the sense memory of the boy he once was, safe and loved, who somehow managed to grow into this mess anyway.

His father doesn't seem to be in any rush to go anywhere, so they sit in the car in silence, looking out the window, waiting for it to rain.

CHAPTER 25

He wakes up paralyzed, his arms and legs frozen. For a few minutes he lies there, convinced that he's died, that this is what death feels like, that the mind stays alive longer than the body, trapped inside, going slowly mad until its life force is completely drained. There was a *Twilight Zone* episode about this. He remembers watching it with his parents in their bed, tucked between them under their comforter, the familiar smell of his mother's lilac-scented moisturizer filling his nostrils. The man in the episode, unable to move, was pleading in a terrified voice-over as they pronounced him dead.

He hopes that his own brain dies before they put him in the ground, because he has never done well in enclosed spaces. He starts to panic at the prospect, and then gets angry at how unfair it is to have to be scared of anything after you've already died. Isn't that supposed to be one of the perks? No more fear and worrying, no more lugging around all the shit that got tangled up in your mortal coil over the years? That's kind of what he's been counting on.

And that's when he realizes that he's been scratching his chest. He does the math, a bit slower than one might think, but ultimately reaches the inescapable conclusion that he's not dead, and not even very paralyzed. He wiggles his toes, bounces his knees, and whistles the theme from *Rocky,* which he mistakenly attributes to *Star Wars* for a few minutes. When they were kids, Chuck and he would play the *Rocky* theme on the living-room turntable and conduct fake boxing matches, hissing out their own sound effects with each blow. He'd forgotten about that, about Chuck, about how it feels to be brothers. It's been a long time since he's thought of himself as someone's brother. He should drop by there like he used to and see how he's doing. He doesn't remember when he stopped.

When he stands up, he briefly goes blind. Everything goes white, and he loses his balance, crashing into the wall before he trips over his sneakers and falls on his face. When he rolls over, his vision has returned.

This is getting tricky.

Casey sticks her head into the bedroom, sees him lying on the floor. The alarm that spreads across her face is both validating and heartbreaking, so he clasps his hands behind his head and attempts a look of casual repose.

"What are you doing?" she says.

"I thought I was dead."

"That's how it looked for a moment there."

She comes over and lies down on her back beside him. They stare up at the same cracked ceiling.

"You thought this was what death looked like?"

"Well, I couldn't see for a little bit."

She appears a little worried about that, and he hates that he's enjoying her concern. "Do you want me to call Rich?" she says.

"I absolutely do not want you to call Rich."

"You sure? If you die in an hour and I didn't call, I'll be traumatized."

"You're already traumatized."

"A little," she admits. "So, what are we doing down here?"

"Just, you know, considering the universe."

"That isn't the universe. It's your ceiling."

"Don't be so literal."

"The universe is one fucked-up place."

"That seems to be the consensus."

He watches her as she traces the long cracks in the ceiling with her eyes. Her horizontal profile makes her look much younger, like a little girl.

"What would you like to do today?" he says.

She gives him a funny look. "What are my options?"

"Sky's the limit."

She considers it for a moment. "Brunch?"

"I say the sky's the limit and all you can come up with is brunch?"

"I'm just not sure we live under the same sky."

He gives her a look. She gives it right back. We could have really had something good, he thinks, regret filling his lungs like water.

"Sometimes I think that too," Casey says, and he realizes that, once again, he's spoken out loud. "But I try not to, because then I get angry at you."

He rolls over and pulls himself to his feet, an act that feels like nothing less than an Olympic event, the blood rushing to his face with a dizzying heat that makes him feel fat and old. "We are going to brunch."

"At Dagmar's," Casey says, popping upright like she's attached to wires.

"Shit, really?"

She gives him a sharp look, one that conveys the many years of shit she is currently setting aside in order to tolerate his presence.

"Dagmar's it is," he says, leaning up against the wall.

"You OK?" she says, raising her eyebrows. "You're teetering."

He nods and steadies himself against the wall. "Aren't we all," he says.

CHAPTER 26

One of two things happens to restaurants in the suburbs: they go out of business, or they remain exactly the same. Dagmar's has been fortunate enough to remain in the latter category. It's one of those suburban nooks with unfinished wooden furniture and the condescendingly healthy menu scrawled like a colorful manifesto across three large blackboards above the counter. The words "organic" and "vegan" are sprinkled generously throughout in bright green. This enables the kids behind the counter to feel even more superior in their checkered shirts and ironic tattoos, and it enables the neighborhood patrons to feel good about paying three bucks for a shot glass of orange juice, so everybody wins.

Dagmar's also happens to be situated in North Point, where Casey and Denise live, and where Silver once lived with them, during that brief hiccup of time when he had his shit together. When he and Denise first split up, he would come every Sunday to have brunch here with Casey, but after a few months of hostile stares from Denise's girlfriends and indifference from their necessarily catatonic husbands, the men he had once considered his friends, it became clear that Denise was the people's champion, and he stopped coming. So the last time he was here was actually with Casey, but it was probably six or seven years ago.

The kid behind the counter greets Casey by name. She says hi back. Both of his earlobes are deformed by large-gauge hoops, the kind that stretch out the lobe to form a hole the size of a quarter. One day he will want to have normal earlobes again, and he'll be shit out of luck.

"You'll be sorry when you're older," Silver tells him, pointing to his ears.

"Shut up, Silver!" Casey says, scandalized.

The kid grins and shrugs. "Like when I'm your age? Odds are I'll be dead long before that."

Silver smiles. "Well played." He likes this kid. Sure he's a fuck-up — no one properly loved would mutilate himself like that — but who is he to judge? In ten years he might be a fantastic husband and father with fucked-up ears. He grows his hair long,

180

and he's good to go.

Silver turns to Casey. "What are you having?"

She doesn't consult the chalkboard menu at all. "I can't decide between the pancakes and the waffles, so I'll have both. Also a tomato-cheddar omelet with hash browns, two popovers, a large orange juice, and a coffee." She smiles wickedly at Silver, daring him.

"I'll have what she's having," he says.

They end up needing a second table for all of the food. The other diners cast sidelong glances at them, but they go about their feast with reckless abandon, their agenda hazy at best, but no less important. They laugh too loud, eat food off the other's plate, conduct entire conversations with dabs of whipped cream poised on the tips of their noses. And beneath it all, the sense that they are trying much too hard to prove something, to themselves and to each other, something for which they have no compelling evidence. Or else they are trying in vain to manufacture a memory, something they will be able to point to in the future and say, "Whatever else, we had that."

The restaurant is filled, and as Casey and Silver play chess with the orgy of food laid out before them, something happens. The room slows down, quiets a little, like the hush before a speech, but no one seems to notice it except Silver. It seems, even as he is fully engaged with Casey, he is able to take note of everyone in the room and, in some superficial but spectacularly clear way, understand them.

The couple at the far table against the wall is ten years younger than him. She was once a beauty, but her age has settled in her cheeks below her eyes, making her look perennially exhausted. He has stayed trim, wears designer sneakers and the jeans of a high school kid, and she quietly hates him for it. Her eyes flit around the room, looking at the other women, measuring herself against them.

One table over sit Dave and Laney Potter. Silver and Denise used to have a standing weekly movie date with them. Now they steal glances at him and whisper to each other, wondering what he's doing here, making him wish he looked a little bit better than he does. Laney is ten years younger than Dave, and a decade ago that didn't matter, but now he's starting to stoop and bend, and she looks young and spry and she must work hard to banish thoughts of younger men and Dave's ample life-insurance policy every time she sees his naked, sagging chest or he farts in bed.

There's a young couple feeding their messy, high-chair-bound two-year-old girl, both parents overly invested in their daughter's meal, loudly micromanaging her, and each other, as they cast wary glances around the room, daring anyone to have a problem with the noise they're making.

At one of the high round tables in the center of the room sit Craig and Ross, Elmsbrook's first openly gay couple. They were fabulous for a while, but now they're just another quietly fading couple melting into the graying tableau.

And off to their left, four women, all friends or acquaintances of Denise's, watching him and Casey, holding high-level discussions about what his presence here might mean, what actions, if any, should be taken. They consult their iPhones, send urgent texts to their commanding officers, await orders. He makes deliberate eye contact with each one of them, and they shy away, feigning obliviousness, as if he's caught them on the one day they aren't going to mentally catalogue and discuss every other person in the place.

He processes these and every other diner simultaneously, at genius speed. And he thinks, I used to be one of them, I used to belong here — and the thought fills him with both relief and regret. There's a modulated numbness to these carefully executed lives, the very numbness that was instrumental in his shameful flight years earlier. And it still scares him now, the muted sameness of everyone. And yet, he wonders, what if he had stayed? What if Denise, Casey, and he were still coming here every week for Sunday brunch? Maybe he'd be looking around, feeling trapped by it all, but maybe not. Maybe it wears you down, like Stockholm syndrome, and then fills you up. Is there really any difference between being fulfilled or just thinking you are? Such questions probably matter less when you wake up next to your wife and the two of you take your beautiful daughter to brunch. He looks around Dagmar's and understands that somewhere he missed a step; he fell behind, and never caught up again. And his life now is every bit as numb as the ones here, except for those moments when the piercing loneliness cuts like a blade right through it.

A small commotion at the entrance; a group of teenage boys walking in like teenage boys do, announcing their arrival with self-conscious bonhomie, rolling their shoulders, swiveling their athletic torsos as they make their way to a table. Silver sees Casey's expression suddenly fall. He follows her gaze, and somehow he can immediately discern which of the boys she's looking at, and in his stroked-out haze of clarity, he immediately knows why.

The boy in question looks familiar, tall and slim and fairly nondescript, your standard-issue college kid, dressed down in jeans and a vintage T-shirt, cracking up at his buddies' jokes. He waits for the urge to throttle the kid to set in, and when it doesn't, he is vaguely disappointed in himself.

When the kid sees Casey, he flashes a broad smile and waves. He has no idea, Silver thinks. She hasn't told him. She waves back, and Silver can tell she's hoping the kid won't come over. But he does.

"Hey."

"Hey, Jeremy."

Jeremy Lockwood, the neighbors' kid. That's why he looked so familiar. Of course, the last time Silver saw him he was a scrawny prepubescent. He has a sudden mental flash of a young boy wearing a cape and a hat, doing magic tricks for them in their living room, something with metal hoops.

"Hey, Mr. Silver."

"You were the magician."

"What?"

"You used to do magic tricks."

The kid thinks about it for a moment then smiles. "That's right. I did. Wow! You have a good memory."

"Sometimes."

"Hey, you know, my roommate was a huge Bent Daisies fan. He played that album almost nonstop. I think I know it by heart."

"College kids are listening to us to be retro. Kill me now."

Jeremy smiles nervously, not sure how serious he is. Silver's not sure himself. So, having paid his lip service to respect, Casey's impregnator turns back to her.

"Have you been getting my texts?" he says.

"Yeah, I'm sorry. We had a bit of a family emergency, and I kind of went off the grid for a few days."

"Is everything OK?"

"Yeah, my dad, he, uh, he was in the hospital."

"I'm sorry to hear that." He turns back to Silver. "You look OK now."

"I'm not."

"Silver," Casey says in a low voice.

"I'm bleeding internally. I could die at any moment."

Jeremy is not sure what to make of that.

186

He's now officially out of his depth, and Silver likes it. It occurs to him, watching the kid squirm, that he feels like a father.

Casey rolls her eyes. "Ignore him."

Jeremy nods, relieved at the direction. "We should get together."

"Sure," Casey says. "I'll text you."

"Great," Jeremy says. "I'll let you get back to your . . ." He sees the piles of food and leaves the rest of the sentence unfinished as he backs away slowly. They both watch him until he's out of range.

"So, that's him," Silver says.

Casey looks instantly alarmed. "What? Who?"

"Casey."

She considers her options. "Not now, Dad, OK?" she says softly. It's the first time today she's called him Dad, either because she's feeling vulnerable or else it's a calculated attempt to distract him with something shiny. If so, it works.

"You OK there, Silver?" Casey says, looking him over.

"You ask me that a lot," he says.

"Well, you are dying — on purpose."

"And you're pregnant — by accident."

"A fine pair we make," she says, thoughtfully licking some whipped cream off her spoon. Then she puts the spoon down with

187

great ceremony and straightens up, becoming deadly serious. "Maybe it happened like this for a reason."

"Yeah? How's that?"

"Maybe we're supposed to save each other."

He considers his beautiful, complicated daughter. How did he ever consider anything to be worth losing her? "Do you believe in God?" he says.

She smiles, like she's the parent and he's the child, and makes a gesture designed to incorporate herself, him, and the world at large. "Who else could throw together such an insane shit show?"

He used to believe in God. When you grow up in a rabbi's house, God is part of the package, an amiable resident ghost, floating about in corners, sitting in the empty dinner chair, peering in through your curtains after you get tucked into bed. He would pepper his father with endless questions: *Does God have teeth? Does He eat? Does He sneeze? Does He watch* The A-Team? His father never tired of the exercise, was always ready to engage in his juvenile theology.

Is He here right now?

Yes.

Where?

Everywhere.

He's in my hand?

Yes. And you're in His.

Silver would hold up his fist, wide-eyed at the notion that the same God who created the world and split the Red Sea could be holed up in his grubby little hand. Then he would open it quickly, like releasing a captured fly.

Does God know everything we think?

Yes.

Does He get angry when we're bad?

He understands humans, because He made them. He knows we're not perfect.

Why didn't He make us perfect?

Because then we'd never try.

Even to his seven-year-old brain, this had the ring of religious propaganda. Unable to confront the idea that his father might be lying or, worse, deceived, he would quickly move them to safer ground.

Does God have other worlds?

He might. We don't know of any.

Does God have a god that He prays to? And does that god have a god?

I don't think so.

Can God die?

No.

And round and round they went.

189

He would lie in his bed at night and picture God, moving about the house like a breeze, making sure they were all tucked in and safe. He can remember talking to Him from his bed, always in a whisper, always with the faintest trace of self-consciousness, finding God's features — His smile, His furrowed brow — in the sand-swirl finish of his ceiling. When the radiator knocked, he imagined God straightening out an errant brick. He saw Him less as a deity than as an omnipotent butler/handyman.

As he got older, God's presence became more intrusive. Silver didn't want Him listening in on his calls, could imagine God's chiding expression when his thoughts turned vaguely and then very specifically impure. You would think having God around would have put a crimp in his burgeoning autoerotic sex life, but somehow, even He wasn't a match for the hormones of a fourteen-year-old boy. You invented this stuff, Silver would remind him on those occasions when he felt himself caught wet-handed.

And then, one day, in his later teens, he looked up at the sand-swirled ceiling and recalled with fond nostalgia how he used to see the face of God up there, and only then did he realize that God was gone, that he'd lost track of Him a few years back. It was like hearing about the death of a great uncle you hadn't thought about in years. You attempt to mourn, settle for nostalgia, and then move on, willfully ignoring the vague sense of unsettlement that lingers, until it gradually fades into one more thread in the tapestry of loss and regret we all weave as we grow up.

CHAPTER 27

Denise is surrounded by Denise. There are three of her, four if you count the real her, the one standing between these angled mirrors in the bridal salon. Four brides, in understated, backless white gowns. She loves the dress — so much more dignified than the frilly gumdrop of a dress she wore her first time around. And yet, somewhere in its ethereal simplicity there seems to lurk the faintest hint of apology; the rueful admission of her marital past.

She is in no state of mind to come to this fitting, but canceling the appointment seemed like a statement of some kind, to Rich, or to herself. She is angry at herself for this sudden bout of confusion, furious with Silver for causing it — at least, she thinks he's the cause — and angry at Rich for . . . no good reason she can think of. After years of Silver's bullshit, and then the divorce, life was like a knot that she had finally, through great effort, managed to untangle, and now here she was tying it all up again.

She turns to study herself in profile. Her stomach is flat, her breasts still poised, her skin smooth. She has held up well. Through it all, she has stayed in shape, healthy, and, dare she say it, pretty. The bride on her right is glowing. But the bride on her left looks like she's been in a bar fight. She runs her fingers along her swollen cheekbone. Two weeks before her wedding. She wants to be the kind of person who can laugh this off, or at last shrug and say them's the breaks. But she's never been that girl. Things get to her. That was why Silver had been so good for her, and so bad for her.

Henny, the seamstress, comes back in and fixes her with a critical eye. "You lose weight since your last fitting." She is Russian, or Ukrainian, or Chechnyan. Something tragically Slavic. Her accent is so thick, it feels like she is forcing her words through a membrane.

Denise shrugs. "Stress."

"Why stress? This is happy time. The happiest." Henny starts to pinch at the material near her waist, and then blanches visibly when she catches a glimpse of Denise's reflection in the mirror. "He hit you?"

Denise laughs. "No! Of course not. I had an accident."

"You don't marry a man who hits."

"He didn't hit me. I got hit by a door." Even as she says it, she knows it sounds unconvincing. There are some things that, for whatever reason, you can't deny without sounding like a liar. "Do you really think I'd be considering marrying someone who hits me?"

Henny nods. "You get married in two weeks, no?"

"Yes."

"So, you are not considering. You are done considering. Right?"

"Right." She wished the woman would just shut up already.

They will be married by Silver's father. She feels bad about that, feels that she is compelling him to betray his own son. But he's the only game in town. She met briefly with Rabbi Davis at the Orthodox shul, but he had a long printed list of requirements — that they use a glatt kosher caterer, that she go to the mikvah the night before and take a dip in the ritual bath, that she present evidence of Rich's Jewish birth — so she politely placed the sheet back on his desk and retreated as fast as she could.

Rabbi Silver, whom she suspected had

always felt some measure of responsibility for her broken marriage, had given her a hug and agreed instantly to marry her and Rich. And even as she was moved to tears in his embrace, she felt guilty, like she was somehow taking a cheap shot at Silver. She wondered if maybe, subconsciously, she was. She didn't think so, but she couldn't be sure. Lately, her subconscious seemed to have an agenda all its own.

Henny is on her knees now, her mouth full of straight pins, which she is pulling out one by one to stab into the fabric at the small of Denise's back. Denise can feel the woman's breath on her spine, and it chills her unpleasantly.

The first time she got married, her mother had accompanied her to her first fitting in this very bridal shop, had cried the first time she saw her in the gown. They had both cried, missing her father, who had died a few years earlier. Then Silver had shown up early to pick her up, and he, too, seemed to be fighting back tears at the sight of her in the white gown. The seat her mother sat in is still there, against the wall next to the couch, but her mother is long gone. Breast cancer. And Silver is long gone, and she hasn't told Rich about this fitting, and besides he's working anyway, and Casey . . .

don't get her started on Casey . . .

"Why are you crying?" Henny says, her accent further complicated by the pins protruding from between her lips like fangs.

And she is, she realizes, turning to see the tears disappearing into the shadows of her bruise before reemerging on her cheek. She is getting married in two weeks, and she has never felt more alone in her life.

"You look beautiful."

The man's voice comes from behind them, startling them both. She turns around to the source of the voice and, seeing him there, she is only surprised that she isn't more surprised. Silver is standing against the wall like he's been there for a while, leaning in that way he has that always makes it seem like he belongs. He smiles at her, a small open smile, and it's been forever since she's seen that smile, and she feels it in her belly. That was how he used to smile at her, before things changed and his expression grew guarded, his eyes unable to rest on hers for more than a second at a time.

"Hi," he says.

"Hi."

"Déjà vu."

She feels herself smiling. It's incredible, she thinks, how worn and dirty love can get. But even as she thinks it, something in her

196

bursts, and she can feel it spreading through her chest, and suddenly she is in motion, flying off the platform, practically knocking the needle-mouthed seamstress onto her ass, oblivious to the stream of Russian expletives that rise up and fill the room. She doesn't remember getting there, and can no longer see him through the haze of tears, but she can feel his arms wrapping themselves around her as she collapses into him, sobbing like a baby.

CHAPTER 28

The baby boy is carried in by his grandmother on a pillow. He is wearing an ornate
white bed shirt and a tiny white skullcap af-
fixed to his head with two white straps. The
crowd gathered in the large, festively decorated living room comes to a hushed silence.
For a moment, there is no sound but the
click and flash of the photographer, shooting the infant relentlessly as the grandmother, who is wearing so much makeup
that she looks like a wax dummy, walks him
into the center of the room. The women
smile and cluck as the baby comes into view.
His mother, looking frail and deflated in
her maternity dress, smiles, but Silver can
feel her ambivalence toward this ritual, as if
it's his own.

Or maybe it is his own, and he's just
projecting.

Denise, holding on to him, her breath lightly

198

tickling his neck, the skin of her back, smooth and warm under his fingers. Casey had gotten moody after brunch, had decided to go see some friends, leaving him to make his way home from the North Point, and as he passed the bridal boutique, he happened to glance in and see that it was Denise up in front of the mirrors. He doesn't know what made him go in — If he understood the thing in him that felt the need to see his ex-wife trying on her new bridal gown he'd probably understand pretty much everything — but either way, he hasn't stopped reliving it since.

"*Baruch Haba,*" the mohel chants. Blessed is the one who arrives. Meaning the baby. Who, at this moment, is anything but blessed.

The infant is just getting over the trauma of his birth, flushed from the warmth of the womb on a harrowing claustrophobic journey through the birth canal, and then thrust mercilessly into the cold harsh light of the world. And now, eight days later, just as he's begun to develop a taste for breast milk and oxygen and is thinking that he might be able to make a go of things here, a strange man is going to pull down his diaper and take a scalpel to his minuscule cock.

Silver has to clamp down on the overpowering urge to snatch him from his wax-dummy grandmother, tuck him under his arm like a football, and run him to safety. The baby's mother, Susie, is on the fence. Silver is almost positive this sort of disturbance will be enough to make her reconsider the whole enterprise. She is in her late twenties, pretty and plump, and he's pretty sure, reading her expression, that this was not her idea. She converted to Judaism in order to marry Evan, which probably seemed like a good idea at the time, but now her son will pay the price. Evan stands at the head of the room, between Ruben and the mohel, in a designer suit and a large black yarmulke, creased and worn askew to demonstrate that he normally doesn't wear one. He watches as his son is carried in, feeling proud and not a little smug in this large, conspicuously expensive house that is a monument to both his wealth and his need for everyone to see it. He is circumcising his son for his father, who circumcised him for his father, who survived the concentration camps. Or else, because Evan feels an innate subconscious need for his son's dick to resemble his own. And thus, the ritual endures, even among the lapsed Jews and their shiksa wives, thanks to a complex, self-perpetuating loop of guilt, narcissism, and daddy issues.

The feel of Denise's body against his, her tears soaking his neck, the overall sense that right there, in that moment, she needed him. No one has needed him for a very long time.

The baby is passed to Evan's father, who sits down on the designated chair while the mohel bends over him, muttering in a slew of Hebrew blessings. Silver looks around the room at the gathered friends and relatives, all smiling and taking pictures, and the absurdity of the entire thing washes over him. A group of civilized, upper-middle-class Americans getting together for some routine genital mutilation, followed by coffee and bagels. He's pretty sure he saw an omelet station out there on the patio as well.

In his admittedly limited experience, he has come to identify two kinds of mohels: those who believe they are carrying out a sacred rite, and those who couldn't get into medical school. The way this mohel snaps on his latex gloves and unfurls his instrument roll with a flourish leads Silver to believe he is definitely in the latter category. He is in his early forties, clean-shaven, and clearly enjoys this moment in the spotlight. He pulls out his scalpel, studies it for a mo-

201

ment, and then leans over the baby and reaches in. The room goes blurry, and Silver realizes that he's in danger of passing out. He leans back against the wall and closes his eyes.

Denise's face, inches from his own, her eyes red, her lips quivering, a trembling in his chest he hadn't felt in years. She was looking at him and he was looking right back at her, and that may not sound like much, but for the first time in years, they were seeing each other.

The first uncircumcised penis he ever saw belonged to James Nevins. He caught sight of it in the boys' locker room while they were changing for gym in the fourth grade. James had his shorts around his ankles — was trying to step into them without removing his sneakers, a task that left him exposed for a good thirty seconds or so. James's thin, flapping member waved back and forth like the pendulum of a metronome, and it looked to Silver like someone had chopped off his tip. He immediately pictured a variety of horrifying, if farfetched, household accidents and, more vitally, wondered how the boy urinated. "What's the matter, you never seen a dick before?" James snapped at him, and he realized he was staring.

"What happened to it?" he blurted out.

"Nothing happened to it, shithead," Jimmy said.

He doesn't remember what he said after that, but it led to his getting punched in the face for the first time. Two firsts in the span of one minute. That was a big day.

Even now, he can taste the blood on his tongue, and he opens his eyes just as the baby starts to wail. The mohel, having made his cut, shouts out a blessing in Hebrew. The father reads one too, his tongue tripping over the Hebrew consonants he hasn't practiced since he was a little boy. Someone produces a silver wine goblet. The mohel dips the baby's pacifier into the wine and then shoves it into the baby's mouth. If you're going to get the baby plastered, why not do it before you cut him? Silver thinks. None of this makes any sense.

And then, just as he was leaning in to kiss her, she turned away, the tip of her earlobe grazing his dry lips with a rough whisper. I'm sorry, she said, although what she was sorry for, like everything else, was utterly unclear to him.

Rabbi Silver addresses the room, attempting to place the procedure into context. "In performing the ritual of circumcision, we have entered this child into the covenant of Abraham and God, and now Susie and Evan will name their boy, as we welcome him into the Jewish community. We are born imperfect by design, and the circumcision is our first step in achieving God's vision for us."

Evan and Susan stand beside Ruben, who begins to chant in Hebrew, and Silver has the baby's cries in his ears and his pain in his crotch and suddenly there's not enough oxygen in the room, and he's sweating profusely. He's either stroking or fainting, or maybe both, but either way, he's not going to do it here, collapsing onto chintzy, overpriced furniture that doesn't look sturdy enough to accommodate a genuine adult body anyway.

He flees, down the hall and through a den, and then descends some stairs into a second, sunken den that they probably call a sunroom, and then out the sliding-glass doors and across the patio, where the catering staff are laying out platters and pouring mimosas.

I am not cut out for this, he thinks, and the cute, skinny bartender with the nose stud and big green eyes looks up and says, "You and me both," which is how he knows that he's spoken out loud. The heat out here is surprising, the sun radiating off the blue-stones, cooking the air at eye level. After the blasting central air inside, it's a welcome respite, like stepping into a different season.

"They wrapping up in there?" the girl says, working the white plastic cork out of a Champagne bottle. Her dark hair is short and uneven, like she cuts it herself, but she's pulling it off.

"Yeah." He can feel himself staring too closely at her.

This is the amazing thing about the male brain, or at least, his male brain, which is admittedly compromised by strokes, and an unrelenting lust that has been nesting there since early adolescence. He can be dying, can be taking in a sacred ceremony that is both deeply moving and somewhat horrifying, can be falling in love with his ex-wife all over again and, at the same time, still have the computing power to consider this hot little bartender, to note the monochromatic tendril of a tattoo creeping around the side of her neck, the way her tongue flicks up to lick her upper lip, to hear the cigarettes in her laid-back, punk-rock voice, and to contemplate how this would all manifest itself in her lovemaking.

She looks at him and smiles, amused and

unthreatened, and he wants to kiss those laid-back lips, wants to run away with her and from her all at the same time.

"You played in that band, right? The Broken Daisies."

"The Bent Daisies."

She accepts the correction. "Cool."

He watches her patiently work the cork, twisting and pulling until it comes out with a soft pop. She puts the bottle down and starts on another.

"You OK there?" she says.

"I'm dying."

She considers the information casually. She is cute, and a bartender, a combination that renders her largely unfazed by default.

"I just needed some air," he says.

"Well," she says, looking around the vast yard, complete with an impressive free-form pool and a goldfish pond, "you came to the right place."

Later, the guests mill about the patio enjoying a late-morning brunch and casting the odd look his way. He is sitting by the pool with his pants rolled up and his legs in the water, drinking Champagne out of the bottle. His father makes his way across the yard and sits down on the ground beside him.

"What happened in there?" he says.

"I don't know, I just . . . I got a little claustrophobic."

He nods. "How's the water?"

"It's nice," Silver says. "Warm."

"Listen," Ruben says, "your mother is beside herself."

"I'm sorry."

"Come for Friday-night dinner. Let her cook for you, let her see you. It will be good for both of you."

"OK."

His father looks at him, kind of measures him with his eyes. There are things Ruben wants to tell him, questions he wants to ask, but he can see that Silver's not up for it right now. Instead, Ruben pulls off his loafers, and then his black socks, pulls up his suit pants, and puts his legs in next to Silver's.

"It's getting so I can't take you anywhere," he says.

CHAPTER 29

Back at the Versailles, Casey joins the men at the pool, which Jack is not happy about. He shakes his head at Silver, like he's just committed the mother of all faux pas.

"What's wrong?" Casey says. "Am I cramping your style?"

"A little bit," he says, then looks at Silver. "Really, Silver. Here?"

"Where he goes, I go," Casey says.

"That sounds like a foolproof plan," Jack grumbles.

"Does my being here make it hard for you to check out the asses of other girls my age? Is that it? Or is it that if I was sitting over there" — she indicates the college girls tanning across the pool — "with those skanks, you know you'd be staring at my ass too, and that's upsetting to you because I'm your friend's daughter?"

"Jesus Christ," Jack mutters.

Oliver laughs.

"Casey," Silver says.

"Sorry, sorry," she says, grinning. "Pretend I'm not here."

"That would be easier if you would stop talking," Jack says.

"What is it with men and younger women?" Casey says.

"There she goes again," Jack says.

"No, I'm serious," Casey says. "I'm genuinely interested."

Jack cranes his neck to look at her, then looks across the pool at the college girls lined up in their chairs like they just came off the assembly line. He looks at Silver, asking for permission, and Silver shrugs.

"I think it's anthropological," Jack says.

"What does that even mean?"

"I mean, we're programmed, in our cells. It's the animal kingdom. The male is drawn to the young, fertile female. It's an instinct. To propagate the species."

Casey shakes her head, smiling incredulously. "So you're just an innocent bystander to biology, is that it? Forces beyond your control."

"You didn't ask me that. You asked me why I'm attracted to younger women," Jack says, turning onto his side to face her. "Control is where I failed. Where you failed too, by the way. We don't get to decide who

209

we're attracted to. Believe me, I wish we did. I'd still be married. And you wouldn't be pregnant." He indicates Oliver and Silver. "None of us would be in this mess." His eyes grow wide, earnest in a way Silver has never seen. "I love my wife. I'd give anything to be with her right now. I mean, look at us. We're intelligent people, but sex has nothing to do with intelligence. It's impulse and instinct and animal attraction and it's built into our cells. I know that's not what they teach you in school right before they give out the condoms, but that's what it is. And I'm not saying I like it. It's a goddamn tragedy, is what it is."

His voice goes up at the end, almost cracking. He looks around at them, suddenly self-conscious. It's the first time Silver has ever heard him refer to his wife like that, the first time he's caught a glimpse of the pain behind Jack's bluster.

Casey seems to sense it too. "That was actually kind of beautiful," she says.

"And strangely articulate," Oliver adds.

"I have my moments," Jack says, already regretting it.

Casey looks over to Oliver. "So, you agree with him?"

Oliver considers it for a moment. "I appreciate his point of view, without necessar-

210

ily endorsing the behavior."

"Oh, bullshit," Jack says, annoyed. "If you could still get it up, you'd be right in there with me."

"I have daughters that age."

"Daughters who haven't talked to you in years."

"Nevertheless."

Jack rolls his eyes.

Casey turns to her father. "What about you, Silver?

"What about me?"

"Come on. I saw you with that girl the other night."

He doesn't want to answer her, but as with everything else these days, he seems power-less to stop himself. "Their skin is tight," he says. "Their asses are round and high, their bellies are smooth and flat, their breasts are full and firm and hang up high where God intended. They smell good, they taste good, and their kisses . . . Their kisses are long and wet and deep, and go on forever. They kiss like they're going to consume you, every single time. You can get lost in those kisses — you can die and be reborn in those kisses. I don't know why that goes away, but it does. . . ."

He looks up to find Casey, Jack, and Oliver staring at him. "What?"

"That was, um . . . comprehensive," Casey says.

"You asked."

"I did."

"Can I change my answer?" Jack says, and they all crack up, for no real reason he can think of, but still, the world feels just this side of OK for a moment.

Later in the pool, something happens. He's floating on his back, looking up at the sky, when there's a flash of light, and then everything goes dark. He is suddenly sinking, feels the water flooding his nose and mouth and then the roughness of the pool bottom, scraping his lower back. He is drowning in darkness and unable to move. This is how it ends, he thinks. Strangely, he is not panicked, just a little bit sad. He tells himself to pay attention. If this is death, it will only come once, and he doesn't want to miss anything. Like he did when he was alive.

Then there are fingers digging into his forearms, hands pressed painfully into his armpits, and then he's shivering in the air, being rolled on hard, gristly pavement. Flashes of color, and then moving shapes. It's like being born, he thinks. He hears Jack's voice: "Come on, Silver! Wake the fuck up," and then Casey's face comes into view, hovering above him, close enough that he can see the thin trickles of water catching the sunlight as they run down her face. "Dad!" she shouts. "Can you hear me?"

He nods, and coughs up a lungful of chlorinated water. He has a vague sense of an assembled crowd, and he is suddenly self-conscious of his flabby gut, hanging out there for all to see.

"I'm OK," he says, rolling over and trying to sit up. He feels a pair of hands behind him, steadying him in place.

"Go slow." He hears Oliver's voice in his ear.

He sits up slowly and looks at Casey, who is fighting back tears. "What the hell happened?" she says.

"I don't know."

"You just went under."

"I didn't mean to."

"Are you sure?"

She looks a little bit off to him, like he can't tell how far away she is. He looks around the pool area, at the men standing around, the college girls, all staring at him. It's like he's seeing them all at a strange angle. In the distance he hears a siren, and by the time the ambulance shows up, he's

figured out that he's gone blind in his left
eye.

CHAPTER 30

"You're going to die," Rich tells him. He is standing over Silver, moving his penlight across his eyes.

"Tell me something I don't know."

Rich retracts the light and looks at him. "What you have is something called amaurosis fugax."

"You see? Now, that I didn't know."

Casey, sitting cross-legged at the foot of his bed, grins and shakes her head at him.

"A small clot breaks off and lodges itself in the ocular vessels. It will probably break down on its own. You're already responding to light."

He closes his right eye and sees a burst of light colors in his left.

"So it will get back to normal."

"Maybe. Maybe not."

Denise comes into the room, looking slightly breathless, like she ran up from the parking lot. They all look at her, and her face goes red. She looks young and shy, and Silver gets that funny feeling in his chest.

"You look pretty."

"Shut up, Silver," she says, but her heart's not in it, and he's wondering if maybe she's been thinking about that hug too. "Are you OK?" she says.

"I get by." It's an old, not-funny joke from the earliest days of their marriage, and he can see it register in her quick, uncertain smile.

Rich stands back, suddenly the interloper in his own hospital, in this family, and the part of Silver that isn't, on some petty level, gloating actually feels sorry for him. You would think that in his dying days he'd be a bigger person than that. You'd be wrong.

"Hi," Rich says to her. He leans forward and kisses her cheek, which looks awkward and wrong because he's wearing his doctor's coat, because there's clearly some tension between them, and because she was Silver's first.

"She was mine first," he says.

"Oh, shit, Silver!" Casey says. "Not this again."

"I know she was," Rich says. "But she'll be mine last."

"Rich . . ." Denise says quietly.

"What?!" Rich says, turning on her. "Isn't

216

that what we do here? We say whatever we think, right? And everyone laughs."

"He's sick."

"He's more than sick. He's dying. And I'm the only one who seems inclined to stop that from happening."

"Which I appreciate," Silver says.

"You're an asshole, Silver."

"I think I'd like a second opinion."

Rich turns around so fast, Silver is sure he's going to punch him. "OK, Silver, here's a second opinion," he spits out. "You don't want to die. You just want a free pass to forgiveness, to undo the fact that you left your wife and neglected your daughter. And you're too self-absorbed to realize that you're just screwing them up more in the process."

"Stop it," Denise says.

"Tell me I'm wrong, Denise!" he shouts at her. "Tell me he's not the reason I'm staying in my old house again."

"You are?" Silver.

"Shut up, Silver." Casey.

"Don't do this here." Denise.

"Where else am I going to do it? It's not like you've been returning my calls." Rich.

Silver rolls out of bed and looks at Casey. "I think we should give them a minute," he says. He heads for the door, but Rich steps forward and blocks his way. Silver looks him up and down, wondering if they're about to come to blows. Rich has a few inches on him but probably hasn't been in a fight in his entire adult life, whereas Silver is a veteran of drunken brawls, none of which he can recall with any specificity, and all of which he lost, but still, being able to take a punch is half the battle.

"You can't have her," Rich says.

"What?"

Rich looks at Denise while he speaks in slow, measured tones. "Denise. You can't have her. She's going to marry me. She may be questioning that right now, but that's how this story ends. And maybe you delay that a little bit, maybe you throw her off temporarily, but in the end, I marry Denise and she and I, and Casey . . . we bury you."

"Unless I have the operation."

"That's right. You can live or you can die. But either way, you can't have my wife."

He's being noble and a prick simultaneously. Later Silver will have to replay this conversation in his head to see how he pulled it off. But for now, his tortured love is filling the room, forcing Silver out.

"Where are you going?!" Denise calls out, alarmed.

"Home."

"You just had a stroke, Silver!"

"Yeah," he says. "But it was a little one."

Out in the hall, he turns to look at Casey. "It's OK, baby. Don't cry."

"I'm not," Casey says, wiping his face with her fingers. "You are."

He loved a girl once. She was pretty and kind, soft and hard, had a quick wit and a killer smile, and for reasons that never really crystallized for him, she loved him back. She laughed at his jokes and craved his body and threw herself into loving him with a blind trust that warmed his heart even while it terrified him. When they made love, they did it with fierce abandon, and it was they who shook, not the earth. And afterward, as they lay together hip to hip, her sweat on his tongue, he would make promises, and she would believe them. It had not been love at first sight, more of a slow burn, but when it hit, it hit like a tsunami. And then, one evening, as they ate ice cream by the wharf, he asked her to take off the Claddagh ring she wore so that he could see it, and when he handed it back, it was a diamond ring. And she couldn't stop crying, and he kissed her tears and promised her that he'd never make her cry again, and that was just one of the hundreds of promises he would break sooner than even he ever would have believed.

CHAPTER 31

Friday-night dinner turns out to be an ambush. Casey and Silver walk in to the shouts and whoops of his nephews, and Chuck and Ruby are on the couch in the living room, in somber conversation with Denise, who looks somewhat ill at ease in the home of her former in-laws.

"Oh, fuck," Casey says quietly.

"Did you know about this?"

"I had no idea."

Ruben comes over to greet them, looking sharp and scrubbed in one of his better suits. He has just returned from Friday-night services. The house is filled with the smells of Silver's childhood: freshly baked challahs, sweetened gefilte fish, and stuffed cabbage. In the dining room, the table is set with an ornate white tablecloth, his mother's silver Shabbat candlesticks standing in the center, burning brightly. This was his childhood, safe and warm and brightly lit, and being here now makes him feel like he died years ago and he's now a lost spirit, stuck between worlds with unfinished business.

"I hope you don't mind," his father says, giving him a hug.

"You could have told me they'd all be here."

"But then you wouldn't have come, and I couldn't disappoint your mother like that."

"So instead, you disappointed me."

He smiles. "I love you, but I sleep in her bed."

"OK, Pops, don't be gross," Casey says, and he kisses her cheek happily.

"Is he here?" Elaine calls out from the kitchen.

"Go say hello to your mother," Ruben says.

"Hey, Ma."

Elaine stands at the center island of her kitchen in a black dinner dress and slippers, slicing a London broil. She must have gone to shul with his father. Silver pictures them, walking home arm in arm after services, breathing in the warm summer air, listening to the familiar rhythm of their heels on the sidewalk, anticipating a lively Shabbat dinner with their children. He can feel their love, their peace, their quiet comfort with their lives and each other. They have done something right without consciously trying, achieved some vital contentment that has fatally eluded him.

"You look terrible," his mother says, putting down her knife.

"It's been a rough few days."

"Come give me a hug."

He is twice her size, but when she hugs him, he disappears.

"Ma," he says as the lump in his throat rises.

"I know," she says, rubbing his back. "I know."

And he almost believes her.

Although the vision has gradually been returning to his left eye, it's still somewhat unfocused, giving him minor balance problems. In the living room, he staggers a bit before sitting down between Casey and Denise on the couch. "You good?" Denise says.

"Good enough."

"I hope this is OK. Your mom wouldn't take no for an answer."

"It's fine."

"And, you know, I miss them."

He knows that's true. Denise's mother died when she was thirteen, and Elaine had always yearned for a daughter. After they got married, Denise had formed an intimate bond with Silver's mother. Silver sometimes wonders whether he and Denise only lasted as long as they did because Denise didn't want to lose Elaine. They still get together for lunch every so often. His mother doesn't mention it to him, but it's a small enough town, and he's occasionally seen them, on sidewalks and through restaurant windows. Getting divorced is a messy business under the best of circumstances, because in some ways, you never stop being a family. The movie stars can pull it off. Everyone else stumbles through it with a sloppy combination of false hope and willful blindness.

At the table he is seated between Casey and Denise, across from Chuck and Ruby, whose two boys sit beside them, vibrating like hot molecules. Zack and Benny, eight and six; they're like cartoon characters who never stop moving. The baby, Nate, is sleeping in his car seat on the floor in the corner. They sing "Shalom Aleichem," and then Ruben raises his silver cup and recites the kiddush, then pours wine from the cup into small silver cups that get passed around the table. The kiddush wine tastes like cough syrup, coating Silver's tongue and throat with its sickly sweetness. They go into the kitchen to wash their hands with a silver washing cup, then return to the table, where Ruben says a blessing and cuts the challah. Then, having dispensed with the rituals, Elaine and Casey bring out the soup.

Ruben tells a condensed version of the story he told at services tonight, and Silver is acutely aware of Denise beside him, listening, laughing, enjoying herself. He would like to hold her hand. So he reaches for it, under the table. She gives him a funny look as she slides out of his grasp, standing up to help clear the soup bowls.

Ruby cuts the chicken for her boys, trading furtive glances with Chuck. Something is going on, there's a plan in place, an intervention of sorts, and there's nothing Silver can do but sit here and wait for them to make their move. He tries to disarm Chuck with a hard stare, but his brother is avoiding eye contact.

"Chuck," Silver says, and when the table falls instantly silent, he realizes that he's said it maybe a bit louder than he intended. Even the boys are staring at him.

"What?" Chuck says.

"Don't do it."

"Don't do what?"

"Whatever this is. Don't do it."

Chuck's face turns red and he looks over at their father, not sure how to respond.

Ruben sighs and puts down his fork. He has spent years counseling families, saying the things people generally find too difficult to say to one another, and for the first time, Silver considers the courage it must take to walk into the emotional minefields of other families, and what sort of toll that takes on a man. His father sits back in his chair, pausing, like he does sometimes in the middle of a sermon, to gather his thoughts, or his energy.

"This is a difficult time for you, Silver," he says. "It's a difficult time for our family. We're all here because we want to understand, we want to help, the same way I know you'd want to help if one of us needed it."

Silver pushes back his chair and stands. "I can't do this right now."

"Come on," Elaine says. "Sit down. We're not going to bite."

"I appreciate what you're trying to do, but —"

"SIT THE HELL DOWN!" his father shouts, bringing his fist crashing down on the table. Everyone jumps in their seats, and the baby starts to cry. Ruby jumps up to grab the baby, and Silver sits down. Denise, back in from the kitchen, sits down in her chair. Beneath the table, she reaches for Silver's hand, clutching it hard against his thigh. They all stare at Ruben, who sits in his seat, fists clenched.

Silver was suspended for cheating on a test in the seventh grade, then again in high school for smoking a joint in the boys' gym shower. He stole the car keys and backed his father's Lincoln through the garage door two years before he was old enough to drive. Once, when he was sixteen, he called God a sick fuck, right to his father's face. And he has never heard him raise his voice like he just did. None of them has, and, even now, Ruben is still trembling from the effort. The dining room acquires a weighted silence, like the silence just before the firing squad fires. Ruben offers a thin, unhappy smile, a tacit acknowledgment of sorts that this just got real.

"I love you," Ruben continues. "But you're being selfish. And cruel. We are your family, and if you're so determined to die, then goddammit, you're going to treat us better than this before you do."

His hand on the table still trembles, causing the knife beside it to vibrate, glinting in the light from the crystal chandelier. Silver closes his right eye and can make out just that tiny crescent of light, waxing and waning in a sea of darkness. When he opens his good eye, the room swims a little before coming back into focus.

Ruben looks over to Elaine, signaling for her to speak.

"I love you, Silver," Elaine says, her voice strangely formal even as it quivers with emotion. "I have loved you from the day you were born. And not once, not when you were off with your band instead of taking care of your family, not when you and Denise were divorced, not when your father and I were spending weekends with Casey because you were off doing God-knows-what instead of being a father — not once did I judge you, not once did I tell you that you were being thoughtless or selfish. And maybe I should have. I don't know. I was just trying to keep you close, so that when you did try to find your way back, you'd still be able to. But now, now I'm going to tell you what I think, and so is your father and Chuck and Denise and Casey and everyone here who somehow manages to love you in spite of you. We're going to tell you and you're going to listen." Her voice is cracking, but she finishes with a defiant nod before sitting down.

Ruben places his hand over hers, nodding his approval, then looks over at Chuck. "Why don't you say something now."

Chuck turns to look at Silver, offering a

sheepish half-smile as he clears his throat. "We were once close," he says. "I don't know what happened. It's like, you moved into that building and you just disappeared. You used to come by for dinner after you got divorced. You'd just show up while we were eating and pull up a chair and talk to the kids and make them laugh. They loved having you around. Then we'd have some beers on the deck, talk about stuff. Do you even remember that?"

Now that he says it, Silver does. But until this moment, he hadn't thought about it in years. Is that the same as forgetting? He guesses that, for all practical purposes, it is.

"I don't know why you stopped coming over," Chuck continues, gathering steam. "Why you stopped returning my calls. I don't know if it was something I said, or did, or didn't do, but we never should have let it drag on like this. I've missed having a brother. I see my own boys playing . . ." His voice cracks a little, and Ruby, shaking the baby in her arms, comes up behind him to rub his back. They form a picture like that, Chuck seated, Ruby over his left shoulder, holding their new baby, like they're being posed for a Christmas card. And looking at them, Silver can feel a familiar, inexplicable anger rising up in him.

"Why is Daddy crying?" Zack says.

"He's not crying," Ruby says. "He's talking."

"No, he's not. He's crying. Look."

"You boys go play in the basement."

Ruby ushers the boys out of the dining room and then comes to stand behind her husband, doing this little dance to shake her baby back to sleep. She rocks on her heels, swaying left and right, and probably has no idea that she's doing it.

Chuck wipes his eyes and takes a deep breath, ready to bring it home. "I don't want you to die," he says. "I think maybe this aorta thing is like a wake-up call for you, a way for you to come back to all of us."

Silver can feel the weight of all the eyes in the room, which move as one across the table to land on him. He fervently hopes he's not about to say what he's thinking.

"You're an idiot," he says.

Shit.

Ruby gasps. Chuck flinches like he would when they were kids and Silver would pull back like he was going to punch him. If he didn't flinch, Silver would hit him.

"And we're off," Casey says, under her breath.

"I'm sorry," Silver continues. "I know

you're being sincere, but I still want to hit you until you bleed for saying it, and I'm not really sure why. I think maybe it's because you have everything I lost, a pretty wife, kids, a home . . . And part of it is because you're so damn smug about it. I stopped coming over because of the way you always made sure to hold Ruby's hand while I was there, and pat her ass, or kiss her when she brought in the brownies. I mean, it was a Duncan Hines mix, for fuck's sake. And I don't know if you were like that because the obvious shittiness of my life made you appreciate yours more, or if it was some subconscious way of throwing it in my face because I was always so much smarter than you — you had all those tutors —"

"I had ADHD!" Chuck says hotly.

"The thing is," Silver continues, "I would always imagine, whenever I left your house, that you'd be up in your bedroom, lying next to Ruby, appreciating how good you had it compared to your loser brother — like I was this cautionary tale that made your life seem better. And after a while, I just couldn't stand that anymore."

"You twisted fuck. I was trying to help you."

"I didn't need your help."

"You needed somebody's help, and you'd

already shit all over everyone else."

"OK, honey," Ruby says, her hand on his shoulder. "We're getting off message here."

"Fuck the message," Chuck says, getting to his feet. "I'm sorry that you took the fact that I love my wife so personally. What an asshole I've been."

"It's not your fault."

"No shit, it's not my fault." He turns to their parents. "I'm sorry, I tried. But there's no talking to him. There never was. I mean, for God's sake, he still thinks he is a rock star." He looks at Silver, shaking his head. "I do feel sorry for you. I pity you. You've pissed away everything good in your life because once upon a time you wrote a hit song."

"It was a bit more complicated than that," Silver says.

"Not by much."

Silver considers it for a moment. "No, not by much," he agrees.

Chuck heads for the door. "I have to get out of here."

"Don't go," Elaine says. "We're eating." She turns to Silver. "Apologize to him!"

"I'm sorry I upset you," Silver says.

"Fuck you."

"Chuck!" Ruby says.

"I'm going to take a walk," he says, heading for the door. He stops to flash Silver one last baleful look. "You're a dick, Silver."

"I know," Silver says. "Where are you going?"

Chuck looks at him, nonplussed. "I don't know where I'm going. Away from you."

Silver nods and gets up from the table, grabbing the bottle of kiddush wine. "I'll come with."

They walk a few blocks in silence, over to the pond behind the Livingston Avenue cul de sac. It's a cool night, the smell of honeysuckle and cut grass wafting across the pond, taking Silver back in time. When they were kids, they would fish out of the pond, pulling in small bass, bream, and the occasional catfish. Silver always had to bait Chuck's rod because Chuck couldn't handle running his hook through live worms. They would sit up on one of the large flat boulders that ringed the pond, and they would invariably end up discussing what Silver came to think of as the three S's: *Star Wars,* sports, and sex. When the pond froze over they would skate on it, and some of the older kids would play broom hockey, but after Solomon Corey fell through the ice and drowned, no one ever skated on the pond again.

Solomon had been a year ahead of Silver in school — a tall, impossibly skinny kid who walked with the jerky stride of a marionette, and his death had weighed heavily on Silver for a while, the impossibility of someone he knew simply being gone. Silver was twelve, and death was a concept that had dwelled at the periphery of his consciousness for many years, but now it had infiltrated his world, and for a while, everything felt unreal. He would lie in bed at night and try to intuit the thoughts that must have flashed through Solomon's head as the icy pond water filled his lungs. Did the reality of his dying occur to him? Or did he pass out figuring he'd wake up in his bed the next morning, same as always?

"You remember Solomon Corey?" he asks Chuck.

"Yeah," Chuck says, tossing a pebble into the pond. They both fall silent for a moment, watching the ripples radiate outward and fade. "I used to think he was still down there. It never occurred to me that they'd have pulled him out."

They are sitting on one of the flat rocks, passing the kiddush wine between them. There are very few occasions where kiddush wine tastes good, but Silver is pleased to discover that this is one of them.

"He was the first person I knew who died."

Chuck nods and takes a long swig of the bottle, cringing as it goes down. "Wow, that's some bad wine."

"I kind of like it."

"So," Chuck says. "What's the plan here? I mean, why are you doing this?"

"It's hard to explain."

Chuck passes him the bottle. "I think you should try."

Silver takes another drink, savoring the wine, the taste of both his childhood and God. He sits back on the rock and looks up at the sky. The pond is one of the darkest spots in the neighborhood, and you can see a greater array of stars than usual.

"They can go in and fix me," Silver says, "but when I wake up, I won't be any better. For the last bunch of years, ever since Denise and I got divorced, I've been treating my life as this pit stop, just kind of regrouping before I move on. But it's been seven years, and I never moved on. I haven't done anything. I just . . . stopped. And now they want to save my life, but if it's just to go back to the life I've been living, well, I've been there for about as long as I can stand."

Chuck nods sadly, absorbing it, and Silver looks away, suddenly unable to maintain eye contact with his little brother.

"But I think that's a good thing," Chuck says. "You've taken stock. You know you need to make a change. So have the operation, and then start making changes."

"Don't you think if I was able to make some changes, I would have already?"

"Things are different now."

Silver shakes his head. "I'm not. I'm the same fuck-up I always was. And I honestly don't see that changing." He thinks about it for a moment. "When I think about having that operation, I think about waking up in a bed, with no one there waiting for me. No one to take me home."

"We'll all be there."

"That's not what I meant."

Chuck smiles sadly. "I know. I know what you meant."

They sit in silence for a while, tossing pebbles into the pond, listening for the splash as the dark water swallows them. Out in the darkness, a frog's plaintive croak reverberates over the water.

"I could help you, you know," Chuck says. "We could come up with a plan, set some goals; a better job, more time with Casey."

"You want to be my life coach?"

"I guess I do, yeah."

Silver shakes his head. He is both moved

and very tired. The wine has worked its way into his system, and he can feel his eyes closing. He wonders if he might die, right here, next to his brother at the pond. There's something about that, a symmetry that makes sense. But even as he thinks it, Silver knows there's nothing symmetrical about death. Just ask Solomon Corey.

"Well," Chuck says. "For what it's worth, fuck-up or not, I still find myself wishing I could be like you."

"Well, like I said," Silver says. "You were never very smart."

CHAPTER 32

Later, he walks Denise home. Casey left while he was out with Chuck — she is stopping by the Lockwoods' for a bon voyage party for Jeremy, who is heading off to his semester abroad with no idea of the mess he's leaving behind. Silver is a bit confused about Casey's motives for attending the party, but he has never really understood women, and now that his daughter has become one, she is every bit as much of a mystery to him as the rest of them.

Denise and Silver walk side by side in companionable silence. She's on his left, so he can't actually see her — his peripheral vision is still compromised — but her arm brushing lightly against his orients him. He can remember nights like this when they were first married, walking home from his parents' house on Friday night, anticipating the quiet warmth of their little house. He realizes that they will pass that old house on the way to her new one, and the thought fills him with a quiet dread.

It's a small house, a Cape Cod with a large family room off the kitchen that was added sometime in the '70s. Once Denise and Casey had moved out, the house became Silver's, until the bank foreclosed on it. Shortly after that, in a drunken pique, Silver had driven his car up the front lawn and through the living-room wall. The criminal charges were eventually dropped, but his car was totaled and he hasn't owned one since.

They reach the corner of their old block, and Denise says, "You want to walk a different way?"

Silver looks down the block. For a while after the divorce, after he had played a gig and loaded his drums into the old station wagon he'd borrowed from his mother, he would find himself driving to the house on autopilot, only remembering as he turned the corner that he didn't live there anymore. The life you build feels like the entire world, and when it's suddenly gone, the world doesn't make sense for a while. Or, in his case, ever again.

"No," Silver says. "It's fine."

Something in him wants to walk past the house with her. He doesn't know if that's because it might heal something or if it's just an extension of the masochistic streak he's cultivated over the years, the need to punish himself for all Denise- and Casey-related matters.

The house is the fifth one on the right. As they walk down the sidewalk, he feels the dread grow in him. He reaches over and takes her hand, feels her fingers wrap themselves around his, anchoring him to the moment. And then they are there, standing in front of the small, white house. It looks exactly the same. He thinks of all the years he walked up those three stairs and through the front door without a second thought, never imagining he'd one day be standing on the sidewalk like this with Denise, the house now nothing more than a monument to all they've lost. This small, dark house that once contained them, its quiet television flickering through the gossamer shades like the last faint sparks of a dying fire.

"It was all my fault," he says.

"We were young."

"Not that young."

There is movement inside. A man crossing a room lit by the large flat-screen television. You catch glimpses of them now in every house you pass, large LCD screens humming away, everyone plugged into the same hypnotic glow. Maybe if they'd had one back then, he'd have been less restless. Maybe he would have succumbed.

Denise looks at him and there's kindness in her eyes and also something else, something familiar that sets the pace of his heart a bit faster.

"Listen," he says.

Denise turns her body, so she is now standing directly in front of him, shaking her head with a sad smile as she reaches for him. He wishes like anything that they could go back to that wedding where they met, and start it all over again. He knows what to do now. He knows the stakes.

"I wish that too," she says, running her thumb across his jaw.

Something is happening here.

She steps into his embrace and kisses his face, underneath his eyes, so that when, a moment later, she kisses his lips, he can taste his tears on hers. The kiss is long and deep and he feels his chest trembling as he pulls her close. He wants to keep kissing her right here, in front of their house, until his aorta snaps and he dies in her arms.

But the kiss ends, like everything else. And he knows that now Denise will say something, something honest and practical and

241

beautiful and devastating, something to move them gently back into their separate orbits again. But instead he feels her lips on his again, and a small groan, almost a sigh, escaping from her as her mouth opens his.

When this kiss ends, he no longer doubts her intentions.

"Let's go," she says.

CHAPTER 33

By the time Casey summons up the nerve to walk over to Jeremy's house, the party is in full swing. She cuts through the yard, past the pool, and up the Lockwoods' sloping lawn. Jeremy has been texting her on and off for days now to come to his party, and so she has, unsure of her agenda.

The music is pumped up loud enough that the bass and drums are escaping through the double-paned glass and floating across the yard before dissipating into the air. A handful of kids are gathered in a small clump at the far end of the pool, surreptitiously smoking a bowl. A couple lies on a single lounge chair in the missionary position, dry humping as they make out. She feels a million years away from all of this.

A small group of adults are sitting on the deck, drinking mojitos and trying to hear themselves above the music. They are either too drunk to register the illicit activities

243

down by the pool or else consider themselves too cool to intervene. Casey sees Rich, leaning back in his chair, nursing a beer. She waves at him, then thinks about sitting at dinner with her mother and father, and feels guilty. She moves around the deck to give him a quick kiss.

"How was dinner?" he asks.

"A clusterfuck," she says.

"You OK?"

"Define OK."

He nods and offers up a small but genuine smile. "Is your mom here yet?"

"She's on her way."

Rich nods and takes a sip of his beer. "Well, you go hang with the cool kids. I won't cramp your style."

"I have no style to cramp," she says, and heads inside.

She comes through the back door and it's every house-party movie you've ever seen: more kids than the house was built to hold, standing in every nook and cranny, drinking, yelling, dancing, making out. She sees a handful of kids from her graduating class, says hi to them, never stopping to talk. Motion is the key here. If you stop, the party will swallow you up. Someone hands her a beer and she takes a nervous sip or two before she remembers that she shouldn't.

But she holds on to it anyway, because holding it makes it a shield of some kind.

Jeremy is leaving for Paris on Monday. He will take a few classes, sit in cafés, start wearing a scarf, experiment with facial hair, develop an affinity for an obscure local cigarette brand that he will express yearning for in the years to follow, and sleep with more than a few of the French girls in his dorm. It will be five months that will feel like a small lifetime, and he will return to the United States believing that he has changed in some fundamental way, but by the end of his junior year, he'll be clean-shaven again and back in his Abercrombie & Fitch, and he'll have stopped Skyping with the one or two girls to whom he had pledged eternal fealty.

We're all clichés, Casey thinks, all following scripts that have been written and played out long before we landed the role.

She doesn't know why she's here. Or, rather, she does know, but doesn't know if it's a good idea or not. Her mother is certain she should have the abortion. She was too, until Silver had his stroke. Then something changed, although she'll be damned if she can say what. It's been strange, spending this time with her father, both gratifying and deeply frustrating. And he's been utterly helpless in this one regard. He will not direct her, other than to say that he has her back either way. She suspects, with budding awareness, that this lack of a firm position on her pregnancy is not unique to her father, might even be a defining characteristic of his. And this realization is both edifying and immensely disappointing. She is seeing her parents not as parents, but as people, and while it has brought her closer to her father, it has also had the effect of making her pity him, which, in turn, profoundly saddens her. She cannot keep track of how she feels from minute to minute. She wonders, briefly, if it might be hormones.

"Hey! Casey!"

She has reached the front of the house and now turns to see Jeremy, in jeans and an undershirt, sitting on the front-hall stairs with a bunch of guys. She says hi and smiles even as she is aware of his friends taking a quick inventory of her: Legs, check. Tits, check. Face, check. Ass, remains to be seen, but can be fairly extrapolated given the evidence at hand.

Jeremy comes off the stairs and joins her on the landing. "I'm glad you came."

"I said I was coming."

"Yeah, sort of," he says. "But your texts

are tricky."

"I don't think so."

"Yes, you do."

He smiles. She smiles back. He has this one tooth, in the corner of his smile, that overlaps the tooth in front of it, and there's no reason that she should find this appealing, but she does.

"So, Paris," she says. "You excited?"

"Yeah," he says. "Truth is, I could use the change of scenery."

"You've been in college for two years."

He grins. "I know. What can I say? I get restless." His face turns earnest. "Can I talk to you for a moment?"

"Sure."

He looks around, then takes her hand and leads her through the throbbing crowd, past wildly dancing morons, girls laughing, guys high-fiving like they invented beer, kids making out on the couch like they're the only ones here, and kids standing around waiting for something else to happen that will send the party into an even higher gear. Everything else notwithstanding, there is something thrilling about the way he has taken her hand and is moving her through this forest with purpose. She feels oddly embraced.

The kitchen is a mess. They step over

crushed plastic cups and plates and through a door to the back staircase, then upstairs to his bedroom, where he closes the door behind them and turns on his desk lamp. She hasn't been up here in years, but it doesn't look like anything has changed. Navy carpeting, matching bed and desk by Pottery Barn, a framed poster of Bird and Magic on the wall, a team pennant from his high school basketball glory days.

He sits down on the bed while she politely looks over his desk, the pretentious college paperbacks — Bukowski, Kosiski — some sports magazines, his Mac and assorted multimedia devices, some decorative water bongs, a few loose pictures of his college buddies, his airline ticket.

"So," he says. "You OK?"

"Sure," she says, leaning against the desk to face him.

"How's your dad doing?"

"I honestly don't know."

"It's weird, you know? I haven't seen him around in years."

"I know."

"I think he was the drummer at my aunt's wedding. Does he still do that?"

Casey rolls her eyes. "What did you want to talk to me about?"

He looks up at her, suddenly ill at ease. "I

know you've had a lot going on, with your mom getting married and your dad's . . . situation. I just . . . I kind of thought, after that night, that we might hang out, you know? And then you didn't answer my texts . . ." He seems lost, tripped up by his own verbiage. "I just wanted to make sure you're OK."

Casey looks at him, feeling both contempt and attraction. She is almost positive that this is a uniquely female combination. "You wanted to make sure that I'm OK, or you're OK?"

He nods, considering. "Both, I guess. I wanted to make sure we're OK."

"Because we had sex."

"Yeah."

She comes over and sits down beside him on the bed. This is her moment.

"I've been going through some stuff," she says.

He takes her hand. "You want to tell me about it?"

She feels his fingers laced between hers, solid and strong. It's his too, she thinks. He has a right to make this decision with me. But she knows that's not true. The decision is hers. She just wants someone to help her make it. And she knows what he'll say; she could probably write the script of their conversation right now and get almost all of it right, word for word. And that's why she came here, she realizes. Because she knew what he would say, and then she could pretend they had decided together.

"Hey," he says, pulling her closer. "You're shaking."

"I need to tell you something," she says.

"OK."

She looks up at him, takes in his round eyes, his earnest expression. She realizes with a start that he is actually somewhat in love with her. Not in a way that matters or lasts, but just in this moment, and there's something warming about that. She now feels herself shaking, almost shivering. He brushes the hair out of her face, and she runs her hand up his arm.

"Casey?" he says, concerned.

"Just . . ." she says. "Can you just kiss me?"

He does not need to be asked twice. And even as he leans in, her hands have found their way under his shirt, sliding up the impossibly long expanse of his warm back. And one kiss becomes two, then three, then one endless kiss, and she feels herself pulling off her own shirt, even as she knocks him down on the bed with unintended force.

She can no longer figure out what her intentions were when she came here, but now that she's lying here, melting into him, she knows she probably never could have brought herself to tell him. The only false note comes when he leans away from her to rummage through his desk drawer for a condom, and she briefly wants to strangle him as she watches him slide it on. But then he's kissing her again, and then he's inside her, and for the next little while they're just two crazy, horny kids on the brink of adulthood, practicing safe sex in his bedroom while, below them, the endless kegger rages on.

CHAPTER 34

Silver undresses Denise delicately, like she might break. He pulls her blouse off and kisses her chest, inhaling her scent, reveling in the familiar topography of her body. The shape of her shoulders, the shallow pockets behind her collarbones, the small scar over her left breast from a childhood fall. It's surreal to be here again, feeling her heat, tasting her skin, realizing that he has carried the sense memory of her inside of him all this time.

He watches her hands undo his belt buckle, and he is suddenly conscious of how his body has changed since the last time they were naked together. He is easily twenty pounds heavier, and the pathetically minimal muscle tone he has accidentally maintained through his drumming appears as nothing more than a shadow beneath the added weight. He thinks of his erectile snafu with the college girl and wonders if he will be able to perform. He can't really feel himself down there, and it's only when she wraps her fingers around him that he registers, with no small measure of relief, that he is hard.

She leads him over to his unmade bed, and he is acutely aware of his bedroom's sparse furnishings, of the clutter on his night table and the floor beside it, of his ragged linens and the fact that he's not sure when he last changed them. He hopes they don't smell.

They come together slowly in his bed. He cannot stop touching her, running his fingers up and down the length of her arms, across her shoulders, down her belly. He opens his mouth against her breasts, kissing and tasting, feeling their familiar shape in his hands, and he considers the possibility that this is all a stroke-induced hallucination, that he'll wake up paralyzed in his bed, or not at all.

Their rhythm starts to build and he feels the force of her beneath him, the growing urgency in her kisses. He always admired her abandon when it came to sex, the way she was able to lose herself in the pleasure. It always aroused him further, even as he wondered why it was never like that for him. He certainly enjoyed sex, but there was always a side of him that stayed grounded, observing the goings-on from a neutral corner in his brain.

"What's wrong?" Denise says to him, panting hard, her breath filling his mouth.

"Nothing," he says.

"Your heart?"

"Broken."

"But beating."

"Yes."

She kisses him furiously, his hands sliding down her back to find the curve of her ass.

"Then can you please get inside me?" she whispers to him.

And so he does.

He wants it to last forever and to be over already so he knows what will happen next. He knows he can't keep her, but he wonders if maybe he's wrong. God knows he's been wrong about things like this before. He can feel everything all at once; her fingernails digging into his skin, her chin pressing against his as she arches her back, the intoxicatingly smooth surface of her ass in the palms of his hands, the first beads of sweat forming on her neck, his heart beating furiously in his chest. Denise rolls in waves beneath him like a storm, lifting him off the bed with her hips, grunting to the beat like a tennis player, and he feels himself build-

254

ing, worries that he will finish too soon. He doesn't want it to end, is terrified of the expression she will wear when they're done. Is this a fundamental change, or is this good-bye? He was both amazed and relieved at how they arrived here in his bed without any discussion, but now he finds himself wishing he knew what the hell she was thinking, or even what the hell he was thinking, for that matter.

Denise comes, crying out with the pleasure of it, pulling him deeper inside of her like she's trying to squeeze the last bit of something out of him. His own orgasm comes on the heels of hers, not nearly as impressive or animated, but it rocks him nonetheless. When he's done, he rolls off of her, closing his eyes as the room flashes like lightning. He feels her hand land on his chest, her finger tracing circles there. She says something, but he can't hear her over the ringing in his ears.

He stares up at the paint swirls on his ceiling and thinks about God, wonders what He might make of all of this. A wave of clarity washes over him, and he has a thought, an epiphany really. Suddenly he sees an answer, not a solution, but a truth floating above him, and he knows he needs to share it with Denise. But even as he starts to speak, the ringing in his ears becomes louder, and the thought dissolves before he can articulate it. He closes his eyes, trying to recapture it, but the darkness is soft and soothing and doesn't lend itself to introspection. He hears a sound, as if from far away, a low rumbling that he only identifies as his own snoring in the instant before sleep consumes him.

CHAPTER 35

Denise lies on her back, listening to Silver snore. She feels guilty, primarily about not feeling guilty, and wonders if that's the same thing. She isn't quite sure when it was she knew that this was going to happen — maybe when he walked into the dress store, maybe when he showed up to dinner at his parents' looking freshly scrubbed and strangely childlike; she suspects it might even have been as early as when he burst into her bedroom that crazy day last week, eyes blazing, looking to somehow reclaim her and Casey. She realizes now that there has been a part of her for all of these years that never stopped waiting for him to do just that.

But whenever it was, she knows this crime was premeditated. Not by Silver, he never planned anything in advance. If he thought about his actions at all, it was always after he had committed them. That was emblematic of their differences in general. Denise considered and planned, while Silver looked back after the fact and wondered what had possessed him.

And yet here she is, lying beside the man who has failed her in every possible way, who has used up the best years of her life, feeling tenderness and . . . loss? It makes no sense, but if there is one kernel of wisdom she does possess on matters of love it is that sense rarely enters into it. Silver was the first man she ever loved, and even now, after all the anger and hatred, she still feels things shifting inside of her when he walks into a room. And that's not healthy, or fair, or right, but there it is.

She rolls onto her side to watch him sleep. His face loses something in slumber, and he looks unfamiliar to her, like a word repeated endlessly until its syllables disintegrate into meaningless sounds. What have I done? she thinks, then chides herself for being dramatic. She moves closer to him and presses her index finger into his shoulder, watching his skin dimple around her finger. She looks around this small, depressing bedroom, with its cracking paint and generic, shit-brown carpeting; the plywood dresser with mismatched handles on its drawers; the random, scattered laundry piles; the lone cell-phone charger plugged into a wall outlet; and the smell of masculine desperation lingering like a base coat beneath the fresh smell of their recent sex. She experiences a shameful pang of vindication, as if these shabby surroundings are incontrovertible proof that the failure in their marriage had been his. But she also feels sorry for him, for the drab and empty life he's been living all these years, and sorry for herself for being here.

What are you doing here? she asks herself. *Do you love him at all?* She does, she supposes, but it's a love, she knows, that's been bent and twisted beyond repair. We don't stop loving people just because we hate them, but we don't stop hating them either. It's just that, ever since he developed this condition, Silver seemed to become more and more the man he was when she first fell for him, the man he still is in her saddest dreams: honest, impulsive, childishly sincere, romantic. The way he spoke to her and Casey that day in her bedroom, the way he reached for her, the way he told her she was beautiful, the way he looks at Casey. He is her Silver again, and even though she knows all of these behaviors are the result of microscopic blood clots and ministrokes, she can't help but be drawn to him again.

She thinks about his aorta, disintegrating inside of him, ready to come apart at a moment's notice. He will either die very shortly or he'll have the surgery and most likely go back to being the self-defeating, disengaged asshole he's been for the last eight years. Either way, there's no version in which tonight's insane indiscretion will ever amount to anything. She knows that for certain, just as she knows that she will grieve him all over again in either scenario.

She is so lost in these thoughts that it takes her a moment to realize that his eyes have been open for the last little while, and he's been gazing up at her.

"Hey," he says drowsily.

"Hey."

"You're still here."

She smiles. The man really takes nothing for granted. "So it would seem."

They look at each other for a moment. There is no time more painfully awkward than the shaky moments after sex that should not have been had.

"What are you thinking?" Denise says.

"I'm thinking that that felt better than anything I can remember," he says. "And I'd like to do it again."

She smiles. "Well, if once was a mistake, twice would be criminal. Besides, I think my twofer days are over."

"You love Rich," he says.

She bristles momentarily at the statement. "Why would you bring him up like that right now?"

Silver shrugs. He meant no harm. "We just had sex, so you must be thinking of him."

She's forgotten how disconcerting his new frankness can be.

"Well, I'm not. I'm thinking of you, actually. Do you really want to die?"

He sighs and looks away. "I really don't like talking about that."

"Tough shit. You had the sex, you're going to have to suffer through the pillow talk."

He smiles at her, his expression so loving that she has to quell the sudden urge to throw herself into his arms.

"I want to have sex again," he says.

"That's not going to happen."

"For sure?"

"For sure."

He ponders that sadly for a moment, then seems to accept it.

"Silver."

"Yes."

"You're just getting to know Casey again. She needs you. You cannot check out on us again."

"I know."

"I mean, I don't know who got her pregnant, but the fact that she won't tell us means she's probably not seriously considering —"

"Jeremy," he says.

Denise falls silent and looks at him. "What?"

"Jeremy Lockwood. She had sex with him."

Denise feels her breath catching in her throat, feels a surge of anger rising up inside of her. "She told you that?"

"We saw him at Dagmar's and I kind of guessed it. He used to do those magic tricks, remember? He would wear this cape and —"

"Silver!" Denise shouts. "Focus, please. Are you sure about this? Did you talk about it with Casey?"

"Yes," Silver says. "She said it was lovely."

"And you've known this all along."

"For a while, yes."

"And you didn't think that was something we should talk about?"

Silver considers the question and shrugs. "We don't really talk so much."

Denise gets out of bed and starts to pull on her clothing. "You're un-fucking-believable!"

"Why are you angry?"

"I'm not angry. I'm upset. My daughter is pregnant."

"She was pregnant before you knew about Jeremy."

"That little shit."

She pulls her bra on and fumbles for the clasps. Silver is sorry to see her breasts disappear.

"I think you should calm down. Come back to bed."

"Sure. Let's fuck again. That will fix everything."

"You need to relax, Denise."

"And you need to get dressed."

"What for?" he says. But, of course, he already knows.

CHAPTER 36

They intersect in the front hallway, Silver and Denise coming through the front door just as Casey and Jeremy are coming downstairs from his bedroom. They stop to consider each other with wary surprise, the air between them charged with panicked thoughts and a complex knot of postcoital guilt.

Seeing her parents together, Casey recalls the years of dreaming that her parents would remarry. She would lie in her bed and dream up elaborately dire scenarios that would bring her parents back together. These scenarios usually involved something bad happening to her: cancer, a car crash, amnesia. She once went so far as to plan her own fake kidnapping, complete with a letter cobbled together from newspaper type. And maybe it's because of that, that seeing them here now fills her with a sense of impending dread.

"What are you doing here, Dad?" she says, trying for all the world to sound like someone who wasn't having sex with the boy next to her ten minutes ago.

"Your mother wanted me to come."

"Hey, Mr. Silver," Jeremy says. "Hi, Denise."

Casey sees Denise look up at Jeremy, and in that moment, she understands what has happened. Whatever it is her mother is about to say, she knows that it will change everything, and while there's a part of her that wants that, she doesn't want it to happen like this.

"Mom," she says.

But before anything else can happen, Valerie Lockwood comes in from the back, followed by Rich.

"Denise!" Valerie calls out, shouting to be heard above the Radiohead that seems to be coming from everywhere at once. "You made it." Valerie, who has always had a tendency to dress too young, is wearing leggings and a sleeveless blouse and waving her half-drained vodka tonic around with a careless abandon that indicates it's been refilled more than a few times. She kisses Denise's cheek, oblivious to the grave, simmering look on her friend's face. Rich steps past them, sizing up Silver. "Hey, Silver," he

265

says. "This is a surprise."

"This is nothing," Silver says.

Casey stares at Silver, her eyes beseeching him to do something. But doing something has never been his thing.

"Is something wrong?" Jeremy says, picking up on the vibe.

"Is something wrong?" Denise snaps at him. "Are you fucking kidding me?"

"Denise!" Valerie interjects, stepping instinctively in front of her son. "What the hell is wrong with you? What happened?"

"Mom!" Casey shouts. "Just stop it!"

"No!" Denise shouts back at her. "I'm not going to stop it."

"They don't know!"

That throws Denise, shuts her up for a moment. A small crowd is gathering in the hall, sensing some drama in the offing.

"We don't know what?" Jeremy says.

Rich leans in to Denise. "What's going on, honey?"

"Yeah," Valerie says, looking pissed. "What the hell is going on?"

And then, to Casey's abject horror, her mother starts to cry, right there in the Lockwoods' front hall, and any lingering hopes of her making a clean escape are dashed. She looks over at Jeremy, standing pale-faced and confused beside her, and feels a surge of pity for him, in these last moments before everything changes.

Denise is suddenly dizzy. She can still taste Silver on her tongue, can still smell the sad, vaguely musty odor of his bedroom — God knows when he last changed those sheets, or what kind of ecosystem has evolved in those filthy brown carpets. The whole episode seems insane to her now, unreal. Did they really just do that? The music washes over her, confusing her as kids slide past her, in and out of the Lockwoods' front door. She looks over at Rich standing beside Silver. For one crazy moment, she imagines that he is sniffing at Silver, that he can smell her on him. The room starts to spin, and somewhere in a room off the hall there's a strobe light flashing in time to the music, and Denise realizes it was a mistake to come here. She wants it to be morning, wants to be lying alone in her bed, watching the shadows slowly retreat as the sun creeps across her duvet. If she can just make it to morning, she'll be able to make sense of all this, get everything back on track. But right now? Now all she wants to do is find a way to gracefully extricate herself from this situation, from this house, without collapsing, or vomiting, or having to make eye contact with Rich or Silver, or Jeremy Lockwood, for that matter.

"I'm sorry," she says through her tears, she's not sure to whom. She is aware of everyone around her looking at her, and she feels exposed and scared. She needs someone to lead her out of here; she doesn't care if it's Rich or Silver. But no one does, and what's the point of having two men in your life when neither is going to whisk you away in moments like these?

"Denise!" It's Valerie, leaning into her. "Are you OK?"

Denise shakes her head, unable to speak. Rich steps forward and reaches for her elbow, to steady her. "What's wrong, honey?"

"Please take her out of here," Casey says, mortified.

"I don't know what's going on," Rich says, sounding lost and, Denise thinks, maybe a little scared. She feels a stab of intense guilt that threatens to double her over. He has been nothing but good to her, he has been loyal, gentle, and unwavering in his love for her, and all she has done lately is put him through the wringer. She pulls him into her and leans against him.

"I'm sorry," she says.

"For what?"

"For all of it."

He gives her a long look, like he's trying to see through her. She looks up at him and wonders what he thinks, what he knows, and what he'll be willing to forgive.

"Take me home?" she says.

But that's not what happens.

Silver looks at Casey and Jeremy standing on the stairs and he can tell, from Casey's posture, from Jeremy's flitting eyes, that they've just had sex. He couldn't say why, but he just knows. He wonders if they can tell the same about him and Denise. He is still reliving the last hour in his mind, the way they came together with no discussion, the way all of the walls between them had somehow fallen away in an instant, as if they'd never been there. There's a part of him that knows he shouldn't make anything more of it than it most likely was — a last communion before the world shifts again. But there's something in him that dares to hope it might have meant something more. He has always had a dangerous tendency to embrace blind optimism in the face of hard facts. He knows this, knows it is largely responsible for the mess of his life these last ten years or so, but even knowing it, he can't seem to shut down the voice in him telling him that everything happens for a reason, that even a stopped clock is right twice a day, that Casey's improbable pregnancy bringing him back into Denise's life just as she planned to marry Rich has a certain karmic potency that seems to have rendered the laws of love and probability up for grabs.

He can't help himself. When he looks at Denise, even now as she sniffles wetly onto Rich's shoulder, he knows that he loves her as much as anyone can love anyone. But she is not anyone, she is the mother of his daughter, and maybe he and Denise walking past their old house, then going home and having sex in his bed, as if that was where they belonged . . . maybe that was all fate, or Providence, or the God of his sand-swirled ceiling righting the old wrongs and setting them all on a new course together. In its own way, sleeping with Denise tonight then coming here with her to collect Casey feels right and portentous, like the start of their family all over again. He looks at Denise and he knows that this is what he had meant to tell her earlier; that lying naked with her, hip to hip, feeling himself inside of her, had felt like coming home after being lost at sea for years. He looks at her and he wants to tell her that, to tell her that kissing her and touching her and fucking her again has woken up something inside of him, the thing he lacked all those years ago when he let her and Casey slip away, and that if she gave him another chance, please, now that he has seen the stakes, now that he's seen all the damage and the pain, all the lost and desolate years, he knows that this time he'd grab hold of them both and never let them go.

He looks at her, wanting to tell her all of this, but then he sees her expression, and the expressions on Rich's face, and on Casey's face, and on every other face staring at him, and he realizes, too late, that he already has.

Denise looks at Silver in horror, then at Rich, who is backing away from her like she's just grown a pair of fangs. A cold sweat breaks out on her back, her stomach churns, and she feels the ground falling away from her, isolating her. She's alone in this, like she was when Silver first left, and what the fuck was she thinking, going to bed with him like that? Pity? Closure? Both are an exercise in futility where Silver is concerned.

"Rich," she says, but she has nothing to say beyond that. Just his name, which rolls off her tongue like a confession. Rich looks at her, his eyes filled with a hurt she's never seen, and she is floating out of her body, observing the whole circus her life has just become from a perch somewhere over her own shoulder. Just as he reaches the front door, he offers her a small, barely perceptible nod, acknowledging all the pain to come, all the things he knows she will tell him after the fact, somehow validating her even as he flees. And beneath the chaos of the moment, Denise becomes aware of a painful truth about herself: she is never as deeply in love with a man as she is in the moment he leaves her. It was true of Silver, and it's true right now. It's the kind of epiphany she'll forget by morning, but right now, with a piercing clarity, she understands this flaw in herself, sees how she will always be doomed by it to some extent.

She should go after him. She knows that. She is supposed to chase him, crying and begging, so that he can yell at her and say things that will cut her and scar her and leave her wailing on her knees while she watches his car speed off down the darkened street. She knows, without ever having been here before, that that's how this is supposed to play out. But right now it's taking every last bit of strength she has to simply exist. Any further exertion on her part, even as little as a sharp breath, and she'll disintegrate like a thousand-year-old fossil.

And then Valerie is standing beside her, holding her up. She must have started to collapse, although she didn't notice.

"Denise," Valerie says.

"I'm sorry," Denise says.

"Just tell me, what does this have to do with Jeremy?"

Denise looks at her friend, at the faint lines starting to break through the Botox barrier of her forehead, at the overdone eyeliner and the makeup flaking out of her crows feet, and feels a wave of tenderness for her. We're all doomed, she thinks. Eventually.

And so she tells her.

This evening began with so much promise, Silver thinks. It was just two hours ago that he was sitting between Casey and Denise in the warm glow of his parents' dining room, enveloped in the aromas of his childhood, feeling safe and loved and hopeful. And then, impossibly, he was making love to Denise, feeling her fingers slide down his spine the way they used to all those years ago, feeling her lips and legs opening for him, taking him back. And now, like he did all those years ago, Silver watches it all come

273

undone. He watches Rich storm out, watches Casey's expression fall, and then fall some more, watches Denise grow pale and collapse a little into Valerie. Valerie, for her part, looks like she desperately needs to sink her long painted nails into someone's flesh, if she could only figure out what's happening here and, more important, who to blame. Silver would like to get out of Dodge long before that happens. He would like to leave the country before he has to look at the next expression on Casey's face, or see the recrimination and regret in Denise's eyes. Everything I touch turns to shit, he thinks, not with self-pity, but with an almost scientific fascination at the truth of it.

He looks up at Casey, who lets go of Jeremy's hand and comes down the last two stairs to stand in front of him. He now sees the tears he couldn't see when she was up on the landing, with Jeremy's shadow falling over her.

"What the fuck, Dad?" she whispers in a voice so low that only he can hear. There's no anger in it, just a pained bewilderment that makes her seem like a little girl.

"It's going to be OK," he tells her.

She shakes her head and smiles bitterly, and now she doesn't look like a little girl anymore, now she looks like every woman he's ever known, shaking their heads in disbelief at what a fucking idiot he is, and at the fact that they ever might have thought otherwise. "Casey."

She shakes her head again, and shreds him with a baleful stare. "I didn't think my life could be any more fucked up than it was," she says. "And then I let you back into it."

He can't look at her, can't bear to see the hate that makes her older and uglier etched into her face, to know that he caused it. "I'm sorry," he says.

Casey couldn't give a shit. She turns and heads for the door. Just before she steps outside, she turns back to him. "If you're going to die," she says, fighting back tears, "I wish you'd just get on with it already." And then she walks out, leaving him hotly eviscerated and vaguely suicidal.

CHAPTER 37

"Hey, Silver? What the fuck?"

Even before he opens his eyes, he wonders at how often people seem to say that to him. What the fuck? It feels like those three words have followed him throughout his adult life. They ought to be carved onto his tombstone, he thinks, a fitting epitaph for the encapsulation of a life that has, from most standpoints, made no sense at all.

DREW SILVER
1969–2014
WHAT THE FUCK?

Yeah. That would pretty much sum it up.

"That would pretty much sum what up? What the hell are you babbling about?"

He opens his eyes to find Jack and Oliver standing in front of him in their bathing suits, blocking out the sun. "Nothing," he says.

"You're soaked," Oliver tells him. "Did you sleep out here like that?"

He feels the wetness of his clothes plastered against his skin, and he shivers. He vaguely remembers standing at the head of the pool late last night, thinking dark, lonely thoughts, but he has no recollection of jumping in, or climbing out afterward. Clearly, he did both.

He shivers in his chair. Now that he's awake, he's freezing.

"What the hell happened to you?" Jack says. He looks worried.

"Rough night," he says. He can feel his jaw trembling as his teeth chatter.

"We have to get him out of those clothes," Oliver says. He leans forward and begins unbuttoning Silver's shirt.

"What, right here?" Jack says.

"Get his belt," Oliver says.

Silver looks down as the two men undress him. He is wearing the same dark pants and shirt that he put on to go to dinner at his parents' house last night. He is wearing one loafer. He remembers buttoning the shirt Oliver is now pulling off of him, checking himself in the mirror. It was less than twelve hours ago. Feels like years. A lot can go wrong in twelve hours.

"Get him in the hot tub," Oliver says.

Jack and Oliver help him up off the chair and walk him over to the hot tub in his underpants. He is shivering uncontrollably now, barely able to stand on his own. The water is so hot that for a moment it burns him, but as he settles into it, he can feel the heat entering his muscles and then his bones, can feel his body relaxing into it. Jack and Oliver take off their shirts and sit down in the hot tub on either side of him.

"Rub-a-dub-dub, three men in a tub," Jack says.

Silver smiles wanly.

"You feeling any better?" Oliver says.

"Getting there."

"There's something in here!" Jack says, alarmed. He reaches down into the frothing bubbles and comes up with Silver's loafer. "Yours?"

"Yeah."

Jack tosses it onto the pool deck behind him. "So, what the hell happened to you?"

Silver shakes his head. Even the idea of recounting last night is exhausting to him. He just wants to sit here and dissolve into the hot water until there's nothing left of him. He closes his eyes and sees Denise, naked, looking up at him with desire. How does something like that happen and disappear so damn quickly? And why can't the bad shit disappear just as fast? What . . . The . . . Fuck?

"Shit," Jack says.

"What?"

He points. "It's the Fucking Coopers."

The Fucking Coopers: Courtney and Shaun Cooper and their fucking kid, Tyler. Through a series of events and misunderstandings that have never been fully explained, the Fucking Coopers thought the Versailles would be a fantastic place to start their young family. Courtney is beautiful in that way Midwesterners are, blond and cheerful, her face always lit up with a relaxed smile. Shaun has a full head of hair and an athlete's physique. And Tyler, well, he looks like a Tyler. Courtney and Shaun look at each other when they talk, and when they lie on their lounge chairs watching Tyler play, she will often have her hand resting on his arm, and they are an oddity here, a freak show, and so effortlessly, casually in love that it's borderline offensive. The Fucking Coopers.

Courtney takes Tyler into the water, where he splashes around happily. Shaun pulls off his shirt, revealing an enviable six-pack, and starts filming them with his iPhone.

"Good morning, guys," he says as he moves past the hot tub.

"Good morning," Oliver says.

"Fuck you," Jack says under his breath, but his heart's not in it. It's hard to hate the Fucking Coopers, which just makes you hate them more. The Fucking Coopers are a fingernail picking and pulling at every hardened, crusty scab on every man in the Versailles.

"One day," Jack says. "One day she is going to fuck a trainer or the goddamn UPS guy, or he's going to fuck someone on a business trip, or her best friend, or maybe her sister. Or he's going to hit her, or gamble away their nest egg, or become an alcoholic, or their kid is going to turn out to be a little sadist who drowns kittens in the bathtub . . ."

Silver stops hearing him. He watches Shaun climb into the water, sees the way Courtney smiles at him, leaning back against his chest while they watch their son swim. He remembers with painful clarity how it felt to be young and in love, with so much living left to do. He would hate them too, he knows, just like Jack, if he wasn't so goddamned tired.

It's late afternoon by the time he gets up to

his apartment. He fell asleep in the sun and can feel the first flickers of sunburn spreading across his forehead like a fever. He steps into his kitchen to find Denise sitting at his kitchen table, in jeans and a black T-shirt that makes her look ten years younger, sipping thoughtfully from a can of diet soda. She has been in his apartment exactly twice, last night being the first time, and her presence here is deeply disconcerting to him. His feelings of shame and exposure were ameliorated last night by the darkness and mutual nudity. But now the sun is out and everyone is dressed, and while he's been known to misread signals before, he's pretty certain that no one will be getting undressed today.

He has lost her, he realizes. In truth, he realized it last night. He saw the look on her face when Rich walked out, and he understood that whatever insanity had moved her to sleep with him last night, it was not love, or, at least, not a love with any practical implications. He thinks about Denise and Casey and feels a sense of grief, and then frustration, because it doesn't seem fair that he keeps losing the same things over and over again.

Denise looks up at him, her expression tired, her eyes red and somewhat swollen.

"You don't lock your door," she says.

"I lost the key."

Denise nods. "Of course you did. I assume she didn't sleep here last night."

He doesn't actually know. He looks around and shrugs. "I guess not."

"She didn't come home."

"Did she stay at the Lockwoods'?"

"No. Valerie has circled the wagons. She's somehow reached the conclusion that her son is an innocent victim in all of this."

"She's just upset."

"Yeah, well. Join the club."

Denise sits back in her chair and looks around his kitchen, taking in the shabby veneered wood of his cabinets, the industrial granite countertops, the crappy appliances, the unwashed dishes in the sink. "I feel like you," she says.

"What do you mean?"

She hesitates for a second. "Last night I sat in my house. Rich was gone, Casey was gone, and I sat there, on my living-room couch, just wishing they would come home, even though I knew they wouldn't. And I felt alone and terrified, and then I thought about you, and I realized, this must be what it feels like for you every day." She looks up at him, her eyes searching his face.

He has no idea what she wants him to say.

He has always felt this way around distressed women, that there is something
they're waiting for him to say, and if he
could only figure out what that is, he could
soothe the thing in them that needs to be
soothed. He has never figured out what
those words are, and he has always believed
that if, just once, someone had given him
this vital piece of information, his entire life
would have shaken out differently.

"Is that how it is for you?" Denise asks
him.

"Sometimes."

"And the rest of the time?"

He thinks about it for a moment. "I guess
I just feel like I've disappeared. Like I'm
already gone."

She absorbs that for a moment, blinking
back a couple of unanticipated tears. "I'm
sorry, Silver," she says. "I'm sorry you've
been so alone."

"It wasn't your fault."

She smiles when he says that. "Oh, I know
that. Believe me." He is struck by how
beautiful she looks. There's a version of his
life that was meant to be spent with her,
and every so often she looks a certain way,
just for an instant, and he sees this version
of her, the one that stayed in love with him.

"I know where they are," she says.

"Casey?"

"And Rich."

"You think they're together?"

"Yes. At the lake house."

"What lake house?"

"Rich has a lake house. Up in Essex. Casey loves it up there. I'm sure that's where they would both end up."

"Are you going to go up there?"

"No." She takes a long, final swig of her soda and gets to her feet. "We are."

CHAPTER 38

The lake house is a haphazard mix of wood and stone that could be kindly designated as postmodern in that it doesn't seem to adhere to any traditional school of architecture or design. But the skylights, the massive bay windows, and high wooden deck facing Lake Kearney render all sins against design forgiven. It's a spacious house, bright, well kept, engineered to let the sunlight in and hold on to it. A narrow dock, stained the same color as the house, extends into the lake like a broken finger directly below, and tethered to the end is Rich's rowboat, retrofitted with a small outboard motor.

Casey has always loved how quiet it is here, how you can step out onto the deck in the morning and feel embraced by the air and kissed by the sun. Being out here, away from the suburban sprawl, surrounded by trees and facing the glistening lake, always calms her and gives her hope for the world. As long as there are still unspoiled places like this, there is the sense that it's never too late for things to turn around.

She sits on the deck, in the porch swing Rich had built for her when she and Denise started coming out here with him. He loved having her here, and she'd intuited, even back then, that it was a little sad to own a house like this by yourself, and that Rich had been lonely here before he'd found them.

She can hear him inside, moving around mugs and spoons, operating the coffee grinder, trying to find some measure of peace in the routine. She'd driven up here alone, after finally managing to elude Jeremy, who was still reeling from the shock of it all, and kept saying over and over again, "What do you want to do?" which was only a slight improvement over the first half hour of "Why didn't you tell me?" Like telling him last week would have made all the fucking difference.

"Go to Europe," she said.

"I can't," he'd said, though he clearly wanted to.

"You can," she said. "I'll let you know how it turns out."

And when he took her hands and said to

her, "We're in this together," it took every ounce of her will to not kick him and run away screaming. Because they weren't. Jeremy would go to Europe, and even if he didn't, she knew enough to know that he was as much a kid as she was, that there was nothing sustainable between them. He was saying all the right things, but the right things didn't matter. No one was in anything together. Not her, not Silver, not her mother, not Rich. Everyone was fucked and everyone was in it alone. She didn't want that to be true, but she was pretty confident that it was.

Rich steps out onto the deck carrying two mugs. He hands one to Casey, and she's touched by his thoughtfulness. She would think he'd want nothing to do with her. After all, she was the one who pulled Silver back into their lives. If she hadn't done that, Silver and her mother never would have hooked up last night, and no one would be in this mess.

For some reason, she hadn't anticipated his being here when she drove up last night. She figured he and Denise would be at their house, saying horrible things to each other. She'd come up here, in part, to avoid that whole drama. She fell asleep on the couch and woke up after noon to the sound of him

287

scrambling eggs. When she came downstairs after showering, there was a plate waiting for her under the heat lamp, but no sign of Rich. Until now.

"I'm sorry," she tells him.

He nods, attempts a weak smile, and then looks away. "It's not your fault," he says.

"Yes, it is."

"Can we not talk about this?"

He holds his coffee mug up to his face, inhaling its aroma.

"What's going to happen?" she says.

"I don't know," he says.

"Please don't hate her."

He looks out at the lake for a long moment, standing absolutely still. Then he turns to head back inside. "I'm doing my best, honey."

CHAPTER 39

Denise drives them in her BMW. Silver inhales the scent of high-end leather as the suspension massages his lower half. Rich seems to dole out cars like Oprah, either as bribes or maybe consolation prizes, depending on how you look at it.

Silver sits in the passenger seat, lulled into a light trance by the thrumming engine and the passing scenery. He has always loved car rides, always felt most at peace on the road, the blacktop churning beneath him, the horizon stretched out to infinity in front of him. He is aware of the obvious metaphor: You can't run away from your problems, but you can definitely put some distance between them and you. He closes his right eye. His left seems to be functioning again.

"I can see," he says.

Denise doesn't say anything. She hasn't spoken since they hit the parkway. She sits erect in her seat, both hands resting in the bottom crescent of the steering wheel — a habit he remembers from their earliest days. Her expression is grimly set, her lips moving almost imperceptibly as she rehearses what she's going to say to Rich. Silver feels bad for her.

"I feel bad for you," he says.

"I feel bad for me too."

It's not exactly anger in her voice, but a not-too-distant cousin — somewhere between a cold shoulder and outright hostility. Silver remembers the disgust and contempt in Casey's eyes just before she ran out last night. He doesn't know if he can bear to see it again.

"So," he says. "What's the plan?"

"The plan," Denise says, "is to ask for and receive exactly the kind of forgiveness that I would never give. I'm counting on the fact that Rich is a better person than me — or you, by the way. And maybe, just maybe, he will still consider marrying me, or at least not dumping me. And while I'm doing that, you will talk to our daughter and do whatever it is that you do that seems to make everyone who by all rights should hate you somehow find you appealing, so we can get her squared away."

"And how do I do that?"

Denise shrugs. "When in doubt, grovel."

■ ■ ■ ■

Silver comes out of the service-station food market carrying two ice-cream cones. He hands one to Denise, who has just finished pumping the gas. She gives him a strange look, but the thing is, Silver knows, when someone hands you an ice-cream cone, just like when someone offers their hand to shake, you generally take it. And Denise does, offering the thinnest smile as she takes a lick.

"I forgot about you and rest stops," she says.

Rest stops have always made him strangely happy. He couldn't say why. Just the idea of everyone on their way somewhere, united by wanderlust, no one belonging more than anyone else.

"And ice-cream cones," she says. "What is it with you and ice-cream cones?"

He licks around the edge of his cone as he considers the question. "I guess no one ever eats an ice-cream cone at a funeral, or a fire. The Red Cross doesn't drop ice-cream cones into third-world countries. If you're eating an ice-cream cone, it's just very hard to believe that things have gone completely to shit. That there isn't still hope."

Denise licks her cone thoughtfully. "So there's still hope."

"I think so, yes."

She nods, and they just stand there for a moment, quietly licking their cones at the side of the highway while the light Saturday traffic speeds past them like missiles.

She looks at him for a long moment, then sighs deeply. "Silver," she says, her voice tinged with a profound sadness with which he is all too familiar. All the things you can't get back, all the things you can never make right. No matter what happens after, you'll always carry them with you.

He looks away from her. "I know," he says. "Believe me, I know."

They exit the highway, driving past strip malls, car dealerships, and department stores until the road narrows and starts to wind through the trees. The sun flickers kinetically through the leaves, like a dying light, hurting his eyes. He didn't think to bring sunglasses. He closes his eyes, feeling flushed and tired from his sunburn, and the car and Denise slip away a bit. He can feel his breath moving up and down his windpipe, can feel the silent, dogged contractions of his heart. It's hard to imagine your heart simply stopping, but at the same time, it's hard to believe that it didn't give up years ago.

"I can't live like this anymore," he says.

He can hear Denise absorbing the remark. "Like what?" she says.

"Like there's some new life that's going to kick in at some point and I just need to hang out in this holding pattern until it does."

Denise looks over at him. "What changed?"

He shakes his head, trying to figure it out. "I don't know. I think I lost track of time. Every day felt the same, so it felt like forever, but also like no time was actually passing. Like the universe was on pause. And then Casey showed up pregnant, and you're getting married, and I realized that there's always been a part of me that thought I would catch my breath and then pick up where we all left off. But then I turned around, and it was too late. You had both moved on."

Denise nods sadly. "You're quite the asshole, Silver," she says, her voice devoid of any anger, like she's just pointing it out to be helpful.

"I know it," he says.

"And now you're just going to wait for

293

your heart to burst and take the easy way out."

"In the absence of any better ideas."

"Well, do me a favor and don't die today, OK? Today I need you. Can you do that much for me?"

He nods and closes his eyes again. "You got it."

They pull up to the lake house at the latest part of the afternoon, just as the light is changing and the sun is starting to dim over the far side of the lake. Casey's white Infiniti is parked behind Rich's Audi. Silver steps out of the car and looks up at the house. "Nice place," he says. He looks over at Denise standing on the other side of the car looking agitated.

"You want me to wait in the car?" he says. "You know, until you've made contact."

She gives him a withering look. "Don't you dare wimp out on me."

"I'm not," he says. "I just thought, given the circumstances, that seeing me here with you might upset him."

"He's already upset."

"You know what I mean."

"He hates me. They both do. How do I even face them after fucking up so badly."

He offers up what he hopes is a slightly

rakish smile. "Stick with me," he says, heading toward the house. "I do it every day."

CHAPTER 40

"You can't come in!"

Casey's voice stops him in his tracks. He and Denise look up to see her standing on the second-story deck, looking down at them.

"Hey, there."

"Shut up, Silver."

"Casey, honey," Denise says. "I was worried about you."

"What about, Rich? Are you worried about him, too?"

"Of course I am."

"Well, don't be. He's fine."

"Honey, why don't you come down here and talk to us."

Casey shakes her head. "So what, you guys are together now?"

Denise looks at Silver then up at her. "No, honey, it's not like that."

"So just a quick lay for old time's sake? And I thought my timing sucked."

"I know, honey. I'm so sorry."

"Don't apologize to me. I wasn't your fiancé."

Denise looks at Silver, her eyes filling with tears. He's been tapped in. He considers faking a heart attack to lure her down, but that seems like a shitty trick to pull on your kid. Still, he sets the idea aside as a last resort.

"Why don't you let us in?" he says.

"It's not my house," she says. "It's Rich's, and he doesn't want you here."

"Then come down. I can't really see you."

"You know what I look like." Casey rests her forearms on the railing and leans forward casually, like she's taking in the view.

"At least she's talking to us," Silver says to Denise.

Denise shakes her head, then goes to the front door and knocks. "Rich, please! Let me in. I need to explain."

Silver thinks he wouldn't mind hearing that explanation himself.

"Come on," he calls up to Casey. "Let's give Rich and your mom some privacy."

"Says the man who fucked up their relationship." Casey boosts herself up onto the railing and swings her legs over.

"What are you doing?" Silver says, alarmed.

297

"Rich!" Denise shouts, pounding on the door.

"He's not going to open it," Casey says.

"I'm not leaving until he does." She bangs on the door some more.

"Why are you so angry?" Silver says.

"Are you seriously asking me that?"

"I am."

Denise stops hitting the door and looks over at Silver, then up to Casey, who slides her legs down until her heels find purchase on the thin ledge between the rail spindles. Then she leans forward into the air, holding on with one hand to the railing behind her.

"What are you doing?!" Denise cries out, alarmed. "Stop it!"

"Casey! Get back behind the railing!" Silver shouts up to her.

"Please honey! Stop this!"

"I AM PREGNANT!" Casey shouts at them, her voice cracking. "I am scared and lost and fucked, and you're both too busy fucking up your own lives to give a shit! I need my parents! Real parents! Not this goddamn freak show!"

She's crying now, hanging off the railing at an angle that scares the shit out of Silver.

"You're right, honey," Denise says, crying too. "I'm so sorry."

"Get off there!" Silver shouts up at her.

298

He can already see her falling, can hear the sickening sound she'll make when she lands.

"Why should I?"

"Please!"

"You think you're the only one who's allowed to play suicide games?"

Silver turns and runs full-speed at the front door, lowering his shoulder as he hits it. The door, though, is not screwing around, and he bounces off of it and lands on his back with the breath knocked out of him.

"Silver! What the fuck?"

Then the door flies open, and Rich is standing there.

"Rich," Denise says.

"Rich," Silver says, getting gingerly to his feet.

"Is everyone done saying my name?" Rich says.

"Sorry about the door," Silver says.

Rich looks at the utterly undamaged door, then at Silver, as if to say, *You're kidding, right?* Then he nods, and then he charges.

What happens next isn't very pretty: two inexperienced, middle-aged combatants, both of whom rely on their hands to make a living and so are unwilling to throw closed-fist punches. Instead, they circle each other, slapping, shoving, and briefly grappling.

Rich takes a running start and kicks at Silver's legs. Silver raises his front leg defensively, so Rich ends up kicking Silver's foot. Silver swings at Rich's face, but Rich is too tall and too far away and so he misses, his momentum spinning him around so his back is to Rich, who gets in a kick to Silver's ass. Silver manages to grab his foot on the way back, and the two of them spin around, Rich hopping as Silver clutches his other foot to his chest. They make their way across the driveway like that, and then onto the dirt in front of the lake, until Silver loses his footing and they both go down in a tangle of flailing arms and legs.

They roll down the small knoll and into the edge of the lake, kicking up water and dark scum as they wrestle. Finally, Silver manages to slip out of Rich's grip and get to his feet, ankle-deep in the frigid lake water. Rich gets up a moment later and they square off, winded and panting heavily. Silver is vaguely aware of Denise and Casey standing together at the top of the knoll, screaming at them, and is relieved that Casey came down off the porch deck.

"Can we just call it a draw?" Silver says.

"You fucked my wife," Rich snarls at him. He tries to kick at Silver again, but the earth beneath the lake is slick and soft, and both feet fly out from under him. He lands on his back with a splash. Silver steps over to him, and offers him a hand.

"Come on," he says. "I'm not the one you're really angry at."

Rich takes his hand and pulls himself to his feet. "No, you actually are the one I'm angry at," Rich says. Then he turns around and throws a punch straight into the center of Silver's face. Silver goes down hard, stunned and tasting blood. Rich stands over him, grimacing as he shakes off his hand.

"Rich!" Denise shouts at him.

"I'll be right there," he says, all traces of his rage gone.

Silver lies back in the water, resting on his elbows. The world has taken on an other-worldly orange glow, and a chilling breeze blows over him. This is death, he thinks. It actually seems perfectly manageable to him. But then he realizes, with something akin to disappointment, that the orange glow isn't death but only the sunset. It would have been a strategically good place to die. He'd been thinking that every time Denise and Casey came up here with Rich, they would look out at the lake and feel him close by, maybe tell each other funny stories about him. He rinses the blood oozing from his nose with some lake water and then gets to

301

his feet next to Rich, who is flexing the fingers of his right hand one by one, studying them.

"How's the hand?" Silver says.

"Looks all right."

"You want to do it again?"

"No. I'm good."

"OK then," Silver says, turning back toward the house. "I'm glad we had this talk."

He steps out of the water and trudges up the knoll, his feet sloshing in his sneakers, to where Denise and Casey are standing, looking on in horror. Denise runs past him and down into the water to where Rich is standing. Silver stands beside Casey and they watch from a distance as Denise talks to him.

"Your nose is bleeding," Casey says to him without a trace of sympathy.

"That's OK."

"Does it hurt?"

"Not yet. But it will."

Denise is crying now, wringing her hands as she pleads her case to Rich. Watching them, Silver understands that they will not come apart over this, and he is both glad and, on some level, moderately insulted.

"We should probably leave them alone," Silver says.

"Yeah," Casey says. "You should probably leave us all alone."

"You're still mad at me."

"What gave it away?"

She won't look at him, and that hurts. Her tone hurts. His bleeding nose hurts. He searches his fuzzy mind for a route to navigate through her anger, but he comes up empty. Lately he has no problem saying all the things he should keep to himself, but when it comes to saying the things that matter, he falls infuriatingly silent.

"Thing is," he says, indicating Denise, "she was my ride. You think Rich will lend me his car?"

She shakes her head. "Jesus, Silver. I can't believe what a douche you can be sometimes."

"I'd think you would be used to it by now."

She looks down at the lake, then back at him, and sighs wearily. "I'll get my keys."

He follows behind her as she heads up the knoll, stopping to pull off his drenched sneakers. He turns to look back at Denise and Rich, still standing knee-deep in the lake, and forces himself to say a mental good-bye to Denise. Whatever happens from here on out, he knows that he can no longer think of her as his anymore. Which you would think should have been obvious all along, but Silver has a long and storied history, has in fact made something of a religion out of ignoring the obvious until it's far too late.

CHAPTER 41

Denise sits on the porch deck slapping at mosquitoes on her arms and neck as she watches Rich fish from his boat. He has been out there all evening, and seems in no rush to come back in. She can't actually see him anymore; the sun has long since disappeared and a thick curtain of darkness hangs over the lake. What she's watching is the small red fishing light of his boat bobbing up and down a hundred yards out in the black nothingness of the lake. The neon bulbs of fireflies periodically ignite, tracing quick, psychotic flight paths that you'd have to be an insect to understand. Lightning bugs. Rich calls them lightning bugs, not fireflies. Rich, who built the dock below by himself, who takes pleasure in catching, filleting, and cooking his own dinner, and who is a man in almost all of the ways Silver isn't, calls them lightning bugs. And sitting there in the darkness, Denise promises herself that from now on she will call them that too. Lightning bugs. It's the least she can do.

She slaps at another mosquito, even though she knows it's pointless. They have the darkness and numbers on their side, and they will have their blood. She should go inside; she knows that, too, but doesn't feel entitled to sit in the warm lights of his home without his blessing. So she sits on the porch deck, drowning the sting of the mosquito bites with the sting of her own slaps, self-flagellating as she berates herself mercilessly for sleeping with Silver. Admittedly, she had drunk a lot of Ruben's kiddush wine, and as the night wore on, Silver had seemed younger to her, more like the man she had lost all those years ago, and the tragic notion that he couldn't land on a single reason to save his own life suddenly seemed unbearably tragic to her. Had she been trying to save him? To trick him into thinking there was hope? Or maybe she was just saying good-bye? She keeps going back to the moment of that first kiss, trying to isolate what it was that had been in her head, but whatever she was thinking then, she can't access it now. Which will make it pretty hard to explain things to Rich when he finally brings the boat in.

When she got back up from the lake earlier, her feet soaked and frigid, her shoes ruined, she was relieved to see that Silver and Casey were gone. Let him sort things out with her. It won't be easy; she knows that from years of doing battle with Casey, who isn't above fighting dirty when she's pissed. But more often than not, Silver seems to get a pass just for being Silver. She chafes at the injustice of his having acquired favored-nation status simply by being an irresponsible asshole of a father, but if she can sail through this one on his coattails, she'll put that in the "wins" column and move forward. More than anything, what she needs now is to right her own ship, to save herself from this terrible mistake.

She becomes aware of the crickets, their low, hypnotic chirping, and wonders idly, as she has before, if what she hears is ten crickets or a thousand. It's one of those mysteries she has never bothered solving. Rich would know. She makes a mental note to ask him the next time they're up here, as if having an agenda might ensure that there is a next time.

She hears the scrape of metal on wood and realizes that Rich is docking the boat. Her perspective was skewed by the darkness and she couldn't tell that the red light had been getting increasingly closer. She heads down the wooden staircase with the cold chill of fear in her belly, and then walks gingerly across the sandy knoll to the edge of the dock. Rich emerges from the darkness, walking down the dock, carrying a string of five or six healthy-sized trout. He sees her waiting for him and pauses for a second, then comes forward to face her. She can feel the dock beneath her shifting with each step he takes. They look at each other for a long moment. The leaves whisper as a mild wind blows through them, and the calls of nocturnal birds haunt the woods around them. She looks out at the dark canopy of trees surrounding the lake, senses the vast array of unknowable creatures living out their lives beneath them. We could live here, Denise thinks. We could make this our home.

"I forgot how peaceful it is here at night," she says.

She thinks that maybe he smiles. It's hard to tell with the shadows playing across his face. Rich holds up his catch; six long speckled trout, gleaming silver in the faint glow of the distant porch lights. "Paperbellies," he says. Fireflies are lightning bugs. Lake trout are paperbellies. He can call them whatever he wants and it will sound right rolling off his tongue.

"Rich."

He shakes his head, not wanting her to say anything more. "I'll fillet," he says. "You cook."

He moves past her and heads up to the house. Denise turns to follow, feeling her heart finally begin to slow down its frenetic rhythms. She feels the dark veil that descended on her future like the night on this lake finally lifting. Rich understands. A small part of him hates her for it, and someday in the future, during an intense fight, he will pull this event out like a chit he has saved and polished for just such an occasion, and he will render her furiously mute. But that future slap will be a small price to pay for his forgiveness today. And they will get past that, just as she now knows that they will get past this. Because Rich understands, maybe even better than she does, that her momentary indiscretion was the end and not the start of something.

And now there is only their own life stretched out ahead of them, a thought that fills her with a sense of peace that for the entire stretch of their engagement, she realizes now, she had been lacking. She would like to tell him this; she thinks it would reassure him, but he has made it clear that he

309

doesn't want to talk about it, and so she must swallow, maybe forever, the elation she feels in this moment, the clarity of her love for him washing warmly over her. She will have to feel it by herself. The thought makes her sad, but she thinks to herself as she follows him up to the house, which is bathed in the warm glow of the incandescent lighting spilling out from the kitchen, there are far steeper prices to pay for forgiveness.

CHAPTER 42

For the first hour of their drive back, Casey drives in silence, refusing to look at him. He tries to wait her out until he can't take it anymore.

"Are you going to say anything?"

"What do you want me to say?"

"I don't know. I just think we should talk about this."

"Which part?"

"What?"

"Which part would you like to talk about? The part where you betray me and tell Mom about Jeremy? Or the part where you betray pretty much everyone by having sex with Mom?"

"Are those my only choices?"

"Joking, right now, would be a serious fucking mistake, Silver. And I say that with the full knowledge of your incredibly rich history of serious fucking mistakes."

"I'm sorry. Tell me what to do, and

I'll do it."

"What I'd like you to do is to unfuck my mother."

"You're not going to make this easy, are you?"

"Fuck you, Silver. I've done nothing but make it easy for you. And in return, you've turned my life to shit. You've turned all of our lives to shit. That's what you do."

"There's a rest stop. Let's pull over and get some ice cream."

"Fuck you, and fuck your ice cream."

"You say 'fuck' a lot."

"Every single fucking 'fuck' is earned."

"You know, what happened between your mother and me isn't really something for you to be angry at."

"No?"

"I mean, if you think about it, it's really not any of your business. It's just a mistake made by two consenting, slightly intoxicated adults. And we'll face the consequences of that mistake, if there are any, just like you have to face the consequences of, you know . . . yours."

"I think you need to stop talking now."

"I wish I could."

"Just hold it in."

"I've been trying all day. It just keeps

312

pouring out of me. It's like something is loose."

"Something is loose, all right."

"I think you should forgive me."

"I've spent my entire life forgiving you."

"And I appreciate it."

"You're such an asshole."

"I am. I know I am. Just tell me what I can do to make it up to you."

"You can stay away."

"What?"

"From all of us. Mom, Rich, and me. We're a family, the only one I've got. And now, thanks to you, that may all fall apart. I've already lost one family, and I can't do it again. Not now. Not ever."

"Casey."

"I'm not saying it to be mean. I just need you to understand."

"Please."

"Do you understand?!"

"I understand."

CHAPTER 43

On the elevator ride up, he collapses against the wall and sinks down to the floor, unable to summon the strength required to remain upright. He is profoundly exhausted, can feel his remaining energy slowly seeping out of him like blood in a horror film. He watches the door open onto his floor, sees the faded wallpaper of the hallway. He's never seen it from this angle before, at eye level with a small constellation of scuffs and tears from the corners and wheels of countless suitcases and pieces of furniture, as sad, defiant, angry, lost men moved in and out of the Versailles. They should leave marks, he thinks. Gashes and smears, scars for all the lives and families coming undone, for all the damage still to be done.

The door slides closed, and the elevator is still. It feels strange to be in an unmoving elevator, like time has stopped. Maybe, when the door opens again, he will walk out into another world, one in which Casey didn't say all the things she said to him on the drive home, things that are now permanently etched into the scuffed hallway walls of his brain.

It's quiet. Someone will push a button soon, and the elevator will either take flight or descend, and life, or whatever the hell it is he's living here, will start again. But for now, there's nothing but the piercing stillness of this immobile box, and the soft, intermittent sounds of his shallow breathing. The elevator would be a strange place to die. On the plus side, though, he'd be found pretty quickly, before he had time to ruin his apartment with the stink of his rot. He'd become something of a legend in the Versailles, the former rock star discovered dead in the elevator. Speculation will run rampant about the fact that he was found barefoot, with his damp sneakers in his hand. And then, after a little while, with a bit of turnover, he will just become one more footnote in the vast compendium of the building's ever-growing tragic lore.

With that in mind, he somehow marshals the strength to pull himself to his feet and stagger down the hallway to his apartment, where he falls down onto his bed, and where, with a surprisingly minimal number of interruptions to urinate, he spends the next forty-eight hours in semiconsciousness and complete silence.

CHAPTER 44

Ashley Ross is celebrating her bat mitzvah at the Stoneleigh Country Club, with three hundred of her parents' closest friends. It's an island theme, and three black men in dreadlocks and robes play calypso music on steel pans in the atrium, which is festooned with fake palm trees and a wall of LCD screens showing a rolling blue surf on a white beach.

The guests have all been given coral necklaces to wear over their blazers and dresses, and a specialty bar mixes Bahama Mamas and other rum-based island drinks. Silver has played functions like this a million times, to the point where he recognizes the steel pan players and the bartenders, the women sitting at a station in the corner putting beaded braids into the girls' hair. It never fails to stupefy him, the things people will spend their hard-earned money on. Still, the Bahama Mamas are hitting the spot, and the buffet is first-rate, so, all things considered, he really can't complain.

He was reluctant to come along, had in fact flat-out refused when Ruben showed up at his apartment to shake him out of his bed and into the shower. "Come on," he said, standing over his bed. "You promised me."

"No, I humored you."

"Same difference," his father said, yanking the comforter off of him. "My God, this thing needs to be burned. Don't you ever send anything out to be cleaned?"

"I'm not feeling well," Silver said, curling up into a ball.

"My heart bleeds pink borscht for you," Ruben said. It was a favorite expression of his, one he used repeatedly in sermons.

"I need to sleep."

"You'll sleep when you're dead."

"Death jokes. Nice, Dad."

"When in Rome."

"Go away."

"Come on, it will be fun. You could stand to socialize a little bit."

"I won't know anyone."

Ruben sat down on the edge of the bed to tie his shoe. "You'll know Casey."

Silver opened his eyes and looked up at his father. "Casey's coming?"

"Apparently she used to babysit for the bat mitzvah girl." He shrugged. "Small world."

Silver sits up, suddenly alert. "Does she know I'm coming?"

"No. We can surprise her."

Silver thought about it for a moment. "I should probably take a shower."

Ruben smiled warmly. "I think that would be wise, yes."

They ran into Casey almost immediately, who took one look at him, then rolled her eyes angrily at her grandfather and said, "Seriously?" before turning on her heel and walking away. And now Silver locates her on the dance floor, falling into step with the younger girls and the absurdly sexy dance motivators, tearing up the floor with "Cotton-Eyed Joe." She grins widely, enjoying herself as she moves across the floor, slapping her heels and spinning around in step, taking great care to avoid any and all eye contact with Silver. For his part, he's happy to see her smiling and dancing, even if there's an ironic texture to her glee.

There is no seat for him; he has crashed the event with his father and mother. But Ruben is almost constantly being drawn into conversations with his congregants, so

Silver slides into his father's seat, next to Elaine, who has pushed her chair back and is taking miserly sips of a colorful drink. She smiles at her son and moves her chair closer to his, so that she can lean against him.

"What happened to your nose?" she says.

"Rich punched me."

She gives him a stern look. "Well, someone was bound to." Then she looks away, forcing herself to change the subject. "It's a bit much, isn't it," she says, her eyes wandering the room. "I mean, what are they going to do for her sweet sixteen?"

He looks at his mother, taking note of how the lines around her eyes now break off and descend in angled streaks down her once plump cheeks. Her lips are thinner than he remembers, as if years of pursing them have worn them down, and her hair, he realizes with a shock, is now completely silver, and he wonders when that happened.

"What is it?" she says, noting his look.

"You look older."

She is momentarily surprised by his candor, and her hand comes up to touch her face. "You try having you for a son."

"I'm sorry, Mom. For all of it."

She takes his hand. Her fingers are cold and damp from holding the drink. "You want to make it up to me? Live long enough to take care of me when I get really old."

Silver nods, and sits back in his chair.

"You're not going to really make me come to your funeral, are you?" she says. "Because I can tell you right now, if you let this happen, I will not come to watch them put you in the ground. I'll go get my nails done. The list of things I wouldn't do for you is pretty damn short, but that's number one on it."

He rests his head against hers. "I understand."

"That's great," she says. "Because I don't understand you at all."

They sit in silence for a few moments, watching Casey do the Electric Slide. "Look at her," Elaine says. "She's a mess."

"She'll be OK."

"No!" Elaine snaps at him, jerking herself away from him. "She will not!"

Silver sits up a bit, surprised by her anger, which has come on without warning.

"I don't need to tell you that you've been a lousy father," Elaine says.

"And yet, you feel compelled to," he says warily.

"Because you still don't get it! Your daughter is eighteen years old and pregnant."

"She's not a crack whore. She made a mistake."

Elaine shakes her head. "I don't know what was going through her head, but I do know that it's your fault."

"Me? What did I do?"

"Exactly. What did you do?"

"Jesus, Mom."

Elaine's face has grown red, her chin quivering with a quiet rage. "You gave her every reason in the world to write you off. And by some miracle, she hasn't. She still loves you and believes in you. Why do you think she came to you?"

"Because she was scared to go to Denise. She figured I'd be more sympathetic."

He is aware that the music has stopped, that the bandleader has announced the next course. He is so accustomed to the rhythm of these affairs that he mentally logs it without knowing that he has.

"You're an idiot," Elaine says, getting to her feet, inadvertently spilling her drink onto the table. The two older couples seated across from them make a big show of not paying any attention to the mini-drama unfolding right there in front of them at Table 16. "She came to you because she's terrified, and she wants her daddy. To make it better."

The truth of what she's just said cuts into him. Casey wants her daddy. He has been an idiot for so long that sometimes he forgets what an idiot he is.

"I'm trying."

"How? By killing yourself? Are you kidding me? What do you think will happen to her then?"

"She's a good girl. She's done fine without me."

Elaine shakes her head at him, stepping away from the table. "You can tell yourself that over and over again, until you're blue in the face. It's not going to make it any more true."

She gives him one last, pained look, then turns on her heel and storms away from him. Silver looks across the table at the two other couples and nods apologetically.

In the center of the dance floor, the DJ is addressing the room. "Ladies and gentlemen, for your entertainment, the Ross family is pleased to present world-renowned mentalist Mr. Dave Zellinsky!"

There is a round of applause as a tall, thin, completely bald man in an expensive tuxedo steps forward and takes the microphone. "Thank you very much, ladies and gentlemen. How about a big hand for our host, Ashley!"

Another round of applause. Silver decides he can't be here anymore in this hot, loud, shiny room full of strangers. He gets up and begins making his way through the tables toward the exit.

"We're going to have a little fun, now," Zellinsky says, moving into the crowd of tables. "I need a volunteer. Come on, people, it's an open bar. Someone here has to be drunk enough to volunteer." The patter of a seasoned professional. This guy has been at it for a few years. Silver wonders, as he always does when faced with the performers who occupy this vast and sad level of the entertainment business with him, what tragic detour landed this guy on the bar- and bat mitzvah circuit. Whatever the story, he thinks he has a pretty good idea of the lonely, self-loathing hell he goes home to.

He is still somewhat stunned by his mother's angry tirade, and so he doesn't realize the unfortunate moment at which he reaches the open dance floor until it's too late.

"Terrific!" Zellinsky says, running over to him. He puts his arm around Silver and leads him to the center of the dance floor. "We've got our first victim!"

"No," Silver says. "I was just on my way
—"

Zellinsky turns to him. "What's your

name, sir?"

"Silver."

"Let's have a big round of applause for Silver!" Zellinsky says. The crowd applauds. Silver sees his father, standing in a cluster of older men, suddenly looking up, his eyes wide with concern. He sees Casey, standing in the back, looking alarmed and mortified at the mess he's gotten himself into.

"So, Silver. Before I read your mind, I just want to get to know you a little bit. What do you do for a living?"

"I'm a musician."

"You any good?"

"I'm OK."

"Yeah, me too. That's why I'm playing a bat mitzvah. It's all about the craft, am I right?"

The crowd chortles appreciatively.

"So, is there anything you'd like to say to Ashley, right now that we have everyone's attention?"

"Congratulations, Ashley."

"And how do you know the bat mitzvah girl?"

"I don't know her."

"What, are you, gate-crashing a bat mitzvah?"

"Yeah. I guess I am."

Zellinsky suddenly looks uncomfortable.

He's not sure how to play this one. He gives Silver an inquisitive look, and Silver shrugs. A quiet falls over the room. Silver is suddenly aware of Zellinsky's flop sweat, trickling down from his bald pate to his temple. He can feel his own sweat chilling the flanks of his back. His eyes fall on Casey, who has stepped away from the wall and is shaking her head, desperately pointing toward the exit.

"Casey," he says, and waves. He had not realized that Zellinsky still has the microphone extended to him, and his voice fills the room. Casey cringes as three hundred pairs of eyes turn to find her. She blushes and waves back, offering a forced but, Silver thinks, still charming smile. Silver takes the mike from Zellinsky, never taking his eyes off of Casey.

"I'm so sorry, baby," he says.

Casey's eyes grow wide, and she starts to shake her head emphatically. *Not now! Please!*

But it's like he's watching himself from the ceiling, from a perch on the grand crystal chandelier that hangs in the center of the ballroom, and there's nothing to do but watch, along with everyone else.

"I don't want to be here," he says. "I don't know why I'm here. I don't mean here at this party, although, to be honest, I don't know why I'm here, either. I don't know these people, and if this ridiculous party is any indication, I'm pretty sure I wouldn't like most of them. But that's not what I mean."

He is dimly aware that the silence in the hall has taken on a new weight, a clarity it didn't possess before. There is not a single clink of flatware on a plate, not a whisper or even a discreet cough. It has been transformed from a polite silence to rapt attention. Casey has stopped motioning to the door. She is now just staring at him, and he can't tell if she's appalled or interested — the lights from the video crew are throwing a glare at his one good eye. But he has her attention and he doesn't know when he will again.

"I don't know how I became this person, this quiet, pathetic waste of space. I've been going over it in my head, trying to find some moment or event where it all went wrong, and I just can't. It's like, I went to sleep one night, and woke up numb." She has moved a bit, stepped between some tables, and he can see her face well enough now to know that she's crying.

"I haven't felt anything for so long, Casey. I forgot what it feels like just to feel something. But then that day I woke up in the hospital, I was suddenly feeling things again. And I have been ever since. I've always known how much I loved you, how proud I was of you, but now I can feel it again, and it's enormous. It fills me up. And that's why I don't want to have that operation. I'd rather die right here, right in this spot, feeling this way, than live another thirty or forty years like I've lived the last ten."

Casey is crying openly now. Behind her, near the ballroom entrance, he can see the man he assumes is Mr. Ross, speaking heatedly with two security guards. The guards begin to weave their way through the tables toward the dance floor. Silver looks over at Zellinsky, still standing next to him, looking like he's going to be sick.

And then, from behind him, the bouncing climb of a familiar bass riff fills the room. A flicker of lead guitar flits in and out, and then the drums kick in as the band starts to play that old chord progression. In an instant the music takes him back to a warm spring morning. He is sprawled on the couch with his new baby girl lying across his chest. He is kissing her bald head, inhaling her baby scent, and humming to her — a loose, free-form melody that gradually takes shape into the thing that will become this song.

Silver turns around. Danny Baptiste is up onstage, grinning at him as the rest of the orchestra takes up their instruments. Silver smiles up at him, grateful that the onerous silence has been broken. Danny leans into the microphone. "Ladies and gentlemen, that's Drew Silver, I'm Danny Baptiste, and we are the Bent Daisies!" The crowd breaks into surprised, scattered applause. The band's intro to "Rest in Pieces" reaches the clattering pause, which was McReedy's cue, but McReedy isn't here. Baptiste looks at him, and nods encouragingly. Silver looks at Casey, brings the mike up to his mouth, takes a deep breath and closes his eyes. And then, he sings. He doesn't possess McReedy's resonance or pitch, and his voice sounds more nasal than usual thanks to the swelling from Rich's punch, but he can carry a tune well enough, and having sung backup on the album, his voice sounds at home in the song.

He doesn't open his eyes again until the guitar solo, and when he does, he discovers he is surrounded by bodies, dancing and clapping all around him on the dance floor. He looks out to see Casey, still standing there in between the now-empty tables, smiling at him through her tears, as she moves lightly to the beat. And then the guitar break is over and he's singing again. The crowd gathers around him, clapping to the beat. They are having a moment, all of them, the kind you can't plan or orchestrate: him, Casey, and this crowd, all connected by the right song at the right time. Every cell in him remembers this feeling. By the time he hits the repeating refrain, he is spinning in circles, disappearing into the music in a way he hasn't for so long.

And someday soon, I'll rest in peace. But till that day does come, I'll rest in pieces.

And a hundred voices sing it along with him, lifting him up, and he hears Danny's voice harmonizing, joining his own, just like old times, and Casey, mascara running in streaks down her face, is singing along like she used to when she was a little girl and he would play the song in the car for her, and the entire ballroom is throbbing. And it would be nice to think that the music has come back for him, to reclaim him, and that everything will be different. But he knows the music will end, it always does, and cold, songless reality will reassert itself. Right now, though, as the buzzing in his ears reaches a fever pitch, he feels more love than he knows what to do with, and there's noth-

ing to do but close his eyes and let it wash
over him for as long as the music will play.

CHAPTER 45

"That was really something, Dad."

"Thanks."

"What's wrong?"

"Nothing, just . . . you called me Dad."

"What should I call you?"

"Dad's good."

"Well then."

"It's just you don't always."

"Really? Huh. I never noticed."

"Well, I like it."

"I can't believe you stole the show at a bat mitzvah party!"

"Yeah, well —"

"That you crashed!"

"I didn't steal the show. I was just a momentary glitch."

"Are you kidding me? The way they all took pictures with you afterwards? You were the highlight of the party!"

"And I'm the only thing they didn't pay for."

"You looked good out there. I never really saw you perform before."

"I was never out front like that. I was always tucked safely behind my kit."

"Well, it suited you. You should think about a comeback."

"Nah."

"Why not?"

"It's a young man's game."

"You're not that old."

"I'm not that young."

"I heard all of those things you said to me — well, to everyone else, too — but anyway. Thank you."

"You're welcome."

"Are you really proud of me?"

"Are you kidding me? You're the greatest proof that my life hasn't been a complete waste of oxygen."

"So, if your life isn't a waste, why not have that operation?"

"It's not that simple."

"You keep saying that, but I'm calling bullshit. You either want to live or you want to die."

"I want to be a better man."

"Well, you're not going to get any better once you're dead."

"You make a good point."

"I'm going to make a better one now."

"OK."

"You left us, Dad. Mom and me. I know you only meant to divorce Mom, but you divorced me, too."

"I know."

"And I forgave you then. Just like I'm forgiving you now. Do you know why?"

"Why?"

"Lack of options. Mom found herself another husband. I don't get another father. And I need one. I mean, look at me."

"Well, thank you. I appreciate it."

"But if you leave me again, I will not forgive you."

"I understand."

"I will hate you. I will get a big 'Fuck-you-Daddy' tattoo across my chest, and I will sleep with an army of losers to get back at you."

"OK. I get it."

"I'm serious."

"I know you are."

"So, you'll do it?"

"I'll consider it very seriously."

"Jesus, Dad."

"So, Mom and Rich?"

"Full-speed ahead. The nuptials are on."

"That's good."

"Despite your best efforts."

"And that's my cue to change the subject.

Can we stop talking about me for a moment?"

"Sure."

"What are you going to do about your situation?"

"I'm glad you asked, because I've actually made a decision."

"Really?"

"Yes. I've decided I'm going to do whatever you tell me to do."

"That's your decision?"

"It is."

"That's ridiculous."

"You know what? I've been functioning without you for eight years now. Eight years that you should have been there, taking the pressure off of me, guiding me, being there for me. The way I see it, you owe me eight years' worth of parenting. So I'm just asking for it all at once."

"That's a good argument, but your logic is flawed."

"How so?"

"You're asking for guidance from someone who, when faced with major decisions, has consistently, almost prodigiously made the wrong choice."

"Well, then it's perfect, because you can't lose here. I know I'm going to regret it either way."

"I need you to know that no matter what you decide, I'm going to support it."

"That's big talk from someone who might be dead tomorrow."

"I'm sorry. I can't make this decision for you. Nobody can."

"Mom can."

"So ask your mom."

"Then what good are you?"

"My point exactly."

CHAPTER 46

This is Tuesday and, it being Tuesday, they are on their way to jerk off. When Silver considers everything that has happened since his last deposit, he is staggered by it. Seven days have passed, but the world has been turned upside down and inside out. Case in point, the backseat of Jack's car now carries an additional passenger. Casey sits on one side, looking pensively out the window, her hair whipping around in the breeze. Silver has adjusted the small mirror on his sun visor in order to watch her. Ever since the bat mitzvah she has been steadfastly, almost insistently upbeat, and it saddens him to watch her straining to keep up the façade. Denise's wedding will be this Saturday, and Casey is clearly worried about its effect on him. He wonders about that himself, but for the most part, he thinks he's fine with it — sad, certainly, but there's something about the finality of it that gives him a sense of peace. Maybe it will finally bring him the closure he needs. Or maybe he'll get himself piss drunk and cry himself to sleep that night. Either way, he's both relieved and insulted to not be invited. In the meantime, he's been trying to figure out exactly what it is Casey needs him to say about her pregnancy, so that he can say it and help her figure things out.

Jack pulls into the Blecher-Royal parking lot. Casey looks around, confused. "This isn't the mall."

"We just have to run a quick errand first."

"What kind of errand?"

"The kind we would prefer to be discreet about," Jack says at exactly the same time that Silver says, "We have to deposit our sperm."

"What?!"

"Jesus Christ, Silver! Is there anything you can keep quiet about these days?"

"Apparently not."

"Wait, Dad. You're serious?"

"It's for medical science," Silver says.

Casey shakes her head. "That's not creepy at all."

"Well, when he says it like that," Jack says defensively.

"Did you really bring me along to wait in the car while my father jerks off?"

Jack flashes Silver an annoyed look as he opens the car door. "I liked you a lot better when you knew how to lie."

"I'm probably disqualified anyway," Silver says. "You have to report any adverse changes in your health."

"Holy shit!" Jack says, stopping with one leg out of the car. "Do you think this stuff had anything to do with your heart thing?"

"I doubt it."

Jack thinks about it for a few seconds, then drops back down into his seat and starts the car. "Fuck that."

"So much for medical science," Casey says from the backseat, and her laugh, gleeful, like a child's, makes him smile and breaks his heart at the same time.

Chapter 47

Silver listens as Lily sings to the kids. "Oh, Mr. Sun," "Michael Finnegan," "Puff the Magic Dragon." She's wearing her hair down today, with no visible makeup, and she looks tired, he thinks.

"So, who is she?" Casey says, coming up behind him.

"Just a girl." He had left her browsing over in the Fiction and Literature section, but she has tracked him down. It's raining outside, a powerful summer rain that batters the bookstore window like applause. Hard rains like this make him miss his childhood, the smell of rubber slickers, the scrape of galoshes on pavement. It's one in the afternoon but it looks like night outside. He is suddenly feeling depressed and irritable.

"She's cute."

"Yeah."

"She's why you come in here," Casey says,

getting it.

"Yeah."

"So what's your status?"

He shushes her, though she is speaking pretty softly. "No status," he says.

Casey looks him over. "How long have you been coming here?"

"I don't know." He wishes he hadn't brought her in here. He feels exposed.

"A few weeks?" Casey says. "A month?"

He looks at her.

"Oh shit," she says.

"You swear a lot."

"Broken home."

"Fuck off."

"Touché."

"Come on," he grumbles. "Let's go."

"Why don't you ask her out?" Casey says, standing her ground.

"I've been waiting for the right time."

"Come on, Dad. When's the last time you asked someone out?"

He rubs the back of his head, still damp from the rain, while he considers. It has been so long since he was in any kind of relationship. He doesn't know how to explain it, this paralysis that takes hold whenever he sees a woman he'd like to ask out. It infuriates him when he considers the years of solitude he has spent because of

341

some latent shyness or fear of rejection he can't seem to overcome when the moment demands it.

"It's been a while," he says. Years, he thinks, although he isn't really sure. Chronology has always been somewhat elusive to him.

"She's a musician, you're a musician," she says. "It's cake. I mean, come on, Dad, you were a rock star!"

"I was the drummer."

Casey shakes her head. "How do you not see the tragic irony here?"

He shrugs. He gave up on irony years ago. It was that or death by prescription pills.

"You were enough of a rock star to completely screw up your life," she says. "And now, when you need to be one, when it will actually help you, suddenly you were just the drummer?"

He looks at his daughter, so pretty and wise beyond her years, and he wants to weep from the loss. Casey seems to sense his mood, and she steps forward and kisses his cheek. He cannot remember the last time she kissed him, and he is dangerously close to dissolving. She places one hand on each of his shoulders and looks him in the eye.

"Dad."

"Yes."

"You're a good-looking guy. You've got that kind of cuddly bad-boy thing going on, like you're dangerous, but only a little bit, you know? You have kind eyes and a killer smile, and life has beaten you up just enough to make women want to save you. Hell, even Mom slept with you again, and she hates you." He gives her a look. "Sorry. You know what I mean. The point is, I always assumed you were swimming in women."

He shakes his head. "Nope."

She nods, understanding, from that one word, the immense loneliness he will never be able to articulate, and he is grateful to her for seeing him.

"OK," she says. "Here's the thing. We are not leaving this store until you ask that babe out."

"Lily," he says.

"What?"

"Her name is Lily."

Casey smiles. "OK then. Go get her."

At the moment he approaches her, she suddenly crouches down on one knee to fix the clasp of her guitar case, and so he is now standing over her. He feels too large and imposing, so he backs away, but now the

343

distance is too great, an awkward distance for conversation, so he takes a step forward, but now he has advanced, retreated, and advanced again, which makes him feel like an idiot, and if she's aware of him standing there, he's sure he looks like an idiot, so he goes back to his original position and waits for her to stand up, feeling much too big and awkward standing here in the Children's Books section, with its miniature tables and the little red chairs with white flowers carved into the seatbacks.

She stands back up and slings her guitar case over her shoulder, only then noticing him standing there. He has never been this close before. She has two faint craters in her forehead just above her left eye, and her eyes in general are bigger than he realized, and a deep green that he finds instantly appealing despite the appearance of dark, tired shadows beneath them. She looks a little sad to him, or maybe just hungover. He has no idea because, despite how long he has been coming here to see her, he doesn't actually know the first thing about her.

"I don't know anything about you," he blurts out.

She nods, considering the information. "There are support groups," she says.

Sarcasm. Or maybe repartee? It's hard to say.

"I'm Silver," he says, offering his hand. She takes it.

"I know who you are."

"You do?"

"You're the guy who comes every week and stands like a spy behind those shelves while I sing."

He can feel himself blushing. "I'm sorry."

"It's OK."

He feels the urgent need to say something clever. "I like the way you sing."

Now it's her turn to blush. "They're just kids' songs."

"I know. Still."

"Well, thank you."

An empty silence descends upon them. How the hell is this supposed to work, anyway? People meet people every day. They talk, they go out, they kiss, they fuck, they fall in love, they make families, and all because they managed to push past any initial introversion and awkwardness to make contact. He wishes they were drunk.

"I'm not good at this."

"At what?"

"At talking to you."

"A lot of people aren't good at talking to me. You should meet my parents."

"I don't think I'm ready for that kind of commitment."

She smiles wryly, then looks up into his eyes, really looks at him, trying to figure him out. "This is a strange conversation."

"I'm sorry."

"No. It's fine."

She is still looking right into his eyes. It's disconcerting, actually. He realizes how rare that is, how few people in his life actually look right at him like that. He suspects this is more his fault than theirs. These last years have buried an aspect of his confidence, and he doesn't know how to access it. But now Lily is looking at him, and there's something both wise and damaged in her eyes, something bold in her shyness, something that feels warm and draws him in the same way her singing does. He senses a profound kindness in her, a softness he wants very badly to know and to protect. *Be a better man.* He could be a better man for her.

Lily looks at him strangely. "You know you're saying this out loud, right?" she says.

He hears his voice retroactively, after she points it out.

"I do now," he says.

He and Casey walk home in the teeming rain, sharing a small drugstore umbrella.

He throws his arm around her and her arm falls easily around his waist, and cars speed past them, kicking up hissing sprays of water from the flooding streets, and Casey is laughing as he replays the conversation for her, and she is beautiful and happy and his, and he wishes he could freeze this moment and live in it forever.

CHAPTER 48

Sad Todd wears black goggles, orange earplugs, a red bathing suit, and blue flippers as he swims his laps. He does this every morning, fifty laps across the Versailles pool, before it gets busy and laps become impossible. Despite his colorful getup, he swims with a power and grace that belies his wallflower demeanor.

Jack, Oliver, and Silver sit out by the pool wordlessly watching Sad Todd swim, the sun just emerging hot and bright from behind the building. They have the pool deck to themselves for the time being, and Sad Todd is like a pendulum, putting them into a trance.

"So, I have cancer," Oliver announces.

Jack and Silver turn to face Oliver.

"Fuck," Jack says.

"What kind?" Silver says.

"The colon kind."

"They can cure that, can't they?" Jack.

"They're guardedly optimistic."

"When did you find out?" Silver.

"About six weeks ago."

"What?!" Jack.

Oliver looks over at Silver and smiles. "You kind of stole my thunder."

"I'm sorry, man."

"You've had cancer for two months and you're only telling us now?" Jack says, irate.

"I've been having chemo treatments. I wanted to see how it played out."

"And how has it played out?"

"The tumor has shrunk significantly. Now they want to operate."

Jack sits back in his chair, disgusted. "Shit! You guys are going to die and leave me alone in this shithole, is that it? Is that the fucking plan?"

Oliver laughs. "That's not the fucking plan."

"So what is the plan?" Silver says.

They all watch as Sad Todd executes a shockingly flawless freestyle flip at the far wall of the pool, cutting smoothly through the water on his way back across. We were all other people before this, Silver thinks.

"I'd like to see my kids," Oliver says. "Before the surgery."

Silver and Jack trade a look. Oliver never discusses his children with them.

"Where are they?" Silver says.

"My daughters all live out west. But my son is in Jersey."

Jack nods and gets to his feet. "OK. I'll drive."

Oliver looks up at him. "What, right now?"

Jack looks down at both of them as he pulls on his shirt. "Damn straight, right now. Between the two of you, someone could drop dead at any minute. I don't even feel safe hanging out with you anymore. It's like a fucking bad-luck convention." He heads for the building. "Meet you in the lobby in twenty."

Oliver and Silver watch him walk away. "Deep down," Oliver says, "he means every word."

Silver laughs. Oliver laughs along with him. In the pool, Sad Todd flips over and turns, just like the world.

Oliver's son, Tobey, lives in Long Branch, on the Jersey Shore. It will take them around two and a half hours to get there. It's a perfect day for a drive in Jack's convertible — the sky is cloudless and the recent rain has drained the air of its leaden humidity — and despite the somber nature of their mission, they can't help but treat this as a road trip. Casey comes along for

350

the ride, sitting in the back with Silver, her face turned up to the sun, eyes closed, listening to music on her phone. Silver sits back, his knees braced against the back of Jack's seat, enjoying the wind coming in waves over Jack's windshield to lightly brush against his face.

When they arrive in Long Branch, wind-blown and dusty, Oliver can't find the house. They drive around for a while, up and down quiet residential streets filled with large, laid-back-looking homes, while Oliver tries to get his bearings. Jack offers to put the address into GPS, but Oliver is adamant that he can find the place, and seems unwilling to have to resort to satellites, as if that would be too much confirmation of this decade-long estrangement. But he finally gives in, pulling up the address from his phone, his faced etched with frustration.

Two right turns later, they pull up in front of a large, comfortable-looking house with an L-shaped addition and the shoreline visible about a quarter of a mile behind the backyard. It's an idyllic house, almost fake in its relaxed perfection. Oliver whistles, impressed.

"Restored Georgian, five bedrooms, three and a half baths, newly renovated, ocean views. That's some serious real estate."

"What does your son do?" Silver asks.

"He writes children's books."

"He must be good at it."

Oliver gazes out from the car, sinking down in his seat. "I think I'm going to be sick."

"You are sick," Jack says. "That's why we're here."

"Nevertheless," Oliver says. Then he cracks open his door and pukes onto the sidewalk.

"Seriously, Oliver?" Jack says, looking away.

Casey leans forward to rub Oliver's back, a gesture that strikes Silver as particularly generous considering she barely knows him, and he feels a warm lump form in his throat.

"We shouldn't have come," Oliver says, pulling himself back into a sitting position, wiping his mouth on a loose napkin from the floor. "I think we should go."

Casey looks over at Silver, her eyes imploring him to intervene.

"You can't be serious," Jack says.

"I'm sorry," Oliver says, still looking a bit green. "This was a mistake."

"Bullshit!" Silver says loudly.

Jack and Oliver both turn around to look at Silver, unaccustomed to such vocal certainty from him.

"This is not a mistake. The mistakes were already made, years ago. We all made them. And we've been paying for them ever since. But there's only so long we can keep paying. I don't know what happened between you and your son. But whatever you did to him, it can't be any worse than what I did to Casey —"

"I slept with his fiancée."

That silences Silver for a moment. It silences them all, even those of them who were already silent.

"Shit, Oliver," Jack says. "Silver had a perfectly good pep talk going there, and you had to go and fuck it up."

"I'm sorry."

"My point still stands," Silver says. "You can't let your mistakes define you. You've paid for it long enough. No kid should be without his father. And if your son continues to make that choice, then that's his tragedy. But it's your job, as his father, to let him make that choice. You can't make it for him."

Oliver looks at Silver for a long moment, then back at the house.

"He'll probably just tell me to get the hell off his property."

"And if he does, you can go home knowing you tried."

Oliver nods slowly, then opens his car door again.

"Good luck," Casey says.

They all watch as Oliver heads up the long, curved walk to the house.

"He's had cancer for six weeks and he didn't tell us. Can you believe that?" Jack says, shaking his head. "What the hell is wrong with him?"

"The same thing that's wrong with all of you," Casey says, watching Oliver ring the doorbell.

"And what's that?" Jack says, turning to look at her, but Casey remains quiet, unwilling to explain what it is she meant.

The front door is opened by a tall, thin woman in exercise clothing. A small boy stands beside her. Oliver is momentarily thrown by the sight of the boy. The woman says something to him, but Oliver can't take his eyes off his grandson. He says something to the boy. The boy responds, and Oliver nods somberly.

The woman looks briefly past him to where Jack, Silver, and Casey are sitting in the car. The three of them smile and wave self-consciously. She waves back — a positive sign? — then disappears back into the house, leaving Oliver to stand there with his

354

grandson. A moment later they are joined by a stocky man in khaki shorts and a T-shirt. This is Tobey. There is no way to miss the family resemblance, down to the same pattern of baldness. Father and son stand there for a moment, each taking the full measure of the other. Like his wife, Tobey looks past Oliver to the car, and the three of them wave again. Tobey doesn't wave back. Then Jack throws the car into gear and pulls away from the curb, tires squealing. Silver and Casey are thrown back against their seats.

"Jack!" Silver shouts. "What the hell?!"

Jack shouts over the roar of his accelerating engine as he steers them out of the neighborhood. "His son would have to be a real prick to kick him out if he doesn't have a ride."

Silver has to concede that maybe he has a point.

Jack finds the beach, and manages to scare up some blankets from his trunk. Silver buys some sandwiches and sodas from the concession, and they eat lunch while they watch the pounding surf. The beach is crowded for a weekday. People are starting to sense the end of summer, still a few weeks away. He looks at Casey pulling her hair into a loose ponytail as she turns her face into the wind, and feels all the usual deep pangs of love and regret. It would have been so easy, he thinks, to do things like this; take her on drives, to the beach, to a movie. Anything. It's not like he was busy traveling the world. He was right here, and nowhere to be found.

He lies down on his back and closes his eyes, trying to shake off the self-loathing that has suddenly descended upon him.

"Don't die," Jack says.

"I'll do my best."

Later, Silver and Casey walk barefoot along the waterline with the sun at their backs. Casey throws bits of bread up to the low-flying gulls, who snatch it out of the air as they bank and swerve.

"I slept with Jeremy again," she says.

He looks at her, at the way she's looking straight ahead, focused intently on his re-action without ever looking at him. It's a strange thing to tell him, but these are strange times between them, and something about the crashing surf seems to blunt the edges of their conversation, making every-thing feel a bit safer than usual.

"It was that night at his party, before you and Mom showed up. I went there to tell him about the baby, and I ended up sleeping with him."

"I figured," he says, remembering what she looked like coming down the stairs with Jeremy that night. "Why do you think you did?"

He worries that he sounds too much like a shrink, but the way she considers the question tells him he was right to ask it. "I guess I just wanted to feel like a regular teenager again, you know? I wanted to feel how it would have felt if I hadn't gotten pregnant, if we'd kept fooling around for a little bit, you know, a summer fling, my first sexual relationship."

"I can understand that."

"Yeah, because, as far summer flings go, I screwed this one up pretty badly."

"There'll be plenty of others."

"Plenty? You think I'm quite the whore, don't you?"

"You know what I mean."

She smiles. "You think Oliver's son will forgive him?" she says.

"I don't know. Not everyone is as forgiving as you."

"True."

"Thank you," Silver says. "For never giving up on me."

"Oh, I gave up on you," she says, taking

his hand. "I just don't have any follow-through."

He smiles and they head down the beach at the leisurely pace of two people who have nothing to do and no particular destination in mind.

When they come to pick up Oliver, he is sitting on the front porch next to Tobey, with his grandson on his lap. Another boy, a few years older, sits on Oliver's other side.

"This looks promising," Jack says.

They watch as Oliver stands up, reluctantly putting his grandson down. He turns to Tobey and they exchange a few strained words and shake hands. Then Oliver reaches out and tentatively touches his son's shoulder. It's an awkward, almost lame gesture, and it makes Silver cringe inwardly in empathy. He knows the broken love that forces the need for contact like that.

Oliver crouches down to hug each of his grandsons. The younger one pulls back and gives him a kiss on the cheek. Even in the car they can hear the kid's sweet, high-pitched voice as he says, "Good-bye, Grandpa."

Oliver gets back into the car, and Jack pulls away. "So," Jack says. "How did it go?"

"He didn't throw me out," Oliver says.

"Baby steps."

Oliver nods, then turns to look out the window as suburbia gives way to strip malls and traffic lights, and then the Garden State Parkway. Everyone is quiet, relaxing into the noisy wind stream of the convertible as Jack pilots it down the highway, and the occasional slight tremor in Oliver's shoulders is the only indication that he is silently weeping against the car window.

They are driving out of a rest stop just north of Newark when Jack asks Oliver if his son is going to come in for the surgery.

"He doesn't know about that," Oliver says.

Jack looks over at Oliver, incredulous. "You didn't think to mention that you're having surgery?"

"It didn't come up."

"How about the cancer? Did that come up?"

"I didn't want to manipulate him."

Jack brakes hard enough that they all lurch forward in their seats. Then he turns in his seat to face them, oblivious to the fact that he is parked in the middle of the entrance ramp. "I just want to go on record as saying that the two of you are handling your respective illnesses with a degree of ineptitude that is staggering. This one can't be

359

bothered to have the operation that will save his life, and this one keeps his cancer a secret from his friends and family. I mean, Jesus Christ!"

Behind them, a car honks, then swerves angrily around them. Jack stands up in his seat to yell an angry fuck-you at the driver.

"Take it easy, Jack," Silver says.

"Fuck you, Silver," Jack says angrily. "Fuck you and your torn aorta and your little emotional monologues that make everyone feel uncomfortable."

"Jack . . ." Oliver says as another car honks and swerves around them.

"And fuck you too, Oliver," Jack says, gathering steam. "Fuck you and your secret-ass cancer and your old-man platitudes. You're fifty-six, for God's sake. Get over yourself." He stares back and forth at both of them, and then sits down, staring forward grimly. "I've got an ex-wife who wishes I was dead, and an eight-year-old bastard kid that has been raised to think I'm the anti-christ," he says. "I don't have a family. You're my goddamn family. And believe me, I know how pathetic that is, but that's where I'm at. And I am sick and tired of you both acting all casual about dying. Death is the least casual thing there is. And if you two leave me alone out here because you

360

couldn't be bothered to take care of your-selves like normal people, I will make a point of visiting your goddamn graves on a weekly basis just to piss on them."

He nods to himself for emphasis, then throws the car back into gear and starts driving again.

"I'm sorry," he says, as an afterthought.

"Don't be," Oliver says.

"It was a good speech," Silver agrees.

"Really? I thought maybe I took it a bit too far with the whole pissing-on-your-graves thing."

"Nah," Silver says. "That was fine."

"You sure?"

"Yeah. You're good."

"It was really more of a metaphor," Jack says, and something in the way he says it sends Casey into a fit of tearful laughter that lasts for a good half mile or so.

CHAPTER 49

Tonight feels complicated.

For one thing, Silver is seeing stars. Not stars, really, but glimmers, like the air is wearing sequins, so from his seat at the bar between Oliver and Jack, everything in the room is glittering. For another, he is on his third glass of bourbon, neat.

He has never been a beer drinker, has always found it to be a sluggish buzz. He sticks to bourbon, always neat, and has learned through trial and mostly error to start watering them down after his third. But still, three shots of Noah's Mill can give him that warm flush, that sense of shifting, as if someone has been making minor adjustments to the gravity in the room.

So there's that.

Also, Lily is sitting on a stool at the center of the small, jerry-rigged stage in the corner of the bar, strumming her guitar and singing a soulful, acoustic rendition of Pat Benatar's "We Belong," which he finds both beautiful and random. He is here at her invitation; it was the last thing she said to him as he clumsily backed away from her in the bookstore.

"I'm singing at Dice tomorrow night. I don't get much of a crowd. You should come by."

He had sensed and been moved by the forced nature of her seemingly casual invitation, tossed out there like it was of no consequence, and now here he is, simultaneously hopeful and angry at himself for being so. Hope has never been a friend to him.

Tonight is also a little bit tricky because Miranda, the mother of Jack's bastard son, Emilio, is tending bar, and she is clearly not happy to see Jack here. Of all the gin joints in all the towns in all the world, Silver thinks. And Jack's not making it any easier, staring her down over the lip of his beer mug.

And Oliver has come along, not so much to provide Silver with much-needed moral support but because today he faced his son for the first time in a decade and met his grandsons for the first time, and he needs to drink his pain, hope, and fear into submission.

And Denise will be getting married this weekend, and the date looms totemic in Silver's mind. He doesn't know if that will be the best or worst thing that could possibly happen to him, if it will save his life or be the thing that puts him over the edge.

So, yeah, it's complicated.

Time is bending. It's slowing down and speeding up with no rhyme or reason. Lily finishes the Pat Benatar and starts singing Chrissie Hynde, but suddenly she's finishing that one and Silver can't remember hearing the song through. Now she's playing "She Talks to Angels," by the Black Crowes — which for some reason is required in every acoustic set played in every bar across the country — and he's hearing every note, seeing the chords as colors in the air around them, flashing and changing through the glittery air.

She never mentions the word addiction, in certain company.

Her hair is down tonight. It's the first time he's seen it like that, and she's wearing a bit of makeup, and a dress and boots that stop just below her knees. Silver is entranced, in a way that makes him pray to God, to himself, to whomever might come through, that he find within himself some basic level of social competence tonight, and maybe, from some forgotten corner of his personality, just the faintest hint of charm. He doesn't know that he was ever charming, but he suspects he may have once been at least a little bit.

She'll tell you she's an orphan, after you meet her family.

Lily's voice, high and soft, pushes past the tin buzz in his ears to land softly in his head. The air shimmers, giving everything a dreamlike quality. Oliver tosses back another shot of Maker's, and Jack curses at Miranda under his breath.

"You got something to say?" Miranda says to him, her voice filled with the threat of violence. She is a short, coffee-colored woman with exquisite bone structure and thick dark hair that falls around her like a mane, and she moves behind the bar with a liquid grace, ducking the lame attempts at protracted flirtation from her patrons, ensuring tips with her easy laugh and the low-cut sleeveless T-shirt proclaiming the name of the bar in bright pink letters. It's easy to see what it was that pulled Jack in.

"No. Nothing," Jack says, slapping down an excessive tip onto the bar. "Another beer, please."

"That guy giving you a problem?" someone says from farther on down the bar. They all look down to see the guy, late twenties, hair locked into place with pomade like it's the '50s, shoulders and biceps rolling off each other beneath his tight T-shirt.

"She's my baby mama," Jack calls down to him.

Silver watches Lily sing, transfixed. It's ridiculous, the love and tenderness he feels filling him up. He wonders if it might be yet another stroke, but then reminds himself that there's been something about her since he first saw her, more than a year ago, singing in the bookstore. He's been around long enough to know that men, or at least men like him, can fall in love like that. He sees something in her, senses it from her crooked smile, from the way she opens her eyes between verses to look out at the back of the room, from the soft uncertainty of her voice, from the songs she chooses. He knows her without knowing her.

"Shut the fuck up," Jack says, although Silver's pretty sure no one has said anything.

"Take it easy," he hears himself saying.

"Peter and Max," Oliver says, naming his two grandsons. "Max looks just like Tobey did at that age."

The conversations have all started to blend together.

"I'm just trying to talk to you." Jack.

366

"Really, the spitting image." Oliver.

"Back off, Jack. I'm not playing." Miranda.

"Tobey looked older than I thought. Did he seem old to you?" Oliver.

"You used to like playing with me." Jack.

"Go easy, man." Silver.

And all the while, Lily's voice is filling his ears as she sings about talking to angels. It is, he thinks for reasons he doesn't fully understand, the perfect song for her to sing.

"Shut up."

"Two boys. Nice-looking kids."

"Fuck you.

"Whatever."

Silver can't follow the various threads of these conversations anymore. He's always been something of a lightweight when it comes to drinking, has often thought of alcoholics with a certain wistful admiration. He could never get there. Dizzy after three drinks wouldn't really bode well for binge drinking. Whatever problems alcoholics might have, commitment isn't one of them. And in this respect, he feels inferior.

Up onstage, Lily starts to play something that he can't place right away. A light, dragging bass line is integrated into her strumming. It's only once she starts to sing that he realizes she's playing "Rest in Pieces." He has never imagined the song this way, and he is stunned by the simple elegance she has brought to the silly pop song he wrote. Was it always there, waiting to be discovered, or has she imbued it with new properties it never before possessed? It seems to him that this is a profoundly important question, one with far-reaching implications, but he is too addled and buzzed and keyed up and lost and found and in love and terrified and tired to figure it out just now.

Lily finishes playing and stands up to a warm round of applause. It was the last song of her set. He wonders what, if anything, that means. He is waiting for her when she comes down from the stage, carrying her guitar. She doesn't seem surprised to see him waiting for her, which he decides he will take to be a positive sign.

"That was really beautiful," he says.

She smiles and looks down at her boots for a second. "I thought you might get a kick out of it."

"So, you know who I am, then." For some reason, he is momentarily thrown by this idea.

She looks at him like he might be joking, sees that he isn't, and she smiles. "You're humble," she says. "I didn't see that coming."

"Not really."

"That's exactly what a humble person would say."

He looks at her and thinks she is beautiful in a way that goes beyond her looks. She is weathered but somehow unbowed, or barely bowed, or maybe she is bowed, but has a sense of humor about it. Time will tell. But she is possessed of an innate kindness that he sees almost like a color coming off of her.

And she is just so pretty.

"You seem like a very kind person," he says.

She laughs, surprised. "You don't have much of a game, do you?"

"No. I guess I don't."

She meets his gaze and holds it, and he holds hers, and it's an effort for both of them, and he feels a thrill building. The air shimmers between them like fairy dust. He wonders if she sees it too. Something is happening here. There are words he can say right now that will elevate them from strangers to something more, and he would give anything to know what those words are. And then they come to him, and he smiles, knowing that he will say them, and she will hear them, and the universe will change in a profound and permanent way.

And that's when Jack sucker-punches the muscle-head at the bar, and a minor fracas breaks out.

No one has patience for another stupid bar fight, and the whole thing fizzles fairly quickly. The guy Jack hit has youth and size going for him, but Jack has Silver, who steps in, looking to break it up, and ends up being knocked off balance and falling down against the bar in a fuzzy haze. There follows a good deal of shouting and jostling, and then, suddenly, in the midst of the chaos, he sees Lily's face, hovering above his, the hint of a wry smile at the corners of her mouth.

"That was fast," she says.

"The good fighters always finish fast."

Her laugh is instant and lovely. Silver looks up at her in a way that makes her look at him funny. "What?" she says.

"I want to kiss you."

She grins. "This doesn't really seem like the right time."

Behind them, he is vaguely aware of Jack cursing a blue streak as management drags him out of the bar.

"It will after the fact," he says. "When you tell the story."

"So there's going to be a story? That must

be some kiss you're planning."

"It might be my last one."

"What, are you dying or something?"

"I might be. It's not clear yet."

She looks at him, really looks at him, trying to understand the things about him that he himself doesn't, and he finds himself smitten anew by her simple sincerity.

"Well then," Lily says. "I guess you had better get to it."

She offers him her hand, and he climbs to his feet. The room wobbles around him for a minute before becoming completely still. He looks at Lily. She has been lonely. He recognizes this as only another lonely person can — that small, almost invisible edge in her expression that comes from too many solitary meals and movies, too much time spent in worthless introspection, too much time spent regretting a past that can't be undone. This is someone who is ready to be loved, he thinks.

"I like you," he tells her.

"It's your funeral," she says with a grin.

"You have no idea." He pulls her close exactly the way someone with confidence would, and he kisses her mouth. Her lips collapse against his in a manner that feels like surrender and conquest simultaneously, and he is flooded with a sweet desire he hasn't felt in years. When it ends, the room wobbles around him for a minute before becoming completely still.

And then he does it again.

He loved a girl once; for no particular reason, just a lot of little ones thrown together. Isn't that what love is, anyway? The sum of a million intangibles that all come together in just the right way at just the right time? Like conception. Or the universe. He loved her before he met her, which isn't as romantic as it sounds, because for some people, loving at a distance comes naturally. And then they did meet, and when she smiled at him through the shimmering air he felt it in his belly. He took her home with him — they didn't discuss it, it just became their presumed destination — and the sex was sex: exciting, intimate, and awkward. These things take time. But afterward, after they had dispensed with it like a formality, they lay in bed speaking in low voices, confessing any sins that came to mind, absolving each other the way only near strangers can. Then it was morning, and she was dressing to leave, and as he kissed her good-bye, he was overwhelmed by the notion that they were, in fact, still strangers to each other, and he couldn't for the life of him see how to get from there to somewhere else. The whole notion of building a relationship from scratch seemed like a vast and complex enterprise, the thought of which was instantly exhausting. And yet . . .

In spite of the strangeness of it all, of the

way they seemed to find even small talk a strain in the harsh light of day, of her quickness in leaving and his desire to be alone with his fears, in spite of all of that, he felt something he hadn't felt in years, a warm energy spreading across his chest, filling him. It seemed equally possible that he might love her forever or might never see her again, but that energy was incontrovertible proof, long overdue, that there was still some juice in that creaky, battered heart of his.

CHAPTER 50

Sad Todd is going home.

They sit in the lobby, Silver, Jack, and Oliver, as Todd moves back and forth, overseeing the two porters who are moving his possessions out to the small U-Haul he's got idling in the driveway. A number of the other men have come down to watch the proceedings. They are all similarly cynical and awestruck.

Reconciliation. The impossible dream.

"So she took him back," Jack says.

"It happens," Oliver says.

"She doesn't need her husband back. She needs reinforcements. I mean, you've seen those kids, right?"

"Maybe she missed him," Silver says.

Jack looks at Silver and raises his eyebrows archly. "You're just not seeing things clearly because you got laid last night."

Silver smiles. He can't really argue. He is still seeing Lily's smile every time he closes his eyes, can still smell her and taste her.

"And you got your ass kicked."

Jack is sporting a nasty laceration under his eye and a bandage across his knuckles.

"Hey, I gave as good as I got."

"How was it with that girl?" Oliver asks him.

"It was good."

He doesn't want to admit, even to himself, that he has no idea how good it was. It was something, and whatever that something was, it was better than the nothing that's been his default for the last seven years.

Sad Todd rolls a cart with his computer supplies across the lobby. Silver pictures the den that will be reclaimed, can feel the sense of renewal that will permeate Sad Todd's house, and he's happy for him.

"He'll be back inside of a year," Jack says.

"Shut up, Jack," Oliver says. "Let's give him this moment."

"Guess we can't call him Sad Todd anymore," Silver says.

The loading is finished, and a handful of men gather around to say their good-byes. Silver, Jack, and Oliver join them, shaking Todd's hand, wishing him well. Stay in touch, Todd says. He does not take a last look around the lobby, doesn't take a sentimental pause, a last breath in these sad environs. He just heads out to the driveway, throws the U-Haul into gear, and drives off.

Sad Todd has left the building. They will never see him again. And in no time at all, he will be largely forgotten. Life swallows people up like that.

CHAPTER 51

Things are starting to speed up. He is losing time. He feels lightheaded more often now, and sometimes finds himself in the middle of a room, or conversation, with no recollection of how he came to be there. He knows that this has to do with blood flow to his brain, with the little clots breaking off in his aorta and shooting up to his brain like microscopic bullets, scarring it like the side of a building after a gunfight.

One minute he is saying good-bye to Lily, and the next he is in the lobby watching the formerly sad Todd take his leave. Then he's in the shower, and now he's out to dinner with Casey. They are at Carlucci's, a family-style Italian place a few blocks over. He doesn't remember making the reservation, doesn't remember the walk over, but here they are, finishing their soups. His is minestrone, hers potato leek. Casey's hair is freshly blown and down, and she looks heartbreakingly beautiful to him.

"So, Dad."

"Yes."

"That woman. The singer."

"Lily."

"Lily."

"How'd that go?"

"Hard to say."

"You going to see her again?"

"I hope so."

"Well, keep me posted as events warrant."

"Will do."

Casey sits back and considers him for a moment. "You seem sad."

"I'm not."

"So what are you, then?"

He thinks about it for a moment. "Waiting," he says.

"What for?"

"Whatever comes next."

Casey spoons her soup thoughtfully, clearly debating whether or not to say something. "You know," she says, "there are some people out there who don't wait for what comes next. They decide what should come next and they go and make it happen."

Silver smiles sadly. It occurs to him that what he has failed to impart through wisdom, he may well have imparted through stupidity.

"You're right," he says. "I think things would have turned out differently if I were one of those people."

"I'm just like you."

"You're nothing like me."

"No, I am. I keep waiting for the universe to decide things for me, and the thing is, the universe has better things to do."

"When did you get so smart?"

She shrugs. "Broken home. You pick shit up."

It occurs to him that there is something wrong with his soup. He takes another few spoonfuls, concentrating. It takes him a minute, but he figures it out. He can't taste it. He leans forward and takes a spoonful of Casey's soup. He eats a piece of the garlic knots the waiter had put out with the soup. Nothing. He can taste nothing.

"What is it?" Casey says, alarmed.

He shakes his head. "Nothing."

He is dying. Bit by bit. He can feel it happening inside of him, small things inside of him starting to call it a day.

"Dad?"

She calls him Dad now, thoughtlessly. And it never fails to bring a lump to his throat.

"What, baby?"

"Are you going to get that?"

380

"What?"

"Your phone. It's ringing."

He almost never carries his phone, which almost never rings. He reaches into his pocket and pulls it out. Sure enough, it's ringing, on a pitch close to the ringing in his ears, which is why he didn't hear it. He looks at the screen and sees a number he doesn't recognize.

"Aren't you going to answer it?" Casey says.

"I don't know who it is."

"You push the button and you find out."

Silver nods and picks up the call. "Hello?"

"I like you too," Lily says.

And then he is in the hospital, sitting in a small room with Jack and Oliver. Oliver is on a leather recliner, the IV needle in his arm delivering his last chemo treatment.

"I still can't believe you've been coming here all this time without us," Jack says.

"Sad Jack hates to be left out of anything," Oliver says, winking at Silver.

"Fuck you, Cancer Boy," Jack says.

They've been calling him Sad Jack ever since Sad Todd left the building, and it drives him crazy.

"When's the surgery?" Silver asks him.

"Next week," Oliver says. "You know, you

could have yours then too, and we could get ourselves a private recovery suite upstairs."

They both look at him expectantly. He isn't ready to talk about this yet. "Denise is getting married tonight," he says.

"Oh, shit," Jack says.

"The wedding day of an ex-wife is always traumatic," Oliver says.

"Even your third ex-wife?"

"Fuck off, Sad Jack."

"Keep calling me that and I'll put an air bubble in your drip."

"Are you going to the wedding?" Oliver says.

"No."

"Why not?"

"What do you mean, why not?" Jack says. "Did you go watch your many ex-wives get married?"

"No, but they all hated me."

"I can't imagine why."

"I'm not invited," Silver says.

They both look at him, and the way they do it makes him feel he has revealed more than he meant to.

"There are plenty of reasons to stay away from your ex-wife's wedding," Jack says. "But that is not one of them."

Oliver nods sagely. "Sad Jack is right."

"Sad Jack is going to jam that chemo bag up your ass and make your shit glow."

Silver laughs. He feels a surge of warmth for these men who have kept him company these last lonely years.

There is a noise behind them, the clearing of a throat. They turn to see Oliver's son, Tobey, standing in the doorway.

"Hey," Tobey says. "I hope I'm not interrupting."

The expression on Oliver's face is something they've never seen before. He opens his mouth to say something, but nothing comes out.

And then Silver is opening the door to his apartment to find his father standing there in his best suit.

"Come on," Ruben says. "Get dressed."

"What are you talking about?"

"The wedding. I can't be late."

"I'm not going to the wedding," Silver says.

"Of course you are. One of every life-cycle event. You agreed to it."

"I'm not invited, Dad."

"That's never stopped us before."

"This is different."

"No, it's not," Ruben says, leaning against the doorframe. "If anything, she'll be happy to see you."

"I think your understanding of women is fundamentally flawed."

"Says the divorced man to the man coming up on his fiftieth anniversary."

Silver grins. "That only means you understand one woman."

"And that's one more than you. So put on that ridiculous tux of yours and let's get moving. I'm on the clock here."

And then he is standing outside Renni's, a large restaurant with an enclosed courtyard. The restaurant has been rented out for the affair, and he can see the guests through the windows, milling about inside. Casey steps outside, wearing a rust-colored gown and heels, looking so much like a woman that when, after a moment, he registers that it's her, there's no choice but to feel old.

"You came!" she says with delight. She takes his arm to lead him inside, but he remains fixed where he is.

"I'm not sure about this."

She turns to look at him, then gives him a quick kiss on his cheek. "Be sure," she says.

CHAPTER 52

They're doing a cocktail hour before the ceremony. Rich, in tails and a white bow tie, stands in a cluster of men near the bar. Silver watches him joking around with his friends. He assumes they're all doctors, but maybe not. Maybe some are bankers, or run hedge funds or technology companies. Either way, they all look scrubbed and polished, every hair in place, every tuxedo perfectly fitted. He instinctively moves in the opposite direction.

"Where are you going?" Casey says.

"I don't think he wants to see me."

But Rich does see him, just then, and while the good cheer that's animating his face definitely falters, he doesn't seem terribly angry. He excuses himself from his golf buddies — Silver has no idea if they even play golf, but that's how he thinks of them — and makes his way across the room to Silver and Casey.

"OK," Silver says. "Be cool."

"I am cool."

"I meant me."

"It's OK, Dad. He's not going to get into it at his own wedding."

"I play about sixty or seventy weddings a year. Trust me, I have seen some shit go down."

Casey takes his arm. "Well, you have me to protect you. Just try not to say anything stupid."

"Have you met me?"

Casey laughs just as Rich comes over to them, still carrying his glass of scotch. "Hey, honey," he says, kissing Casey. "You look magnificent."

"Why, thank you."

Silver extends his hand. "Congratulations, Rich."

Rich hesitates just long enough to make him anxious, then he takes the hand and shakes it. "How's the nose?"

"It's OK. How's your hand?"

"It's fine."

Rich looks at Casey. "I'm sure your mom would love your help getting ready," he says.

Casey looks unsure. "We'll check on her in a few minutes."

Rich smiles. "It's OK, honey. Silver and I will be just fine, won't we, Silver?"

"You'd know better than me," Silver says.

Casey looks torn, but then nods. "OK. But you two behave, OK? No drama."

"No drama," Rich says.

Casey casts a last anxious look in Silver's direction, then turns and leaves. Silver turns to Rich. "So, I'll let you get back to your guests."

"You are my guest," Rich says. "You may have crashed, but that doesn't mean I wasn't expecting you."

"If you don't want me to be here, I can go."

"I don't want you to be here. What man in his right mind would want you to be here? But Casey wants you to be here. And she may be your family, but she's mine too, and I won't be the one who disappoints her."

"You're a better man than me," Silver says. "They're both lucky to have you."

"You're damn right I am," Rich says, more angrily than he'd intended to. He takes a breath and checks himself. "The thing is, Silver, I can get past that bullshit with you and Denise — some last, crazy impulse — she's getting married, you may be dying . . . I recognize that there's a lifetime of unresolved issues that were there before I came along. I don't like it — believe me, I don't

387

like it — but I can't change it, and I'm smart enough to know that."

Silver nods. Rich leans in and looks him square in the eye. "Now you have to be smart too, and I know that runs contrary to your general MO, but you have to know what it is that you can't change."

"I do."

"Are you sure?"

"Yeah. And I know it's kind of late for this, but I'm very sorry for all the trouble I've caused."

Rich looks at him for a moment, then takes a long swallow of scotch. "I used to like you, Silver. I don't know why, and I don't anymore. But on the subject of things you can and can't change, you need to have that operation. I'm not going to beg you. But whatever it is you've lost, you still have a family."

"Thanks, Rich," Silver says. "And I do hope you and Denise will be very happy together. You both deserve it."

Rich searches his face for any trace of sarcasm. Finding none, he nods and allows a small smile. "Thank you."

"And thanks for being so cool about me crashing your wedding."

"Thank the Xanax-scotch cocktail," Rich says, holding up his glass as he backs away.

"Do me one favor?"

"Sure."

"Don't fuck up my wedding."

Silver smiles. "You got it."

"Seriously, man. Don't."

The ceremony takes place in the courtyard. The guests sit in rows of chairs facing the chuppah, which has been rigged to four white columns festooned with roses. Silver sits in the back next to his mother, feeling highly conspicuous as he sweats into his shirt.

"Breathe," she tells him.

The Scott Key Orchestra is playing. Silver saw them at cocktails, and he nods a quick hello to Baptiste, who is playing a standing bass for the small combo that will be handling the processional. The music starts and, as always, Baptiste throws him a quick little riff. Silver nods his thanks.

They are playing Clapton's "Wonderful Tonight," a foolproof, if somewhat sappy, selection. Casey walks down the aisle with a poise that puts him on the verge of tears. She turns to look at him and flashes a wry smile. She will be OK, Silver thinks to himself.

"Breathe," Elaine whispers again.

"I am," he tells her, too loudly, and she

389

shushes him.

He can see Rich up front, greeting Casey with a hug and a kiss. He is jealous and grateful and flushed with shame, all at once. He failed, as a husband and father, and this better man has stepped in and cleaned up his mess. And it's while he is awash in these feelings of shame and regret that all the guests rise, and Denise steps into the room.

Silver looks at her, luminous in her white gown, her hair teased into unfamiliar, luxuriant curls that frame her face, her eyes as wide as her smile. He can see, beneath her makeup, the faintest trace of the bruise from where the door hit her what seems like a lifetime ago. She takes her first step into the room, and he can feel his face grow hot. The last time he saw her in that dress, a few days ago, she had fallen into his arms, and he'd entertained absurd notions of getting her back, of turning the last seven years into a bad dream. Now, looking at her face, filled with joy and purpose, he understands that that was never an option. Forgiveness has its comforts, but it can never give you back what you've lost.

As Denise passes his row, Silver fades back, trying to confer on himself a form of invisibility, but something makes Denise stop and turn. Their eyes meet, and he feels his legs begin to tremble. She looks at him for what seems like an eternity, then she turns and steps out of the aisle and into his row. It's happening, he thinks for one insane moment.

The people standing between them in his row back up to make room for Denise, their chairs scraping noisily against the stone floor of the courtyard, and he is aware of small, hushed whispers breaking out in the crowd.

Her ex-husband.

I don't know, he wasn't invited.

The Bent Daisies. The drummer.

Silver.

And then she is in front of him, and even now, here, knowing what he knows, he wonders if she'll ask him to run off with her.

She smiles, and puts her hands on his shoulders. "Silver," she says.

"You look beautiful," he tells her.

Her smile grows wider, even as tears form in her eyes. She pulls him into a hug, and he feels the skin of her back against his fingers one last time.

"We need you alive," she whispers to him, even as he feels things inside of him dying.

And then she's back in the aisle, although he can't remember letting go of her. And then his father is chanting a blessing, and then rings are being exchanged, and then Rich stomps on the glass and kisses his bride as the courtyard erupts into applause and cheers. Denise is married. And even though nothing has changed, not really, in that moment he feels like he has lost her all over again.

The reception is in high gear, and the family has converged on the dance floor in a wild and sweaty horah. Silver watches from his seat as they go around in a tight circle, holding hands and laughing. Denise, Rich, Casey, Rich's two sisters — tall, gangly women who could, at best, be referred to as handsome — Rich's parents, who are surprisingly small given their towering offspring, Denise's father, whose face remains without creases from a lifetime of not smiling, and Ruben and Elaine, who don't seem at all put off by the fact that they have just married off their ex-daughter-in-law. Ruben, in particular, has his face raised to the ceiling, his eyes closed, and an almost rapturous smile on his face as he moves around the circle, holding Elaine's hand on one side and Casey's on the other.

Casey momentarily steps out of the circle and comes running over to Silver, grabbing both of his hands. "Come on, Dad."

She called me Dad.

"I think I'll sit this one out," he says, but even as he says it she is pulling him, off his chair, onto his feet, through the throngs of onlookers clapping to the beat, and into the center of the dance floor to join the circle. It's Denise who breaks ranks to let him in, so he ends up holding her hand on one side and Casey's on the other as they dance the horah, pulling one another around in an accelerating circle. Ring-around-the-rosy at high speed, Silver thinks. Denise smiles happily at him and squeezes his hand. He is happy for her, even as her joy leaves him dented.

Around they go, and even as they pick up speed, keeping time with the band, he feels everything slowing down. He is aware of Casey, her fingers in his hand as she laughs, trying to manage the excessive folds of her gown while keeping up with the tempo. He remembers her as a little girl, squealing with glee as he held her hands and swung her in circles around the room. And here they are now, older and sadder, but still spinning.

He sees the band, playing this strange hybrid of a traditional Jewish horah fused with jazz, sees Baptiste, like him, years away from their brief moment in the sun. He wonders if Baptiste's life after the band has mirrored his own. They've never really talked about it. He sees Dana, standing with a second backup singer he doesn't know, remembers her toes curling up on his comforter that last sad, sexless night they spent together.

He sees his father and mother looking over at him, the love in their eyes tempered with concern and confusion over what he's become. He'd like to tell them how grateful he is to them, how none of this is their fault. He should tell them that, as soon as this dance is over. That they did everything right and he turned out wrong anyway. Just like he did everything wrong, but Casey will turn out right.

He sees the beads of sweat forming on the highest peaks of Rich's forehead, where his hair is beginning to recede more aggressively. He'll be bald within a few years, but it will only make him look better, more dignified. Silver always reserved a quiet contempt for men like Rich, straight-laced, earnest, uncomplicated. Content. And now he'd give anything to be like that, to have always been like that. Instead, he was blinded by the flare of fleeting, accidental stardom, and when it was over, he never stopped seeing spots.

Silver sees all of this in an instant as he dances around in the circle, his feet stomping the ground, the sweat dripping down his face. And then he lets go of Casey and Denise and finds himself in the middle of the circle, spinning counterclockwise, like an inner wheel within their wheel, spinning and sweating and laughing and crying. He feels the love around him, feels the people in his life swimming past him in a blur, feels the grief and regret crashing down on him in waves. He spins. Faster and faster, his feet keeping time in half beats, quarter beats, eighths. His hands come up to his sides, then higher, reaching up above him. He is faintly aware of clapping and cheering, catcalls and whistles as he spins, eyes closed, the lights flashing like lasers behind his lids. He remembers going to the planetarium in high school to see a laser light show set to rock music. Pink Floyd, Led Zeppelin. Sneaking in a joint and getting high as the lights exploded across the ceiling. There was a girl. He held her hand. He can't remember who she was, but he has a sense of her smile, her clean white teeth, the smell of her shampoo as they rested their heads together, the erection he hid artfully under his shirt until the marijuana calmed it down.

Silver spins and sees his life in its entirety, laid out before him between the crunching beats of the music; all of the joy and pain and anger and lust and love and song and sex and regret. All of the points at which he should have turned right but instead went left, the places he should have stopped but instead kept going, and the cost of it all. A deep sob escapes him and he opens his eyes. He sees the ceiling, high and ornate, a painted fresco, spinning above him, making him dizzy. And then he sees it: a cluster of bad spackle work to the side of the chandelier fixture, a sand-swirl finish that reminds him of the ceiling in his childhood bedroom. And just before everything goes down, Silver remembers God, and surprises himself by offering up a lightning-quick but no less heartfelt prayer. Then he closes his eyes and surrenders to the incessant buzzing in his ears, which continues to rise to an ungodly decibel until everything goes dark.

CHAPTER 53

He opens his eyes in a hotel bed. The room is dim, and the first hints of morning are starting to come through the window. He rubs his eyes, feeling the incipient throb of a hangover behind them. He had some wild dreams last night, intense and vivid, only now fading into vapor. He turns onto his side to study the woman asleep beside him. Denise. The wedding. He remembers now. He smiles.

She stirs beside him, her arm sneaking out from underneath the comforter, flailing until it finds his chest, where it comes to a rest, and he savors the warmth of it as he relives the night. His cousin Bruce's wedding. She was the slightly sad bridesmaid. They had danced and laughed, then come up here and had much-better-than-expected sex. And now she's asleep beside him, and he has a chance to study her face. She's prettier than he remembers, a rare feat in these situations. There was something about her, a warm wit that he had enjoyed. He runs his fingers gently up her back. He likes the way her skin feels beneath his fingertips, hot and so incredibly smooth. He does it again. She makes a sound, like purrring, and rolls herself closer to him, nestling into the curve of his body.

"Silver," she whispers to him.

"Yes."

"Keep me warm."

Something about the way she says it moves him profoundly. He wraps his arms around her, her back pressed against his chest, and presses his lips against her shoulder, and, as he listens to her soft, shallow breathing, decides that that is exactly what he will do.

CHAPTER 54

When he opens his eyes again, he is lying on a couch in the small back office of the restaurant, and Rich is taking his pulse.

"I'm OK," he says.

Rich shakes his head, trying to conceal his anger. Or annoyance, really. "You are a lot of things, Silver, but OK is not one of them."

Silver sits up, to prove him wrong, or to prove to himself that he still can. He feels a wave of dizziness and almost lies down again, but he fights through it.

"Where's Denise?"

"She's outside. You know, at her wedding."

"I'm sorry," Silver says. "I didn't mean for this to happen." He could be summing up the moment, or his entire adult life.

Rich fixes him with a hard look, and then sighs, his expression softening. "I know you didn't."

"Get back out there. You can't miss your own wedding. I'll be fine."

"Casey went to get you a drink. I could use the break anyway."

They sit in silence for a moment. The office is small and musty and smells of dog, with messy stacks of paper on every available surface. Silver can't imagine any real work getting done in here, but then again, what does he know from offices? Or work.

"Hey, congratulations," Silver says.

Rich smiles archly. "Thanks."

"I thought I was dead."

"You're not too far off."

Silver smiles grimly. He has run out of time, he can feel it. "You've got a wedding full of doctors here. Why are you the one in here with me? You should be out there, enjoying yourself."

Rich gives him a funny look. "Because you're family," he says. "You're a colossal pain in the ass, but you're family."

Silver nods. He still feels the urge to hit Rich, and maybe on some level you never stop wanting to inflict some kind of pain on the man your ex-wife loves, no matter how decent a man he is. But beyond that, he feels the simple, effortless generosity of Rich's statement, including him in the family he has lost any right to claim. He doesn't like to be pitied, will go to great lengths to avoid anything resembling it. But the sense

400

he gets from Rich is that, despite his consistently bad behavior, Rich would like to be his friend, and for some reason, this notion, as strange as it may be, fills him with something that, if pressed, he would define as hope.

The office door swings open and Casey comes in carrying a glass of water. "Hey," she says to Rich. "How's the patient?"

"Breathing," Rich says, giving her a quick kiss on the cheek. "What's your mom doing?"

"Circulating."

Rich and Casey share a knowing grin. Silver can see that they have a shorthand between them, and he feels that familiar sense of loss tweak something in his belly.

"I'll go check on her," Rich says. Then he turns to Silver. "We're supposed to leave for Turks and Caicos tomorrow. But I will gladly shift that by a day or two if you would agree to let me operate on you tomorrow."

"That's very nice of you, Rich."

"I need to know, today."

"I understand. Thank you."

Rich nods and leaves the office.

Casey comes over to Silver and sits down next to him.

"He's a good guy," Silver says.

"Yeah. How are you feeling?"

"Suitably embarrassed."

"They'll edit you out of the video."

"And I was trying to be inconspicuous."

She smiles and hands him the glass. "What do you do when you're trying to get noticed?"

Silver grins and takes a greedy gulp of the water, then immediately gags and spits it out, coughing violently.

"Shit! What the hell is this?!"

"Vodka rocks."

He clears his throat, panting heavily as the vodka burns his throat. "Jesus Christ, Casey. I was unconscious five minutes ago."

"I know. I figured you could use a stiff drink."

He looks at her through the haze of the shock-induced tears brought on by the drink. "And why is that?"

"Because it's time to decide."

"Me or you."

She gives him a serious look, and he can see in it the formidable woman she will be. "Both of us."

He takes her hand in his and pulls her against him. "I missed you," he says.

"When?"

"Always."

He can feel her vibrating against him, and when he turns to look at her, he is surprised to see that she is crying.

Be a better man.

Be a better father.

Fall in love.

He understands now that they're all the same thing, all connected, all about this beautiful young girl he doesn't deserve to have sitting beside him, her robust tears leaving a gentle trail on the smooth surface of her gown.

"Did you know that your mother was a bridesmaid when I met her?"

She turns to look at him, curious. "No. You tend not to ask your divorced parents how they met."

"Well, do you want to know?"

She leans her head against his shoulder. "Yes, please," she says in a voice so soft and high, she could be seven again.

So he tells her. And when he finishes, they decide.

CHAPTER 55

Silver sits behind his kit, giving his drums a workout. He has set up two bass drums, as he always does when he's looking to sweat. He plays in common time, bass-comping wildly, shifting in and out of broken-up beats, luxuriating in the solid *thunk* of his beaters against the bass-drum skins. His hands are a blur, his left rolling and sliding across the snare, his right tapping out a separate rhythm on the cymbal bell of his ride. He shifts rhythms thoughtlessly, starts his fills three measures back, so that by the time he crescendos they've told their own story. He jumps out of the beat, keeping it in his head while he goes into a complex drag sequence, and then diving back into it seamlessly. He can play like this for hours, with no accompanying music, no audience, just him and the beat, keeping time. His tinnitus comes from his years behind the crashing cymbals, but it is only here that he

404

can drown out the ringing in his ears.

He plays himself into a frenzy until he reaches the place where all sound retreats, and he is completely absorbed into the rhythm. It's here, in this sweet spot, that he has always found his peace. And now he plays with ferocious intensity, feeling each stroke, each beat, trying to internalize it. For all he knows, this might be the last time he ever sits behind his kit.

He has already begun to drive himself crazy with thoughts like that. It's around five in the afternoon and he is walking around his apartment, just as he has for the last seven years. But tomorrow he could very well be dead. And within a week, the apartment will have been repainted, and some other poor loser already moved in, still falling asleep every night to the hum of the thruway, reassuring himself that it's only temporary, a minor setback. There is a fair amount of turnover at the Versailles, and when it happens, it happens fast. He briefly pictures Jack and Oliver sitting at the pool, Jack watching the college girls, Oliver napping, Silver's empty chair between them as a memorial.

He goes for a walk as the sun is setting. There's a faint chill in the air, barely noticeable, but he can feel the ghost of the colder season to come. He nods a greeting to everyone he passes, returning any smiles that come his way, overcome with sentimentality. He would like to be remembered, he thinks, and then panics that he won't be. Now that he's decided to live, he's terrified that he will die. He is painfully aware of his every heartbeat, wondering if this will be the one that tears his aorta, draining his heart as it floods his organs. He realizes that he didn't shave today, and wonders if they shave you postmortem. The idea of being buried with stubble is disconcerting.

He turns onto a block, just prior to the business district, with a long row of two-family town houses. Lily is sitting on her porch beside a decrepit-looking dog as she waits for him. She smiles as he comes down the block, not the radiant smile that he hopes she will one day hold in reserve for him, but it's still a warm smile, and he welcomes it.

"Hey," she says, coming down the stairs.

He wonders if they're at the stage where a kiss hello is called for, and then, after a moment's hesitation, he remembers that he might be dead tomorrow, and he leans in to kiss her mouth, softly and decisively. He feels her lips part beneath his, and knows he's made the right choice, so he stays there for a while, until the need for oxygen becomes imperative.

She looks at him inquisitively. "So, what's new and exciting?"

"I don't want to die."

"Good, because the ability to breathe is definitely something I look for in a man."

"Anyway, I can't really stay. I just wanted to tell you that I'm going to have that operation. And that I haven't stopped thinking about you."

She nods, and then takes his hand in hers. "I know we just met, really, but do you have people?"

He was right about her. It's nice to be right about something like that. "Yes," he says. "I have people."

"OK, because, you know, I'm around."

"I appreciate that. But I think I need to do this part on my own. I just came to tell you that that's the only reason I won't be calling for a few days. But if you're up for it, I'd really like to call you once I'm back on my feet."

She fixes him with another warm smile. "I'm up for it."

"Good."

He kisses her again, and feels momentarily reborn when her fingers gently graze the side of his face. He steps back and stupidly kisses her hand before backing away. She laughs. "You've really got no game at all, do you?"

"Maybe. Or maybe having no game is my game."

"Well, whatever it is, it's working for you."

He grins and takes in the sight of her one last time. There's very little he knows about her, and the whole thing could either fizzle or go up in flames, or he could die tomorrow and never find out. But right here, in this moment, he feels himself falling in love with her, and that feeling alone is a perfect little miracle.

"Hey," she calls out to him as he heads up the block away from her. "Are you going to be OK?"

He turns back to her and smiles. "That's the plan," he says.

Chapter 56

In order to fix Silver's heart, they first have to shave his groin. He didn't see that coming. He lies in bed while an Asian nurse shaves him, first with an electric trimmer and then with a disposable razor. He finds the whole process a bit of a violation. The nurse wears a surgical mask as she shaves him, which seems somewhat extreme, but he doesn't mind, since he really doesn't want to know what she looks like.

He leans back on his pillow and counts his heartbeats. Yesterday he watched his wife marry another man. Today, the groom will insert a catheter arthroscopically into Silver's freshly shaved groin and guide it up to his damaged aorta, where Rich will repair it by inserting a stent in precisely the right spot. Done correctly, this will save his life. Done incorrectly, Silver will most likely not survive the surgery. He stupidly went online last night, where he discovered that the mortality rate for this surgery is roughly thirty percent. Those are some pretty rough odds.

At this moment, Silver is filled with the psychic certainty that he is going to die today. He can't stop shaking, although that might be from having his groin exposed in the cold, sterile room, his cock shunted off to the side under a paper pad like a vestigial appendage. He wonders if he is being punished. He looks up to the ceiling, but there is no sign of God. Still, maybe a quick prayer, something simple and heartfelt, just to let Him know that he'd like to do better.

Casey sits in her car, in the parking lot, her legs shaking restlessly. She looks at her watch. They'll be getting Silver ready now. She came into his bedroom last night and found him lying on his side, shaking visibly.

"Are you OK?" she said.

"I'm sorry," he said.

She lay down beside him and put her arm over him, trying to calm him. "It's OK, Dad," she told him. "It's going to be fine." She was glad that he was scared — it gave her hope — but it was unnerving to see him like that.

She takes a deep breath and looks out her window. The sky is overcast, and there are tiny droplets forming on her windshield. It's going to rain hard when it comes. She closes her eyes and allows herself a single tear.

Rich comes in, already in his scrubs, and checks Silver's vitals.

"They shaved my balls," Silver tells him.

"They shaved your groin," Rich says as he reads Silver's chart. "And you're welcome. You ready for this?"

"No."

"Well, I am, and if one of us is going to be, it should probably be me."

Silver smiles. "You sound confident."

"Bad for business if I don't." Rich puts down the chart and smiles. "The anesthesiologist will be up in a few minutes." He pats Silver's shoulder.

"Hey, Rich?" Silver says.

"Yeah."

"I don't want to die."

Rich nods and smiles warmly. "I'm glad to hear it."

Casey grips her steering wheel, watches a flock of geese fly past. She rubs her sweaty palms on the leather of her seat, and then turns off her car. It's time. She steps out of the car and feels the humidity enter her pores. Off in the distance, the faintest roll of thunder, and it calms her. Sunshine today would be unbearable.

She locks her car and heads across the parking lot, then stops short when she sees Denise, standing at the clinic entrance, waiting for her.

"Hey," Denise says.

"I thought you'd be over at the hospital."

Denise looks at her with so much tenderness that Casey can feel herself coming apart right there on the sidewalk. "Silver asked me to be here for him."

Casey thinks about it for a moment. "He'll be OK, right?"

"I think so, yes." Denise puts her arm around Casey and kisses her lightly. "You ready to go in?"

Casey leans her head against Denise's shoulder, and takes a last deep breath. Then she takes her mother's hand and they head inside.

The anesthesiologist is a thin, quiet man with salt-and-pepper hair that Silver finds reassuring. He sets up his various drips, humming lightly to himself.

Jack and Oliver come in one last time, to wish him well. Oliver talks in low tones while Jack paces nervously, touching all the equipment.

"Will you stand still?" Oliver says. "You're making us all nervous."

"I'm sorry. Hospitals make me nervous," Jack says. "You sure you can handle this now?"

"It's fine," Silver says. "I don't really have to do anything. They'll wake me up when it's over."

"Just don't die," Jack says.

Oliver turns to fix him with an incredulous stare. "That's great advice, Jack. Why don't you go downstairs?"

Jack nods and turns to leave, then comes back and leans over Silver, giving him a quick kiss on the forehead.

"Now I know I'm dying," Silver says with a grin.

"Fuck you."

"I'll see you on the other side."

"OK."

Jack looks at him for a long minute, then turns abruptly and leaves the room. Oliver smiles apologetically. "He's just worried about you."

"I know."

"I'm not going to kiss you."

"I appreciate that."

Oliver pats his leg. "We'll be waiting downstairs."

Silver is momentarily overcome and has to look away as Oliver leaves the room.

And then he is being wheeled down the hallway on his bed, with his mother and father on either side of him, just as they walked him down the aisle at his wedding. Elaine smiles down at him, and he can see the tired strain in her eyes. Ruben is inconspicuously saying a prayer under his breath, and Silver knows without hearing him that it's Psalm 121, which has always been his father's go-to prayer.

I will lift up mine eyes unto the hills, from whence cometh my help.

Silver feels the roll of the wheels beneath him, the light bumps every time they hit a seam in the linoleum flooring.

My help cometh from the Lord, which made heaven and earth.

They have reached the end of the corridor. His parents can go no farther. Elaine leans over to kiss him, fighting back the tears. "Be good," she says.

He smiles. "Always."

His father finishes his psalm and kisses Silver's cheek, and he can feel the tears threatening. "I'm sorry," Silver says. "For everything."

"You're going to be OK."

"Is He here?" Silver says.

His father looks at him. "Who?"

"God."

Ruben smiles. "He's around here somewhere."

The nurses push Silver through the swinging doors, and even though he can't look behind him, he can nevertheless see his parents, coming together in his wake, watching him go.

Inside, just before they put the mask on him, Silver looks around the sterile, metallic room. For some people, this is the last room they will ever see. They ought to make it look a little nicer, he thinks. Give it some warmth.

Then the mask is on him, and Rich is hovering over him.

"You good, Silver?"

Silver nods, no longer able to speak.

Rich pats his chest. "OK then. I'll see you in a bit."

The anesthesiologist is suddenly there, fiddling with a knob beside Silver's head. "Just breathe deeply," he says, and then the room begins to shimmer and fade before disappearing into a deeply textured blackness.

And then he is standing beside the small

house he lived in with Casey and Denise. He looks down at his feet, barefoot on the lawn, which has been recently watered and feels cool and damp against his toes. A pair of birds fly past him and, much higher up, an airplane, too far to be heard, leaving a white vapor trail as it crosses the sky.

He hears laughing and turns to see Casey, six years old, running around the house from the backyard.

"There you are!" she says, her voice bubbling with excitement. "I found you."

"Yes, you did," he says, smiling at her.

"It's your turn," she says. "Come with me."

"Where?"

She gives him a mildly impatient look, like he might be teasing her. "To the swings."

She is wearing a red T-shirt, white shorts, her legs skinny and scraped, her feet in a pair of white flip-flops. She always loved flip-flops, loved the accompanying noise they made as she walked. He remembers that now. He remembers everything.

He is not really here. He knows that. And yet, somehow he is. He can see the water droplets on the grass tips, can see the browning on the white siding of his house, can hear kids riding by on their bikes, calling out to one another. Somewhere in the distance, he hears the musical chime of the ice-cream truck making its rounds.

"Daddy?"

She calls him Daddy. Of course she does. That's who he is.

"What, baby?"

"Come on!"

She is walking backward now alongside the house, leading him past the rose bushes to their small backyard, which glows orange in the evening sun. He wonders if he's died and she's there to lead him to the next place, or if she's simply there to lead him back. Either way, he knows nothing will ever stop him from following her again.

He catches up to her and takes her hand in his, reveling in the way her fingers unconsciously wrap themselves around his hand. She looks up at him and smiles. He smiles back.

"Let's go," he says.

ACKNOWLEDGMENTS

My heartfelt gratitude to:

Mom and Dad, for always being there, but especially now. Ben Sevier, for your patience and guidance — you definitely earned your paycheck on this one. Simon Lipskar, for your expertise, acumen, and steadfast support. Kassie Evashevski, Tobin Babst, David Park, and Fred Toczek, for keeping all those plates spinning. The infinitely generous and talented Laura Dave and Josh Singer, for their indispensible friendship and counsel. Dr. Abraham Schreiber, for all the medical consults, and Greg Yaitanes, for shooting my new author photo.

ABOUT THE AUTHOR

Jonathan Tropper is the internationally bestselling author of five previous novels: *Plan B, The Book of Joe, Everything Changes, How to Talk to a Widower,* and *This Is Where I Leave You.* His books have been translated into more than twenty-one languages. He is also a screenwriter and the cocreator and executive producer of the HBO/Cinemax television show *Banshee,* which will air on Cinemax in 2013.

www.jonathantropper.com
www.twitter.com/jtropper

did a jig right there in the lobby when he took up residence in the Versailles.

"You look at them," Oliver grumbles from beneath the crumpled baseball cap resting on his face. "I'm napping here."

Oliver is in his late fifties, tall and beefy with loosening skin, tired eyes, and an ocean of whiskey under his belt. He is one of the few men who doesn't have to live there; he is rich enough to live anywhere, really, but he likes the camaraderie. He has been married — count 'em — three times, has grown children who don't speak to him, grandchildren he has never met. Oliver is fourteen years older than Silver, and Jack is an oversexed misogynist, but somehow, in a way he couldn't retrace if he tried, they have wordlessly become a unit.

And here they lie, every day baking in the sun: Jack, long and lean, only now beginning to lose some of the definition in his abs and chest. Silver, thickened everywhere, like an aging baseball pitcher, and then Oliver, long gone to seed, his sagging beer gut rounding him out into something vaguely pear-shaped. Jack and Oliver are like Before and After pictures, and he is the softening middle stage, the moment it all went wrong.

"Sure, there's the obvious," Jack says, ignoring Oliver. "The anatomical advan-

31

tages go without saying. But go deeper. Look at their eyes, the way they move, the way they laugh. They're brimming with this . . . unspoiled sexuality. They still love men. They're at least a thousand fucks away from the bitter, cynical women they all eventually become."

"Or one night with you."

"Ah, fuck you, Oliver."

"They're kind of young for you, aren't they?" Silver says.

"Fuck no," Jack says. "Who do you think is going to gratify these girls, college boys? Think back to when you were twenty. Sure, you were a walking hard-on, but were you any good? Did you really know how to please a woman? Did you even care to? No, all you knew was where to stick it, and nine out of ten times, you were finished before she'd even gotten started."

Silver thinks of a girl, he can't remember her name, lying beneath him in the sweaty confines of her cramped dorm single, her wide eyes looking up at him with unrestrained desire, and he feels something he's become accustomed to lately, a dull, humming grief for all the things he can never get back.

"Forget what you think you know." Jack is gathering momentum now, which is never a good thing. "These are not the girls you and I went to college with. This is an evolved species. They love sex. They love it and they want it, and they feel it's their inalienable right to have it. These girls are feminists, God bless 'em."

"Will you quit speechifying?" Oliver says. "I'm trying to relax over here."

"Come on, Oliver, you know you'd take any one of these girls. A bottle of wine, a couple of Viagra, you're good to go."

Oliver pulls the cap off his face and squints at Jack. "But would any one of them take me?"

"What are you talking about? You're a handsome man."

"I am old and fat, and I survive by knowing my role in the jungle."

"And what's that?"

"The rich old toad who pays to occasionally have his cock munched," Oliver says, pulling his cap back over his face. And right at that moment, Silver thinks, there is something vaguely toad-like about him.

The girls stretch and roll on their chairs, expertly opening the clasps on their bikini tops to avoid tan lines. They swing their legs, they rub lotion into their cleavages, lick their lips, play with their long hair. Jack lifts his Ray-Bans to squint at them, then laughs at the wonder of it all. "God in heaven," he says.

Oliver farts, long and high, like air escaping from a pinched balloon.

"Christ, Oliver, take a pill," Jack said.

This is what passes for his friends these days.

They are still sitting there, two hours later, when Casey shows up. The sun is high above them, the smell of tanning oil sizzling on the skin of the college girls wafting across the pool to tease their senses. Heard from a certain vantage point, the tractor-trailers thundering down the interstate can sound like the pounding surf. Silver is, as he so often seems to be these days, adrift in a hazy fog of memory, fantasy, and regret.

"Silver."

And maybe, on his better days, the faintest glimmer of hope.

"Silver!"

Casey is walking purposefully toward him, in shorts and a breezy halter top, her almond-colored hair pouring down her back and billowing slightly in the faint summer breeze. As she gets closer, he can see that her face is lightly dusted with a horseshoe-shaped constellation of freckles. Jack grunts, making a big show of not checking out his